"I want to get married, Lewis."

"Are you sure about this, Phoebe?" he asked.

"Absolutely," she answered. She looked at him. "Are you?"

He nodded. "Yes. I love you. I'd do anything for you. *Anything*."

She'd lost him for years and now she'd found him again. She wasn't letting him go back to Edmonton and maybe find some other woman. Besides, she was tired of always being the good girl in her family, tired of always having to be sensible.

But how to explain this sudden urgency? The sudden overwhelming desire she'd felt this morning, watching him sleep, to be his, really his. In the most sacred, profound way. *Marriage*. "I know it seems kind of crazy, but doing it like this cuts out a lot of trouble. You know what I mean?"

"Uh-huh. Your folks." His dark eyes were steady on hers.

Phoebe glanced away. "Them. And everyone else. They don't know you the way I do. They'd bring up all kinds of complications. They'd think we should get married in a church. All that fuss. Weddings are stupid, anyway! *Being* married is what counts."

"Is it?" He turned to study her. "You know I'll do anything you want, Phoebe, even sneak off like this and marry you. But we can't hide forever."

"It'll just be a secret for a while," she told him. "*Ours!*"

Dear Reader,

Writing a collection of books set in and around the small
town of Glory, Alberta, has been a challenge and a source
of joy for me. I have lived in so many small towns myself
that Glory has come to reflect everything I like and dislike
about small-town living. No one can say there aren't
disadvantages—lack of privacy, interfering neighbors,
limited shopping. But there are great advantages, too—
a sense of community, parents looking out for their
neighbors' children, knowing that you'll always find help if
you ask for it.

Lewis Hardin, a young man in trouble in my first MEN OF
GLORY book, *The Rancher's Runaway Bride*, has always longed
for something we all cherish: a home of our own. In this
story, with childhood sweetheart Phoebe Longquist's help,
Lewis discovers his special place in more ways than one.

I hope you'll enjoy the love story between Lewis and
Phoebe. It was a wonderful book to write, and brings the
folks of Glory full circle, back to the beginning. The place
we call home.

Judith Bowen

P.S. Let me know how you've enjoyed the MEN OF GLORY
books and thank you for your many, many letters over the
years. You can reach me at P.O. Box 2333, Point Roberts, WA
98281-2333. Or check out my MEN OF GLORY web page at
www.judithbowen.com.

MEN OF GLORY titles in Superromance:

A Home of His Own
Judith Bowen

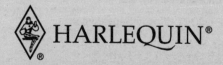

HARLEQUIN®

TORONTO • NEW YORK • LONDON
AMSTERDAM • PARIS • SYDNEY • HAMBURG
STOCKHOLM • ATHENS • TOKYO • MILAN • MADRID
PRAGUE • WARSAW • BUDAPEST • AUCKLAND

ISBN 0-373-70950-1

A HOME OF HIS OWN

Copyright © 2000 by J. E. Corser.

This edition published by arrangement with Harlequin Books S.A.

® and TM are trademarks of the publisher. Trademarks indicated with ® are registered in the United States Patent and Trademark Office, the Canadian Trade Marks Office and in other countries.

Visit us at www.eHarlequin.com

Printed in U.S.A.

A Home of His Own

CHAPTER ONE

THE FIRST TIME Phoebe saw Lewis Hardin she was maybe ten. She'd gone out to the Hardin place, at the top of Bearberry Hill, with her mother to deliver some parceled-up goods from the parish. The Hardins weren't Catholic, as far as Phoebe was aware, but that didn't matter: they were poor.

That afternoon, bored with the adults' visiting, Phoebe had climbed a massive poplar in a copse near the Hardins' old post-and-beam barn, then had daringly crawled onto a ledge that led to the loft. The loft contained very little hay. The roof, under the rafters, was thick with the nests of barn swallows; it echoed with the squeaky shrills of the parents swooping in to stuff their offspring's bellies with mosquitoes, then out again. There were no animals in the barn, only a few badly rusted farm implements. She'd heard a rhythmic *rap-rap* sound below somewhere and had crept from one side of the loft to the other, peering through the square holes in the floor cut out for hay and straw to be thrown down to horses or cows.

She was afraid, but she was thrilled, too. This was

an adventure. Even dangerous, up here with the stinky hay and the uncertain footing. By herself, too—no Jilly tagging along. The fun of having a new little sister had worn off long ago.

Finally, almost on top of the *rap-rap* sound, Phoebe cleared the hay cautiously from the place where the wall of the barn met the floor of the loft and peered down. She spotted a boy, about fourteen or fifteen, hammering on a homemade punching bag made from an old feed sack, it looked like, filled with straw. He jabbed at the bag, grunting at the effort, his skinny body gleaming with sweat in the shafts of afternoon sunlight that lazily probed the deep gloom of the barn's interior. The punching bag hung in one corner of a box stall that had been fixed up with a bed and pallet and a rickety-looking table and bench. There were candles set into pop bottles, on the table, a knife, chunks of wood and several plastic bread bags. Was there food in them? It seemed that the boy lived in the stall, or at least slept there part of the time. A few boards pried out of the barn siding provided an exit.

Phoebe held her breath, rapt. Finally, with a last vicious series of jabs and a shout that thrilled her blood, he swung away from the bag and sank heavily onto the wooden chair. After a few moments of hard breathing, he retrieved his T-shirt from the adjoining pallet and put it on, then picked up the knife and a piece of wood from the table and began whittling.

She was certain he hadn't seen her, not with the racket from the birds above. She was just thinking of how she could inch her way back, desperately afraid she'd sneeze or something, when he looked up and grinned. "Here you go, you little peeper!" He tossed something at her and she ducked. When she raised her head again, he was gone. She felt around in the hay until she found what he'd thrown. It was a small wooden frog, crudely carved.

Five years later...

SHE'D THOUGHT it was beautiful and had kept it on her windowsill ever since. She'd gone back up to the house to join her mother and the Hardin women that day, but the boy had not appeared.

Now, at nearly fifteen herself, on another such mission of charity, with her mother and her aunt Catherine this time, Phoebe thought about that silly wooden frog. It was grubby from handling, and once she'd actually thrown it away; the next day, she'd dug through her bedroom trash basket and retrieved it. It brought her luck. Or happiness. Something that didn't bear thinking about.

Saint Augustine's kept a list of the families they helped in the area, and Bearberry Hill was within the parish. Nothing remained there but a white-painted clapboard church with a windblown cemetery at the brow of the hill and the ramshackle settlement that marked the Hardin place. If there'd been a husband for the older woman, Mercedes Hardin, he was long gone and forgotten by the community. Her daughter, Billy, lived with her, a young-old woman of perhaps forty. She was not right in the head, some said, and others said she was peculiar by choice. Mercedes looked older than her sixty-some years, with flyaway white hair and watery blue eyes. Because of a hip broken years earlier, she favored one leg and walked with a cane, which had always made her seem older. There was another member of the family, Phoebe knew—the son, Lewis. He was in jail.

Ever since Lewis Hardin had gone to jail for rustling cattle the year before, Cal Blake, the rancher who lived up the road a few miles, had kept the Hardins supplied with beef and firewood. He'd promised Lewis they'd be taken care of, according to a neighbor, which was strange, considering it was Cal's beef that Lewis and a gang of n'er-do-well cowboys had stolen.

"I hear Mercy still keeps a fine garden," her mother said, from the driver's seat. "And no one can say they're afraid of work, the two of them, living like they do."

"Nan," her aunt sniffed. "Be sensible. It's no way to live, two women out here alone. They ought to move to town."

"Mercy was born on the place and she'd told me

once the only way she'll be leaving is feet first,''
replied Phoebe's mother.

Feet first, Phoebe knew very well, meant *dead*.
Phoebe sat in the back, between two large sacks of
used clothing from the parish thrift store, which had
been chosen with the Hardin women in mind, and a
box of groceries on the floor of the station wagon,
which had come from the Glory food bank. Canned
goods, mostly—ham and soup and condensed milk—
although Phoebe could see several boxes of pasta
and, oddly, a flat, paper-wrapped tin of anchovies.
Anchovies!

A view of the azure blue Pacific off Peru, silvery
with the tiny fish, flashed through Phoebe's mind…

''And that boy of hers—ooh!'' Her aunt shuddered
and made a face Phoebe could see in the rearview
mirror. ''Thank goodness he's where he belongs—in
jail! He's been nothing but trouble since he was born.
Imagine another one coming so long after Billy? It
makes a body wonder who the father was…''

''Oh, Catherine,'' her mother murmured, driving
slowly and carefully. ''I don't suppose anyone cares
about all that. Not now. Not after so many years.''

How many years? About nineteen or twenty,
Phoebe guessed later when she came across him at
the bottom of the orchard—mainly twisted crab apple
trees and blighted russet pears. He frightened her,
sitting there on a long-downed tree trunk, so still and
so alert at the same time. He blended into the dry

grass. If she hadn't smelled the cigarette smoke, she might not have seen him at all. And that thought scared her more.

She'd asked Mercy Hardin if she could go and see the sheep that she'd noticed from the road when they turned into the lane. Since that first long-ago visit, the Hardin women had acquired a scruffy clutch of sheep, black and brown and white, that they kept for who knew what reason. Meat, perhaps. Or wool.

Two of the Hardin dogs, who'd barked madly at the car as they drove up to the house, lay at the man's feet.

"Come here," he said quietly. At first she didn't realize it was Lewis. He was supposed to be in jail. "Are you afraid of me?" His eyes narrowed through the cigarette smoke. He wore an old shirt and jeans, no jacket, even though it was cold enough that Phoebe had worn the new wool coat her mother had bought her for school in September. His boots were black, sturdy and plain. Government issue.

"I'm not afraid," she said, picking her way toward him through the fallen branches and frozen windfall fruit. It was true; she wasn't. She stood in front of him. "You shouldn't smoke. It's a filthy habit."

He laughed and threw the stub of a cigarette away. It smoldered in the frosty grass. "Who's up there?" He frowned and hunched one shoulder toward the house.

"And you shouldn't throw away lighted butts like that. You could start a forest fire."

"Aw, can it, kid. Who's up there?" he repeated.

She frowned. "At the house, you mean?"

He nodded impatiently.

"Just my mother. And my aunt Catherine."

"That's all?"

She nodded and he patted the log he was sitting on. "Have a seat. I'm not gonna bite you."

She sat beside him. He edged closer to her, against her, and she realized he was shivering. "How're Ma and Billy?"

"Why? Haven't you seen them?" She was thoroughly confused. What was he doing here in the orchard, anyway?

He glanced over his shoulder in the direction of the house. "Naw. Not yet. I'm supposed to be in jail, didn't you know?" He smiled briefly. His features were harsh and pinched. All these years she'd remembered a dark intensity, a passion, to his thin face; what she now saw was hunger and a certain grim determination.

"Well, why aren't you?" Later, when she thought about it, she wondered at her nerve.

"I left. Got tired of the food they shove at you in there." He winked and put his arm around her shoulders in a sudden, impulsive gesture, and held her close against him. "Man, it's cold! I could use a cup of coffee and a bellyful of beef stew. Some nice warm Parker house rolls. Ma done her baking to-day?" He had a wistful look in his eyes, then came the knowing, self-deprecating laugh again.

Phoebe stared at him. She shook her head. "I don't know." She unwrapped the scarf from around her neck, the one her grandmother had knitted, and gave it to him. "Here, this will make you a little warmer."

He buried his hands in the scarf. "You're a good kid, you know that?"

Phoebe shrugged. "Well, I guess I'd better go back to the house." She made a move, as though to get up, but he bumped her with his shoulder, on purpose. She could feel her thigh warm against his. Her thigh and her arm and her shoulder.

"You won't say nothing?" He shot her a penetrating look. "About me down here?"

She hesitated. "They'll get you, you know. Eventually, you're going back to jail. For even longer."

He laughed again. "Yeah, yeah, I know that. I just needed a break, y'know? Little holiday. I wanted to see how Ma and Billy were getting on. When your ma leaves, I'll go up to the house, say hello." His face was so close to hers. He hadn't shaved in a while. She couldn't think of any of her friends who wouldn't have been scared to death in her situation. Natasha Jarvis, her best friend, would have died. *Imagine*—she was talking to an escaped convict!

"I—I hate it there," he burst out. "You can't understand, a kid like you, what it's like to be trapped, spied on—'' He clamped his jaws closed, as though he'd stopped himself from admitting something. *That he missed home. That he longed to be free.* Then he shocked her. ''Listen, you ever kiss a man?''

''N-no,'' she said slowly, shaking her head. She began to get up. He grabbed her arm and she shook him off.

''Boys? You ever kiss boys?''

Phoebe decided to lie. ''A few,'' she said airily.

He stood up suddenly and put his arms around her. ''Kiss *me*.''

Then his face was right up against hers, and he nuzzled her nose and forehead, as though she were a kitten. He kissed her, softly at first, and then more and more intensely, and she felt rivulets of something weird shoot through her body, through her legs and arms, through her stomach. His mouth was wet and soft and faintly, disgustingly, smoky from his cigarette. But oh, so warm and exciting! Phoebe kissed him back, as well as she knew how, which wasn't very well at all.

His arms were tight around her, iron bands. Then she felt his hands, cold and hard, under her coat and slipping up under her sweater against her hot skin. She moaned and shivered and pressed herself against him. Suddenly he released her and she nearly fell backward. His eyes were dark and flat. He pulled her sweater down and fastened her coat. "You'd better go, kid. Before we're both in trouble."

She began to make her way, stumbling, across the orchard. He called after her, "Hey, kid!"

She stopped. She needed to, anyway, her heart was pumping so hard.

"What's your name?"

She hated her name. It was a stupid, old-fashioned, ridiculous name. "Phoe—" She couldn't get the whole word out of her throat, couldn't shout it back to him.

She turned and ran toward the house.

Later her mother had asked what happened to the scarf Granny Longquist had knitted, the one that matched her new mittens. Phoebe said she didn't know. That she must have lost it somewhere. But she fell asleep dreaming that her scarf was wound around his neck or warming his hands—as she'd seen him do—and that he'd really meant it when he said she was a good kid.

Of course, it was a sin to lie. Especially to your own mother. But somehow this was different. Somehow this mattered less—and, at the same time, more.

When Phoebe was nearly seventeen...

THE NEXT TIME Lewis Hardin went AWOL, he came to Swallowbank Farm.

She and her sister Jill were picking raspberries at

the back of the garden behind the house. Her mother wanted to make a shortcake. Normally Phoebe would have resented having to help with the garden, but today she was glad to be outside. It was a glorious late-June day and she'd been studying hard for her final exams. One more year of high school, grade twelve, and if her marks were good, she'd be in line for a decent scholarship. If that didn't happen, she wouldn't be going into the science program she wanted. She'd be taking a hairdressing course. With four brothers and sisters and a father confined to a wheelchair, there was no extra money for things like a college education, even with student loans. Not unless the Longquists won a lottery. And her mother, of course, didn't buy lottery tickets—they were the devil's work, she said.

So that was that. It was "be a good girl, get good marks and everything will work out." She knew if she worked hard and did her part, her parents would support her any way they could.

They were good parents. She loved them both dearly. Her father had been injured in a farm accident working for her uncle Joe, her mother's brother, who owned the place where they lived, Swallowbank Farm. Uncle Joe had kept her father on, doing the books and helping out with other farm chores that he could handle, but it was tough supporting two families on one hay-and-grain farm. Now that Uncle Joe was married, and his wife, her aunt Honor, worked two days a week at the law firm in town, things were a little easier. But not easy enough that anyone—the Gallants or the Longquists—threw money around.

In fact, her mother had told her this morning that she and Jilly could pick extra raspberries, if the crop was heavy, to sell to summer tourists at the neighboring farm's roadside stand. But Phoebe was past that. She'd earned money doing that as a kid, but no way was she standing at the side of the road selling berries at nearly seventeen. She had a job lined up at the town library for the summer, although that didn't pay much, either. It was depressing.

She thought of the little frog she'd had for so long. "Bring me some luck," she muttered to herself, hunched over in the hot sun trying to fill her dishpan, which seemed to have a hole in the bottom of it. "I sure could use some."

Phoebe had made several passes back and forth along the rows, looking for ripe berries, before she realized she was hearing something peculiar. It wasn't the magpies chattering on the fence posts, although they did seem unusually agitated. It wasn't the distant sound of Uncle Joe working in the fields on his new John Deere tractor. It was something else. Phoebe stopped, straightened and adjusted her hat, resting her dishpan half-full of berries on one hip.

"Pssst!"

She frowned. She could see nothing at all. Only the raspberry canes, stretching up six feet or more, thick and green, the white-painted fence behind them and then Uncle Joe's hay field stretching out for acres and acres beyond that. Not even a tree to break the horizon.

She bent and began picking again, reaching through into the center of the rows to where the big fat berries hung, among so many still underripe. It looked like her mother's prediction was good: there'd be a bountiful crop this year.

"Pssst!"

Phoebe glanced toward Jilly, who was at the other end of the garden. Naturally her little sister wasn't helping at all. She was sitting on the edge of the strawberry bed, gazing up at the cloudless blue sky, her arms clasped around her bare knees. Daydreaming again.

"Pssst! Phoebe!"

Phoebe caught her breath. She didn't know what to do. Someone must be nearby, but it was so weird that she couldn't see anyone at all. Probably a wacko. Out here on the prairie? And how would a wacko know her name? Phoebe considered going into the house to tell her mother, then curiosity got the better of her. Whoever it was had to be hiding in here somewhere.

Probably Trevor. Her brother was a prankster. He could get up to anything.

She set down her pan of berries and moved quietly to the back of the bushes. She began to push her way behind the thicket, where the canes had grown up and intertwined with the fence, when she felt something—or someone—grab her ankle.

Her tiny shriek blended with his, "Shhhht!"

"Lewis!" She looked down and saw a male hand clutching her ankle, and a laughing, darkly handsome face. He was lying flat out in the long grass—no wonder she hadn't seen him—and had snaked one hand under the fence to grab her as she'd crept along.

He let go and raised himself on one elbow, a finger to his lips and a significant nod in the direction of her sister.

"What are you *doing* here?" She leaned on the fence, ignoring his invitation to join him on the other side. But she wanted to giggle. Imagine!

"Come on over," he urged.

She set her jaw stubbornly. "No! I want to know what you're doing here."

"Scared of me, huh?"

Phoebe answered by placing one sneaker on the lower rung of the fence and swinging herself over. She tossed her braids back—braids! He must think she was a real kid.

He sat up, grabbed her hand, and first thing she knew, he'd pulled her down beside him. "Careful! Don't want anyone to see us."

She did giggle then. She didn't dare laugh too loudly in case Jilly heard her and came to investigate, but she was pretty sure it would take an earthquake to interrupt her sister's daydreams, and even then Phoebe wouldn't count on it.

She stopped laughing abruptly and turned her head to look at him. He was staring straight up at the blue sky, a stem of timothy grass in his teeth, looking very pleased with himself. His hair was too long, but he was so handsome, grown-up and handsome. "What *are* you doing here?"

"You really want to know?" He shot her a searching glance, then smiled. "Hey, you're looking good, Phoebe. Real good. I like freckles."

She wanted to hit him. Her freckles were the bane of her existence. Everyone had told her she'd grow out of them, but they seemed to go with her auburn hair, and so far there was no sign of them fading.

"How did you know my name? How did you know where I lived?"

"Asked Ma and Billy. They know all about you and your ma and your family. Think you're wonderful folk." There was a bitter edge to his words. "Wonderful *kind* folk."

He was no doubt referring to the good works her mother and aunt carried out on behalf of the parish. Phoebe ignored the comment. She sat up, crosslegged, then remembered that they were supposed to be hiding and ducked down again. The crushed grass sent up a glorious green sweet scent.

"That's better." He grinned at her and she felt her heart lurch around unsteadily. He looked so good in his white T-shirt stretched across a man's chest, his worn jeans. Her breath hurt in her throat. She remembered the last time they'd met—how he'd kissed her. She'd fantasized about that kiss for months, relived every second of it, until finally she'd had a few dates and got a boyfriend of her own and realized that kissing was no big deal.

"So, are you working around here?" She held her breath.

"No, uh…" He poked his head up over the grass and looked around quickly, then lay back down. "I'm still a special guest of Her Majesty."

"In *jail?*" Phoebe felt her skin tighten and her hopes crush.

"I left in the laundry truck," he said, grinning at her again. She did not smile back. Scratch "grownup," she thought sadly. He was still acting like a kid running away from home.

"When was that?" She felt sick inside. She didn't really want to know. And yet she desperately wanted to know. *She wanted to know everything about him.*

"Four days ago. I know they're looking for me. That's why I couldn't stay out at Ma's anymore. I suppose I'm ready to go back. But, hey! I wanted to see you while I had the chance."

He was teasing her. No question of that. She started to get up. "Well, now you've seen me. I've got some berries to pick and I guess you can just head back to the slammer. Or are you waiting until they catch you?''

''I don't know,'' he said. He plucked a new stem of grass and stuck it in his mouth. ''Haven't made up my mind yet.''

''Why do you *do* this, Lewis? Don't you realize it doesn't do your mother and sister any good? Don't you want to *make* something of yourself? Turn your life around? *Be* somebody?''

He frowned up at her. ''For what?''

''For...'' She felt angry, really angry. *For me.* ''For them. For yourself. For...oh, I don't know!'' She plucked a stem of grass and stuck the succulent end in her mouth.

''Hey,'' he said, reaching for her hand. She shook him off. ''*You* care, don't you? You care what happens to me?''

''No, I don't,'' she said, throwing down the blade of grass and preparing to get up again. ''Most definitely not. I don't care a *damn* about you or if you want to throw your life away. I don't even know you. I just don't think it's fair for your sister and your mom, alone up there on the hill.''

He sat up with her, apparently no longer caring if they were seen. He grabbed her hand and held it this time. ''That's not true, Phoebe. It's *me* you care about.''

She couldn't meet his gaze. She glanced down.

She felt his free hand caress her cheek, then his fingers under her chin, forcing it up. "Right?"

She nodded mutely, her eyes filling with tears. Damn him anyway!

"Oh, man, you are such a sweet kid…" His voice was hoarse. He bent and kissed her and, heaven help her, she kissed him back, with every ounce of pent-up feeling she'd had for him since that day so many years ago when she'd spied on him and he'd caught her and had tossed her the little wooden frog.

She reached to put her arms around him as his arms were around her, and they tumbled back down and he rolled and shifted his weight onto her. It felt good! She gave herself up to the sensation of Lewis stretched beside and above her and the warm grass and the bright sky and the soothing buzz of grasshoppers nearby. And kissing. Everything was so peaceful. Except this—what was happening between them.

His breath was hot on her face and neck as he kissed her all over, making appreciative little sounds, working his way down to the open neck of her sleeveless shirt. He kissed her breast through the cotton cloth and she gasped and squealed and felt him put his hand across her mouth to silence her. She bit his hand and then took his head in both hands and pulled him up so she could kiss him on the mouth again.

"Hey-hey-hey…" He laughed, a low, sexy, vibrant laugh. A laugh full of pleasure and boldness.

Phoebe couldn't believe how quickly her feelings were aroused. Sexual feelings. She'd never ever felt this with any of the boys she'd necked with. Maybe kissing *was* a big deal, with the right person.

But Lewis Hardin was not the right person. He was an escaped convict. A two-bit rustler. A dropout. A small-town loser. A Peter Pan who refused to grow up. Not her type at all.

"Pheeeeb!"

Phoebe froze. Jilly! What if she discovered them like this? What if she told their parents about Lewis, hiding out here in Uncle Joe's hay field?

"I've got to go," Phoebe said, urgently, straightening her blouse and her shorts and brushing the grass off her bare legs. She fanned her blouse from her body, back and forth, hoping the telltale damp mark he'd made on her breast would dry quickly. "I—I hope everything works out for you and—"

He grasped her hand as she stood. "I'm not going anywhere. We need to talk. Meet me tonight behind the—" he glanced around "—chicken house. I'll be the tall one wearing shoes."

Despite herself, Phoebe giggled. "Okay." What was she doing promising to meet him later? She must be nuts!

She crawled back over the fence and hurried to where she'd left her dishpan. She caught a last glimpse of Lewis nearly hidden from sight in the grass, arms behind his head, ankles crossed, smiling at her.

"Phoebe! Where are you?"

"Here!" she called back. She tackled the raspberries again, picking furiously to make up for the time she'd missed. Pesky younger sisters. Lousy raspberries. Stupid job at the library this summer.

She hated being poor. Her life was poor and boring. A scholarship was her ticket out. Maybe Lewis Hardin was a loser, but at least he had some excitement in his life. Some adventure.

CHAPTER TWO

PHOEBE HAD NOT SET a time for her meeting with
Lewis, and in late June the sun didn't set until nearly
half-past ten. When it was finally dark enough to
sneak out, it was quite late. Well, she wasn't really
sneaking out, she convinced herself. She'd been
studying all evening and told her father, who was
still up watching television, that she wanted to get
some fresh air. Jilly was at a friend's house for a
sleepover, and Trevor was out. Since he'd acquired
his driver's license that spring, he'd been out most
evenings. Her mother and the baby, little Renee, had
already gone to bed.

Harry Longquist looked up and nodded sleepily.
Phoebe adored her dad. She felt momentarily
guilty—really, she *was* sneaking out, wasn't she?—
and walked over and dropped a kiss on her father's
cheek. "'Night, Pops." She squeezed his shoulder.

"'Night, honey," her father said with a smile before returning his attention to the baseball game. The
Jays were taking on the Mariners in Seattle.

Well, she *was* getting some fresh air.

She made a trip through the kitchen to collect a

few leftovers. It had occurred to her when they were having their raspberry shortcake that evening that Lewis must be hungry. She filled a paper bag with a banana and two apples and loaded a plate with potato salad, sliced ham, two buttered rolls and some bean salad. At the last minute, juggling her load, she snagged a quart of milk from the fridge and let herself out the back door.

She set the food down carefully on the outside step, with a hiss at Gerald, the dog, who'd begun to thump his tail happily against the porch boards in gratitude for her apparent offering. Gerald looked offended and sloped off the porch and around the corner of the house. Phoebe reached back inside and grabbed an old windbreaker that belonged to Ben, her older brother. Ben was away, working for Adam Garrick at his ranch west of Glory, as he did every summer. He'd never notice the jacket was gone.

There was a moon overhead, waning now, and a few clouds, so that sometimes she could see nearly as well as daylight and other times she had to be careful not to stumble.

Lewis was waiting for her behind the chicken shed, as he'd promised.

"Oh, baby!" he said when he saw the food she carried. "Man, I was hoping I wouldn't have to settle for sucking eggs tonight."

"You wouldn't!" Phoebe handed him the plate.

She'd forgotten to bring cutlery, but it didn't seem to matter.

"Oh, yeah, I would." He scooped the potato salad up with a piece of ham and chewed hungrily. "Thanks," he mumbled, his mouth half-full, waving around the chicken yard. He bowed slightly and took a step backward. "What's this?" he asked, tasting the bean salad gingerly. "Bean salad?" Before she could say anything, he'd tipped it off his plate, onto the ground. "I hate that stuff. Treat for the hens tomorrow," he said, grinning at her. "But thanks all the same."

She held out the jacket and he took it with a smile. "Good girl. You thought of everything. Let's sit down."

Phoebe looked around. The chickens were all inside their shelter, roosting for the night. "No thanks. Come on." Phoebe led him out of the enclosure, shutting the gate behind her, and they sat down on the dewy grass between the chicken coop and the garden.

"I brought you some fruit, too," she offered. "In case you get hungry later." She gestured toward the bag, then gripped her knees with her forearms and watched him eat. He popped the lid on the milk jug and drained half of it in one long swallow. Phoebe smiled to herself. She was pleased she'd remembered to bring food. And the jacket. She'd done the right thing.

When he finished, he patted his shirt pocket absently. "Damn, I forgot. I quit smoking."

"You did?" Phoebe was happy to hear that.

"Well, sorta." She could hear him grinning in the semidark. "I ran outa smokes. And money, too."

"I'll feed you, but I won't buy you cigarettes," she said firmly, leaning back, then felt his hand on hers in the grass.

"C'mon, Phoebe. I haven't got much time. Let's talk."

"What do you want to talk about?" She felt shy suddenly.

"You. Me. Everything." He hunched closer to her and she felt the warmth of his shoulder against hers. She shivered and he put his arm around her. It reminded her of the time he'd first kissed her in the orchard.

"Cold?"

"A little. It's damp here." She wasn't shivering because of the damp and she knew it. "Let's go over behind my uncle's house," she whispered. "There's a hammock." She needed to buy a little time, and it worried her that anyone could look out the back of the house and spot them sitting there on the grass. Still, she surprised herself with her own daring, suggesting a more private tête-à-tête. "My aunt and uncle are away." She glanced first toward Lewis to gauge his reaction, then at the darkened side of her own house. People slept with the windows open on summer nights. She'd die if her mother heard her talking and came out to investigate. Or if Trevor came home and caught them.

"Okay." He stood and slung the jacket over his shoulder, then stooped to pick up the milk and the bag of fruit. He took her hand and pulled her up beside him. They left the plate in the grass. "Lead the way, princess."

Princess Phoebe. That was a good one.

LEWIS MUNCHED on the apple. Phoebe could hear the strong crunch of his teeth every time he took a bite, although she could barely make him out in the near pitch-dark.

It had to be close to midnight. They were still in Uncle Joe's hammock, behind his house. They'd sat on it for a while, swinging their feet. Then—she wasn't quite sure what had brought on the change— they'd swung their feet up and lay down side by side. Other than sliding his arm around her, so that she could rest her head on it, and occasionally hugging her, he hadn't tried anything funny. Not that Phoebe was worried; she was quite confident she could take care of herself if the need arose.

But his quiet, just-friends behavior surprised Phoebe, considering their hot kisses that afternoon. Maybe she ought to give Lewis more credit than she had so far. Maybe he wasn't just out to get whatever he could, whether from a girl or from the system he seemed to despise so much.

"Tell me about your mother," she said. "Don't you worry about her living out there alone?"

Lewis thought about the question for a few minutes. Then he sighed. "I do. It's just that...I don't have much in common with them. Billy's more like an aunt or something than a sister. She's sixteen years older than me and she never talks, never says boo. You know what she's like. Ma? Well, she's kind of weird...."

His voice trailed off. Phoebe realized he was being excruciatingly honest with her. He was right; his sister and his mother were pretty weird. Still, they were his family, he must feel something for them. "Did you send them money? Before...you know?" Phoebe knew that neither woman had an outside job.

"Before I went to jail? Yeah." Lewis seemed a little agitated. He swung the hammock vigorously with a foot he had extended to the ground. It was fairly cold now, and Phoebe felt clammy from the dew settling in the air. She was glad she was snuggled up beside Lewis. His body was warm, even hot, and he didn't seem disturbed by the damp. "I gave them money when I was working. Even that rustling business..." He laughed, a short humorless sound. "That was to try and get a decent stake for them. I sold a couple of the steers we stole and made some serious money. I knew it couldn't last..."

"It was stealing, Lewis," Phoebe said. "It's wrong."

"You can say that. You've never been hungry," he responded bitterly. "You don't know what it's like to have do-gooders coming out to visit, figuring if they leave off a bag of grub they've got a right to take up your time. Like they own you. Or the religious busybodies…"

Phoebe raised her head to look fully at him. "I hope—"

"No," he broke in. "Not you or your folks. Your ma's a pretty nice lady. I know Ma and Billy think the world of her."

Phoebe lay back down, mollified. He had a point. What about the other side of it? It was one thing to help people out, but what was it like to be always having to accept help?

"How about your dad? You ever hear from him?" Phoebe had never heard anything about a man in the Hardin family, other than Lewis.

"Could be dead for all I know." Lewis shrugged. "Some drifter, probably. I have no idea who my father is. Do you believe me?"

Phoebe was stunned. "Oh, Lewis…" She turned to him, into his shoulder, and her eyes sought his in the semidark. It had grown lighter now that the cloud was moving off the moon.

"You don't need to feel sorry for me, Phoebe. All I know is, every once in a while, back when I was

growing up, Ma or Billy would find an envelope
stuffed with cash in the mailbox. Used to be just like
Christmas.'' She heard his smile. ''I'd get new
clothes, Billy would order a bunch of seeds from the
seed catalog, Ma would buy a new coat, if she
needed one. Or a pair of boots. I never knew where
the money came from, but I used to pretend it was
my father, looking after us, you know? Maybe it was.
But maybe it was just some do-gooder. It was always
cash. No return address.''

Phoebe nodded.

Lewis laughed that bitter laugh she was beginning
to recognize and dread. ''I figure the bastard must be
dead. Hasn't left us any money for quite a few years
now. *If* it was him in the first place.''

Phoebe didn't know what to say. She couldn't
imagine life without her parents. They were both so
understanding, so supportive. A father, especially.
How could Lewis have managed with no father in
his life? A lot of people thought Harry Longquist was
gruff and grumpy since his accident, but Phoebe
knew better. He was an old softie inside. It sounded
like Lewis had brought himself up, really. She remembered that spare room fashioned out of a box
stall, the first time she'd ever seen him. He'd been
trying to build up his muscles, working out with that
makeshift punching bag. She could still see the sin-
ews in his skinny back, hear the shout of frustration
when he gave it up.

Phoebe reached up and put her hand on Lewis's chest. She touched his throat, bare and warm in the cold night air. "I'd better go, Lewis. I—I'm glad you talked to me. I really hope things work out for you—"

"You mean that, don't you, Phoebe?" His voice was raw.

She nodded. "I do."

"Kiss me, Phoebe. Kiss me one more time before I leave. I'm going to start walking toward town. Someone will pick me up—I'm not worried about that. And tomorrow, I'm going to turn myself in to the cops. Finish my sentence."

"No more sneaking out in laundry trucks?" she asked, running her fingertips along the line of his throat, where his T-shirt met his neck. She felt him shiver.

"Nope. I'm gonna do my time, put it behind me. Start looking after Ma and Billy again. They need me. They got nobody else. And, Phoebe, I want you to…" He paused and turned to her, fingering one of her braids. "Ah, hell, never mind. Just kiss me!"

Phoebe kissed him. She was hoping he'd ask. She wanted to lose herself in the luxury of his arms, his warmth, the skill of his kiss. Lewis was no rank beginner at the art of love, as she was.

He pressed her close against him and she could feel the bulge of his erection in his jeans. He made no attempt to conceal it. Her pulse shot into overdrive, but she knew they had to stop. This...this wasn't right. She pushed back, gently.

"What...what were you going to say?" she managed, wiping her mouth with the back of her hand. Her breath was out of control, her breasts were swollen and aching.

"What about?" he murmured, kissing her neck and throat.

"When you said...something you wanted me to do..." She lay back in the hammock, every nerve in her body singing, every muscle mad with need.

"I wanted to say..." He kissed her deeply, reverently, then raised his head and stared down into her eyes. Phoebe could see him clearly, since the moon had emerged from behind the clouds. "I wanted to say that I wish you'd wait for me. But I know that's crazy." His voice was deep, every word he said so...so tender! Just like in the movies. "You've got your own life to live. There's no future for the two of us. You and me. We're...we're just...I don't know—accidental friends, I guess. If you'd never come out to the farm with your mother..." He shrugged.

"You gave me a frog," she told him softly.

"I did?" He sounded amazed.

"Yes. Remember that first time, when I was up in the hayloft at your place? You threw a wooden frog up to me."

He grinned. "That's it, kid. I'm the frog and you're the princess. Like I said, no future."

He sat up and swung his legs over the side of the hammock. Then he climbed out and helped her down. Phoebe felt cold now that she was separated from him. She was still wearing shorts, although she'd put on a long-sleeved shirt before she'd left.

He shrugged on Ben's windbreaker and picked up the paper sack with the fruit in it. They walked toward her house, hand in hand. Phoebe noticed that her father's truck was parked outside the garage. Which meant Trevor was home. She hadn't heard him drive up.

"You're a good influence on me already, Phoebe. You know that?" He stopped and pulled her into his arms and brought her hips close against his. Phoebe was glad of the darkness, because she knew she was blushing.

"Oh? In what way?"

"If I wasn't trying to turn over a new leaf, I'd be tempted to hotwire that truck over there and drive it to town. Maybe get another six months tacked onto my sentence."

Phoebe was shocked. How naive was she? Of course. Lewis Hardin had been on his own, looking after himself all his life. These were the kinds of things he did.

"As it is, I'll just walk out to the main road like a decent, law-abiding citizen and hitch a ride."

Phoebe laughed. "You're sure you'll be all right?" She wondered if she should offer to give him a lift. But if she started the truck, someone would be sure to come out and see what all the activity was about.

Lewis drew her close and kissed her again, one last, lingering kiss. Then he grinned at her. "I'll be fine—now." Phoebe thought she'd weep at the sweetness of his farewell. *It was so romantic....*

Then he stepped away from her and started walking down the dirt road that led to the farm. It was only half a mile or so to the paved secondary highway. He turned once and raised his hand in farewell.

Her highwayman was leaving her.

Phoebe felt her lower lip tremble, then realized her face was wet with tears. She raised her hand in return. "Goodbye," she murmured, catching back the "godspeed" that had trembled on her lips. She realized she'd read too many novels. "Don't worry, I—I'll wait for you, Lewis Hardin. *Forever.* I promise."

FOREVER WAS a very long time.

That summer Phoebe started dating one of the boys who'd graduated the year before but returned to Glory to work for the summer in the town office. His kisses weren't anything like Lewis's, but on the other hand, he was ambitious and smart, and everyone said he was bound to go far.

Go far. That was what Phoebe wanted.

She worked hard in her senior year and graduated at the top of her class. Her parents were ecstatic. Two scholars in the family! Ben, her brother, hadn't achieved marks as spectacular as hers, but he was doing well at his course in university, working part-time during the school year and saving every penny he made in the summers to put himself through.

Phoebe got a scholarship from Cross-Canada Pipelines—their big scholarship, which they awarded to only one student in each Western province. She wouldn't have to worry about money. All she'd have to do was keep up her average…and the future was hers.

In Glory, her path only crossed Lewis Hardin's again once. After grade twelve, she gave in to curiosity about Lewis, and what he was like now, and bid on him at a bachelor auction in town. He was out of jail by then and working at a ranch west of Glory. She didn't know what had possessed her to do such a crazy thing.

Phoebe shuddered when she remembered the disastrous evening she'd spent with him. Any silly romantic dreams she might have had about Lewis Hardin had died a swift death. How could she have been so wrong about anyone?

She never heard from him again while she lived at home. Then, in her first year of university, she got a letter forwarded by her mother, with a note attached expressing her amazement that Phoebe was corresponding with "that Hardin boy." Phoebe had never talked about her feelings, had only confided a few girlish yearnings to her brother Ben. She knew now that what she'd felt for Lewis was nothing more than a crush. The note told her, with many misspellings and scratched-out phrases, that Lewis had given up ranching and taken a job on a wildcat rig up north. Somewhere up by Fort Chipewyan.

A long way from Glory. A long way from the University of Alberta in Edmonton, where she'd begun her science degree, specializing in organic chemistry. Phoebe had reread the letter, alarmed that her first sense of relief had given way to something else. An ache. A yearning. A wondering—what was he like now? Had he ever changed…for the better?

She'd never know. And she had too much to think about these days to wonder for long about the life and prospects of Lewis Hardin, ex-convict. Lewis— along with the wooden frog, which she'd left at Swallowbank Farm at the very back of the closet in her room, taken over now by Jilly—was part of the past, of her childhood.

Phoebe was twenty now. And she had serious prospects of her own.

CHAPTER THREE

Three years later, the present…

LEWIS WIPED his face. Or attempted to wipe his face.
His sleeve was as muddy as the rest of him. The roar
of machinery and the dull sound of the diamond bit
far below the earth's surface, coupled with the shouts
and curses of tired, overworked men, filled the early-
morning air. There was no time to appreciate the full
richness of midsummer, the cries of the black-capped
chickadees with their nesting songs from the willows.
Or to notice the sharp scent of the poplar trees, white
and black, gorged and green with summer sap.

All Lewis smelled was drilling mud, male sweat
and the sudden stench of fear in the hot summer sunshine.

Men were shouting. They'd lost pipe! Discon-
nected steel shafts and rogue chains whipping across
the base of the drilling tower could be lethal. Slip-
pery drill mud made for treacherous footing, even in
steel-toed, caulk-soled Grizzlies. Last night's rain
hadn't helped.

But the crew was seasoned. Lewis knew they
could handle anything that came up on the site, in-

cluding this kind of setback, which had happened just as they approached their target depth.

Drilling for oil and gas was a twenty-four-hour-a-day business with big money at stake. The Calgary syndicate that had put together the cash for this venture expected returns, and they expected them fast. Anything Lewis's crew wanted, they got. Whether it was racy movies or porterhouse steak served twice a day. Lewis's employer, F&B Drilling, drew the line at bringing in women, but everything else was possible. Nothing mattered except getting the job done.

The job? To get in and get out as soon as possible with the kind of drill samples that could send a syndicate's shares soaring on the exchange or crashing through the basement. If the news wasn't good, it wasn't unusual for the principals or the good friends and wives of the principals to bail out before the news spread. It was illegal, of course—insider trading, or the nearest thing to it—but that couldn't always be proved. Nothing grabbed an oilman's blood like the fever for black gold.

A tight hole meant approved personnel only on the site. Other companies, competitors, were not above sending in spies. A tight hole meant a security check on each and every pickup that drove in. Every delivery. Every visitor. The big sign out front at the secondary road, where the raw, freshly bulldozed and graveled rig road led to the site, meant exactly what it said: *Tight hole. No admittance. That means YOU.*

Tight holes and the security that went with them were Lewis Hardin's particular specialty. No one got into a site, drilled and got out faster than Lewis Hardin's crews. He'd begun as a roughneck on the drilling platform, the roughest, meanest, dirtiest job in the business. He'd moved his way up to tool-push, the captain of the project. His rise had been spectacular, and he had men on his crew—men who respected him—who were nearly twice his age. The partners who owned F&B were urging him to join them as a full partner, sweat-equity. Other companies had been courting him, too, incessantly, annoying him more than anything.

But Lewis wasn't sure that partnership—or switching to another drilling outfit—was a move he wanted to make.

He was twenty-seven and getting restless. He'd never stayed at one job as long as he had this time with F&B, which was the hottest medium-size drilling company in the province. He sure wasn't going back to ranching—not until he had the stake to set up his own place—but he was getting tired of the oilfield. Two, sometimes three weeks on the job, twenty-four hours on call, then a week or two off, if you had an assistant push. If not, you stayed until the job was done. It was a cowboy, Dodge City kind of life: work your guts out, then spend your paycheck in town and start all over again, broke. For most single guys, the money made it all worthwhile.

But after a while, even the toys began to pall—the brand-new four-wheel-drive vehicles, the snowmobiles in winter, the prize shotguns and the best dogs in duck season, the dirt bikes and ATVs in summer. Lewis used to enjoy it, but the last few times he'd taken time off, he'd driven five straight hours to do some fishing by himself down in Glory country, back where he'd been born and brought up. He spent a few days helping Billy and Ma, fixed a squeaky door, spaded a new garden patch, tacked down some roof shingles. Keeping up the fence alone was a mammoth task, and he'd almost decided not to bother. What was the point? The Hardins had no animals but the few sheep they kept in the derelict orchard. A dozen or so scrawny chickens in the henhouse. There was no haying or farming going on. Never had been, in Lewis's memory. But the two women who'd raised him, his mother and his sister, wouldn't hear of giving up the homestead. Last time he'd been home he'd convinced them to lease some of their grown-over pasture to a neighbor. At least that meant a little money coming in monthly, besides what Lewis sent them.

How did they live? Lewis really had no idea. Of course, they had no mortgage. No debts.

No expectations. No hope.

They kept a garden and had a few eggs from their chickens. The only cash they needed was to pay their electric bill each month and their taxes once a year.

Mercy sold the quilts she made, several a winter, to a craft store in town. Billy sold garden produce at a roadside stand, but mostly, she just gave it away. They bought tea and flour and sugar. Dog food. Feed for the sheep. Ma and Billy both wore secondhand clothes, and their Ford pickup was ancient. It shouldn't have been running at all, but somehow Ma kept the old wreck going with a little haywire and a lot of luck.

Glory.

The town was like a great big bad dream. He'd thought he'd left the place behind him for good when he'd quit Adam Garrick's place that first terrible summer after he'd gotten out of jail. But maybe he hadn't. Something always seemed to pull him back like an invisible line, especially lately. A thin, taut line, a strand of twisted steel that never let him go. A yoke. The farm itself, he supposed, was one thing. It had been in Ma's family forever. The Rockies, the foothills? Maybe. He loved the wide-open country. It was a place where you could breathe. *Something* pulled him back.

Phoebe Longquist? Ha. He'd never forgotten her, but she wasn't much more than a fuzzy memory now, just a kid dressed in shorts and a home-knit sweater. Some hot kisses. A few quick gropes in her uncle's hay field. The kind of heart-to-heart midnight talk that had embarrassed him the next day, in the hard light of noon. *Girl talk.*

He'd had half a dozen girlfriends—maybe a dozen—in the years since he'd last seen Phoebe, the late-summer night she'd come out of nowhere to spend her hard-earned money on him in a charity auction. What a disaster that had been. He hoped the experience had cured her of any romantic notions, if she'd needed curing. She didn't need a guy like him in her life, and he was pretty sure she'd got the message that night.

He'd balked at joining the other cowboys in the auction right from the start. Publicity of any kind was the last thing he wanted, either to remind the town of him and his prison record or of his long-suffering crazy family living out there on Bearberry Hill. Adam Garrick, who'd hired him when he got out of jail, had told him the auction was for a good cause. Not that a good cause normally would have pulled any weight with Lewis, but he owed Adam and this was as good a way as any of repaying him. Adam had taken him on at the Double O, albeit reluctantly, when few other ranchers would even look at him. A cowboy who'd gone to jail for stealing his boss's steers had few prospects of employment in ranch country, no matter how shorthanded an outfit might be. Country people had long memories.

YES, GLORY WAS on his mind, but damned if he was going back there this time. It was a good three-hour drive to Edmonton, with an eye out for radar traps, and he intended to spend the first couple of days in the province's capital city. He kept a studio in an apartment-hotel, right downtown on Ninety-Eighth Avenue. Bed, table, stove, fridge. He never cooked, but the fridge was handy for beer and leftover pizza. He wasn't sure why he rented the apartment, since it was expensive for the use he got out of it—maybe a week a month, if that. But Lewis liked having his own place, no matter how barren and impersonal. Ma's run-down homestead, a cell in the lockup at Fort Saskatchewan, cowboy bunkhouses, mattresses on the floor at various friends' places in town—most of his life had been spent under someone else's roof.

One day Lewis intended to change all that. The apartment was a start.

This weekend was the big event that Bethany had been waiting for. He'd known Bethany Cook for six months. They'd been lovers for four, although Lewis was aware that the relationship was cooling off. Bethany, he knew, saw other guys when he was out of town. Which was okay by him. When you were contemplating a split, it was always easier when the other person had been no saint, either.

He'd offered to help Bethany with her deliveries and setups this afternoon for the big riverboat event. She ran a small florist shop on Whyte Avenue— Bethany's Blooms—and this reception on the *Alberta Queen* for the new dean of science at the University of Alberta was a huge coup for her, one she hoped would lead to more university business.

Miles of lonely muskeg and thickets of black spruce swept by on either side of the highway. It was a grim landscape, but Lewis barely noticed. He was used to it. Once in a while he'd catch sight of a coyote skittering off into the ditch. Or a deer or moose. Sometimes he'd see a black bear browsing in the lush grass beside the road; it wouldn't even look up as he drove by. He'd driven this road a thousand times, it seemed, in the past few years.

As he got closer to Edmonton, the scruffy forests gave way to cleared land, first bare-knuckle little farms and ranches, scraped out of the muskeg and trees, then more verdant hay and grainfields, fenced pastures with cows. There was no cattle ranching here on the scale of southern Alberta, but the district grew plenty of grain and hay to supply the ranchers and feedlot managers. Wheat, too. Some of the fields showed tall stands of winter wheat, almost ready for harvest. Lewis noted the mallards and pintails that had already raised their families in the weedy shallow sloughs that lay in the hollows of the hills; they were still hanging around, resting up, building reserves for the long flight south.

Summer made him restless. The truth was, every change of season had that effect on him. Closer to the provincial capital was plentiful evidence of Alberta's new emphasis on agribusiness. Telltale clutches of feed silos marked the windowless, vented barns of broiler and hog operations nearby.

Poor trapped creatures, Lewis thought. Never even glimpsed that high blue sky. Just scrapping for their share of chop, chewing on each others' tails and ears out of boredom, then the short one-way ride to the slaughterhouse.

Nothing like old Molly Baskins, the black-and-white Berkshire sow he remembered Ma keeping when he was a child. Old Molly Baskins had just lain down in the orchard one day with a great sigh and never got up again. They'd had to dig a hole right there and roll her in and cover her up, Ma bawling her head off the whole time. That sow had had the best possible life a pig could have. Table scraps, rotten apples, oats and barley chop, pleasant afternoons spent rooting through the orchard for succulent roots and smelly old fungi. An ancient collie for a pal in her last years. A mud puddle to lie in on a hot day in August.

Lewis grinned. Quite the life, all right! Then he frowned—why the hell had they called her Molly *Baskins?* Probably one of Billy's crazy ideas. Who ever heard of a pig with a last name?

Finally Edmonton loomed on the skyline—a spread-out prairie city located on the wide winding valley of the North Saskatchewan river.

Was this home? It didn't feel like it. Somehow

he'd never felt really comfortable living anywhere he couldn't see the Rocky Mountains.

BETHANY AND HER PART-TIME helper had really outdone themselves. By the time Lewis got there, ready to help load and deliver the flowers, the floor of the small shop was crowded with arrangements and loose, freshly cut flowers in buckets, ready to go to the riverboat where the reception was being held. The *Alberta Queen* was a recently launched tribute to the old-time riverboats that had once plied the North Saskatchewan from York Factory to Edmonton, delivering freight and passengers. This modern riverboat delivered Dixieland jazz and passengers up and down the river on scenic cruises, for a price.

"Oh, Lew!" Bethany flew into his arms and kissed him. "Thank goodness you're here. I just said to Reg—" Reg was her assistant "—that it'd be just like you to get here two minutes before the reception—"

"I told you I'd be here," Lewis said firmly, with a smile at the overwrought Bethany and a nod to Reg. "And here I am. Ready to help."

Bethany kissed him again in a frenzy of new energy, and Lewis grimaced as he stepped back and removed his jacket. Bethany Cook in this mood was, well, hard to take. She was a fine woman, but her constant and varied enthusiasms wore him out. He liked a little more quiet in his social life, a little less excitement. Reg, nineteen and a floral-arts student at the local community college, fed Bethany's flames with his constant reminders of potential disaster. His *what if*s and his *did you remember to*…s drove Lewis nuts. They were quite a pair.

Lewis loaded the van without saying anything else. He took the map Bethany had drawn and studied it for a moment or two before getting into the driver's seat. Then he dropped it on the passenger seat beside him; he knew where the riverboat dock was.

The reception, Bethany had told him, was scheduled for four o'clock. Apparently the high-up civic muck-a-mucks and the university crowd were going to munch and nibble during a river cruise. Speeches, probably. Smoked salmon. White wine. He could imagine the type of thing. B-O-R-I-N-G.

It was two o'clock now. Plenty of time for Bethany to get set up. She and Reg were coming behind him, in her little car, with some of the other arrangements. He, Lewis, had instructions to unload the flowers. Period. Bethany and Reg would do the arranging.

Which was fine by him. Flower arranging wasn't one of his specialties.

He had the flowers unloaded by half-past two. Where was Bethany? He waited for her in the van, watching as a few early birds pulled into the riverboat parking lot and got out for the short walk through the trees to the actual dock. The nervous types, worried they'd be late. He watched them go, women in fluffy jackets, short skirts and pearls, men in navy blazers and gray flannel pants. All laughing. All merry. All looking forward to a pleasant outing on the river.

Lewis idly wondered what could shake up their worlds. Losing a job? A call from Revenue Canada? A botched dry-cleaning job? A daughter caught stealing lipstick at the local drugstore?

"Lew!" Bethany jumped out of the small red car that had just pulled up beside him. "Omigosh! We're late. We couldn't find the new carton of floral clay I'd ordered and—can you hang around and help us, Lew? I really need your help!"

How could he say no? So Lewis got out of the van, locked it and helped Reg and Bethany cart the special arrangements down to the boat. These were small arrangements that she apparently wanted on each table. The loose flowers were to be arranged in large vases on the decks and under the canvas awnings.

Lewis wasn't happy. This was typical Bethany Cook. Bad planning. Lousy logistics. It was the kind of thing that bugged him because organization was so critical to his own job. What if he forgot to order some crucial element on a two-week drilling job? Say, dynamite. Or grease guns. Or extra chewing tobacco in case the men ran short. He'd be out of a job so fast he'd have a headache.

But he knew Bethany—somehow she'd muddle through and it would all come off just fine in the end. He had to admit he admired her grit and persistence.

"That's it?" They were finally done. A few more couples had arrived and were standing around in small knots, talking and laughing. Lewis knew Bethany was a little embarrassed because she'd intended to have all the floral arrangements in place before the guests showed up.

"I think so. I need to talk to the steward for a minute..." Bethany and Reg moved off, and Lewis stepped behind a large fake potted palm that was part of the boat's everyday decor.

His heart stopped. That woman—that woman in the black dress. The one with legs that went on forever and russet hair that brushed her shoulder blades on her very bare back. Her very bare *freckled* back. Lewis had only caught her profile for a flash before she'd turned away from him.

He watched her accept a glass of something that a tall, weedy blond type had plucked off a tray and handed to her with a smile. The guy wore glasses, the old-fashioned horn-rim kind, but they were probably cutting-edge fashion now—with a certain type of man.

Lewis's heart started to beat again. Nah, couldn't be....

But hadn't he heard that she'd won some big science scholarship? That she was studying pond scum or fish or bugs or some damn thing at the university? Who could have mentioned it to him—Ma? Billy? He knew that his mother and sister thought highly of the entire Longquist family.

She turned again, this time straight toward him. Lewis's heart lodged in his throat. Yep. Same nose, same eyes...same freckles everywhere. It was Phoebe Longquist.

Had she seen him? He hoped not, but then he noticed that her hand had tightened on her drink and her companion had turned in Lewis's direction, too, as if aware that his date's attention was suddenly elsewhere.

"Lew!" Bethany rushed up to him. Thank the Lord for small mercies.

"What is it, Beth?" Lewis couldn't keep the irritation out of his voice. It was one crisis after another with this woman.

"You've got to go back to the shop—here, take the key!" She thrust a key on a chain attached to a wooden daisy at him. "I forgot the most important arrangement, the one for the buffet table."

"What about Reg?" All Lewis wanted was to go back to his apartment and turn on a baseball game.

He was tired of the florist business. Tired of everything.

He didn't dare look toward Phoebe Longquist. His brain was still churning, trying to think of what he'd say if she approached him. If he couldn't avoid her entirely.

"Reg can't drive and I've got to finish up here. Pleeease!" Bethany had tears in her pretty blue eyes.

"Hey, of course I will," Lewis said soothingly, taking the key chain and feeling a little foolish for even thinking he'd rather be watching a baseball game. He'd intended to help her all along. Trust Bethany to hire an assistant who couldn't drive.

"I'll be right here, Lew." She glanced at her watch. "You're going to have to hurry. The boat's due to leave in less than half an hour. We've got to be finished and out of here by ten to—"

"Don't worry." Lewis impulsively dropped a kiss on her nose. She smiled and looked slightly relieved. Lewis desperately wanted to see if Phoebe had noticed. Why had he done that—kissed Bethany? Except to hope that Phoebe noticed.

All the way back to Whyte Avenue, Lewis cursed himself for a fool. Phoebe Longquist was long out of his life. And he was long out of hers. But he could still see her tender smile, her shining eyes the night she'd raided her mom's kitchen for him and they'd talked until past midnight on her uncle's hammock in the backyard. He'd felt her genuine goodness warming him through and through. He'd believed that she really, truly cared for him—a stranger—the way no one had ever cared for him before. Not Ma—who'd always been old and preoccupied, as long as Lewis could remember. Not Billy—who kept to herself and was so much older than he was. She was kind, but he sometimes felt he barely knew her. She never talked to anyone if she could help it, anyone except Ma.

Lewis had a hard time getting the key in the front door of Bethany's Blooms. And then when he did, it wouldn't turn. Cursing, he tried the old Yale lock on the back door. It fit—just. Naturally Bethany hadn't mentioned which door the key was supposed to open. Once in the small shop, he looked wildly around for what might be the missing arrangement. There were all kinds of small stock arrangements in the front of her store. Potted baskets. Violets with ribbons. The sort of thing people took to hospital patients.

The cooler.

That made sense. There was a huge, spread-out arrangement of fall flowers in the cooler. That had to be it. And if it wasn't—tough.

Lewis loaded the arrangement into the van, taking care not to bruise or break any of the stems. He checked his watch. Still fifteen minutes before the boat sailed.

He made the trip back to the dock in record time and leapt out of the van. It was difficult carrying the awkward arrangement with any speed along the footpath, but somehow he managed, sweating and cursing the entire way. It would be a long time before Bethany Cook roped him into something like this again.

So where was she? Lewis hadn't thought to look for Bethany's car in the parking lot and now, aboard the *Alberta Queen,* she was nowhere in sight. Nor was Reg.

Lewis slammed the floral arrangement down on the buffet table in the space that had obviously been left for it, ignoring the scowl of the steward. Or whoever the dandy was, outfitted in a penguin suit and visor cap and looking as if he was in charge. Lewis ripped off the cellophane covering the flowers and thrust it at him.

"Any sign of the flower lady?" he asked, noting that the steward had speedily handed off the plastic wrap to a surprised underling, who stuffed it in the nearby trash container without comment. There was obviously a chain of command here.

"*Flower* lady?" The steward gave him an icy stare.

"Oh, never mind." Lewis stalked off. He headed toward the open foredeck, screened from the afternoon sunshine by a big blue-and-white canvas awning. He scanned the deck. Lots of guests, chatting and sipping their wine, but no sign of Bethany or Reg.

Lewis wheeled, intending to leave the boat and give Bethany a piece of his mind as soon as he located her. He stopped.

Phoebe Longquist was standing right in front of him, with the worried-looking blond man at her side.

"Lewis…"

Lewis took a step back. "Hey," he said, taking a deep breath and nodding. "Phoebe."

"I…I *thought* I saw you earlier, bringing in the flowers…" Her eyebrows rose delicately over green-blue eyes. The color of a mountain lake at sunset. God, she was beautiful!

"Yeah, that was me, all right," he admitted. "Helping a friend." He looked around and frowned, saw the light in Phoebe's eyes dim slightly. Man, he could be an unsociable jerk sometimes. Where were his manners? "So, uh, how are you?"

"Fine. And you?"

"Great. I see you've still got your freckles."

Her eyes flashed dangerously. "And I see you've still got your bad attitude. Lewis, this is a friend of mine. Boyd Paterson. Boyd—Lewis Hardin."

Against his will, Lewis found himself shaking hands with the weedy academic type.

"*Professor* Paterson," corrected the blond man, nodding vigorously. "Ha-ha. Just recently appointed to the department." He turned to Phoebe. "Old friend of yours?"

"You could say so," Phoebe murmured. Lewis

saw that she was ruminating over the word *friend*. "We're from the same district in southern Alberta."

Yeah, well. Lewis glanced toward the open deck. He wanted out of here. Fast.

"Are you in the sciences, too, Mr. Hardin?" the professor asked, the sun glinting off his lenses as he inspected Lewis's casual attire. He'd obviously missed Phoebe's comment about the flower delivery earlier. "Freshwater algae, perhaps, like our Phoebe here?" He laughed. A rather stupid laugh, Lewis decided. *Our Phoebe*. What did she see in a goof like that?

"No, I'm in oil," he said abruptly. "Oil and water don't mix, as you know." The date hooted with laughter.

Just then Lewis realized that the sound of the boat's big diesels had changed. The boat was moving. Damn it! He looked around.

"Lose something?" Phoebe muttered, adding just for him. "Something with, er, long black hair in designer jeans?"

Lewis cast her a sharp glance. She'd noticed that he and Bethany were together. "You could say that," he replied smoothly. "How long is this cruise supposed to go on, anyway?"

"Four hours," she said, tipping up her glass to finish the champagne, then handing it to the professor with a charming smile. He moved off with the empty glass. She knew damn well Lewis hadn't planned to sail with the boat. "The dean is over there." She pointed to a middle-aged man in the middle of the deck, looking very flushed. This was his big day.

"They docking anywhere else?" He could hope.

"Not as far as I know," she replied, still smiling. She seemed delighted to see him in this predicament.

Lewis stepped over to the side of the boat. He hadn't made it as far as he had in a tough business by letting petty details stop him. They were only seventy yards or so from the dock, upstream. It was doable. And the south bank of the river was even closer.

"Lewis!"

He grinned. He'd shocked her, after all, right out of her creamy smooth, Phoebe Longquist, algae-specialist self by stripping off his T-shirt and tossing it to her. She caught it by reflex. He kicked off his sneakers. He'd buy a new pair.

"Sorry, Phoebe, *Professor* Paterson," he said, stepping up to the railing. The professor had returned with two full glasses and was regarding the crumpled white material in Phoebe's hands with an expression of horror that might ordinarily be reserved for, say, a rattlesnake. "Sorry, folks, can't stay. I've got other plans."

And with that he dived smoothly into the North Saskatchewan River. When he surfaced, he laughed and waved at the boat. Dozens of screaming spectators leaned over the side and the boat's steam whistle shrilled. He saw Phoebe in the background, waving back. He'd swear she was giggling.

Lewis sputtered. It was tough to swim and laugh at the same time. Then, with steady, powerful strokes, he set off for shore.

As he'd told her, he had other plans.

CHAPTER FOUR

WHEN LEWIS GOT BACK, Bethany and Reg were kissing and cuddling in the tiny crowded office of Bethany's Blooms.

He was astonished. "I thought Reg was gay."

"What!?" With her hands on hips, disheveled as hell, Lewis had to admit Bethany looked as if they'd been having a good time. Her face was flushed and her eyes were soft. Funny, it didn't hurt at all. In fact, Lewis wanted to laugh. Loverboy was hiding in the office—the coward—with the door closed, while Bethany confronted Lewis in the shop.

"Yeah. I thought—"

"You thought he was gay? Just because he works in a florist shop? Just because he loves flowers the same way I do? Just because he's a fine, sensitive, artistic young man? Lewis Hardin! You should be ashamed of yourself. You're just one cliché after another."

"*I* am?" Now Lewis *was* hurt. "He's six years younger than you. He can't even drive!"

"So what? He has many other fine qualities. And, yes, you are one testosterone-loaded, macho-oilfield cliché after another, with your…your big muscles and your smelly boots!'' With that final salvo and one long manicured finger indicating the door, Bethany asked him to kindly leave her establishment, which Lewis did, shaking his head. *Smelly boots?*

It was true. He'd found some steel-toed boots in his Jeep and had put them on when he got back to where he'd left his vehicle, in the alley behind her shop. He'd also found an old shirt to wear. His jeans were soaking wet. Bethany hadn't asked how they'd gotten that way. Hadn't she even noticed? Just before he climbed into the Jeep to leave, Bethany ran out and hugged him and thanked him for all his help with the riverboat. The flip-flop was pure Bethany. She was a good kid, underneath all her craziness.

''Where were you, anyway?'' he asked when he got his breath back. ''Why'd you leave the riverboat?''

''We were worried you weren't going to make it in time so we…we thought we'd hurry back to the shop and see what was happening.'' Bethany looked doubtfully at him. ''I had to drive.'' He figured she knew very well that she was making no sense. He handed her the keys to her van.

Whew! Some females. Lewis got into his own vehicle and left. He felt better than he had in a long, long time. *His big muscles and his smelly boots?*

Bethany and little Reg. Well, hot damn. Who'd a thought…

PHOEBE STUFFED Lewis's T-shirt in her bag and asked the boat's steward for a plastic bag so she could take his sneakers, size twelve, home with her, too. She'd return them to Mercedes and Billy Hardin next time she was in Glory. They could make sure Lewis got them back. No point wasting perfectly good clothing.

Boyd quizzed her about Lewis as he drove her home, but Phoebe's mind wandered, and she realized she wasn't paying as much attention to him as she usually did. Generally she enjoyed the young professor's conversation and his company. He'd been the one to insist she go to the reception today, telling her it couldn't hurt to be seen at a few department events. It was sincere and well-meant advice. But somehow today, since she'd seen Lewis peel off his shirt and take that flying leap into the icy North Saskatchewan River, Boyd seemed…well, pale. Thin and pale and not nearly as interesting as she'd found him in the past.

When he kissed her at the elevators that led to the third-floor apartment that Phoebe shared with another graduate student, she didn't invite him up. Men were allowed on the women's floor between 8:00 a.m. and 10:00 p.m. Phoebe and Lindy Sokoloski were "floor mothers" in the undergraduate girls' residence, Hanratty Hall. It was a job, extra income that paid for her accommodation, which meant she could use all her scholarship money for school and books. Well, most of it. She looked down guiltily at the little black dress she was wearing. It had been on sale, she reminded herself, or she'd never have spent the money.

And now that she'd graduated at the top of the dean's list and been accepted into a very limited postgraduate program, she had a certain amount of socializing to do, even within the department, as Boyd had reminded her. She needed clothes, besides the jeans and T-shirts she wore to classes and in the field. She had a career to develop. There was politics in the sciences, just as there were in the arts. Maybe more, with everyone jockeying for publishing credits and grant money. Boyd Paterson's specialty was studying the sediments at the bottoms of lakes. It was a subspecialty of geology. Pond science, she called it privately.

Algae was her particular passion. Chemistry and plant science. She was excited about the work she'd be doing this year with algae. New breakthroughs in DNA technology had opened up possibilities for the simple-celled organism to supply all kinds of useful products—starches for the food industry, waxes for cosmetics, enzymes that might prove useful in medicine, even oillike substances that might help replace fossil fuels someday.

''Lindy?'' No answer. The apartment had an empty feel, and Phoebe was a relieved. There were disadvantages to sharing such a small space; lack of privacy was one.

She went into the small alcove that served as her bedroom—Lindy had one on the other side of the tiny living room—and folded Lewis's T-shirt carefully, pausing to stroke the soft, overwashed texture of the cotton knit. How would she have explained pulling *this* out of her purse if her roommate had been home? Plus a pair of men's sneakers? Lindy might not have asked. She was pretty easygoing, one of her qualities Phoebe admired most. Lindy was practical; she'd just assume Phoebe had a good explanation for bringing home a pair of men's size-twelve sneakers and a T-shirt. Otherwise, or so Lindy would reason, why would she have them?

Phoebe buried her nose in the soft folds of the T-shirt and breathed deeply. A faint musky scent lingered in the fabric. *Lewis.* That summer so long past came rushing back—the scent of the crushed grass, the taste of Lewis's kisses, the warm strong feel of his arms around her. *His laughter.*

She sat down on her narrow bed and gave herself up to the flood of memories.

The way he'd looked at her back then, the way no man or boy had ever looked at her before or since. As though this magical thing between them, this thing that had just *happened,* would go on forever and ever. She'd been half in love, no question. Her girlish, sensitive heart had been terrifically impressed with him. He was the romantic hero of all the novels she'd read in her quiet bookish childhood.

And, then—that horrible evening after her high-school graduation when she'd impulsively bought him at the charity auction. He'd insisted on replacing the money she'd spent, over her protests. She didn't understand the fine cold anger on his handsome face. He acted like a stranger. Didn't he want her to "buy" him? Did he think she was chasing him? Didn't he want to see her again?

Apparently not. The rest of the evening had been a nightmare. They'd spent a very uncomfortable hour or two—at least for her—in the tavern of the Glory Hotel with the friends Lewis had met. Losers and drunken cowboys, every one of them. Phoebe didn't like beer. He drank several glasses, but before they left, she saw him go up to the hotel bar and purchase something else.

They'd left and, without even consulting her, he'd driven his truck to the town dump. He'd parked right in front of the dump, rather than at the nearby lovers' lane. By then it was dark. He kissed her, his kisses rough and hard, not at all like the Lewis she remembered. These were a man's kisses—a frustrated, demanding, *powerful* man. She was frightened. When she came back to the truck after going out to the bushes to relieve herself, he'd started drinking whatever it was he'd bought at the hotel. Rye whisky, straight out of the bottle. She thought hotels were only allowed to sell beer, off-license. What did she know?

He didn't offer her any. Not that she would've been interested. In fact, he barely spoke to her, just flicked the truck's lights on once in a while and watched the skunks and possums scatter before switching the lights off again, grinning. Some inner joke, she presumed. It was sick. She didn't find the scavengers or the spotlight he put them in the least bit amusing. Finally she realized he was too drunk to drive; too drunk to do anything. She considered getting out and hitching a ride back to town, but that meant she'd have to walk to the main road first, at least half a mile in the dark.

When he got out to relieve himself—she noted that he didn't bother to move more than ten feet away from the pickup door, although he did have the decency to turn around—she slid into the driver's seat, grabbed the keys out of the ignition and locked the door. Lewis had to make his way around to the passenger door, cursing and staggering.

As soon as he got in, he passed out. *Thank heaven.* Phoebe had driven him back to the Double O ranch, had opened the passenger door and, with a combination of pushing and pulling, managed to flop him onto the porch at his boss's place, dead drunk. Then she'd driven his truck back to the Glory Hotel where she'd picked up her car, leaving his keys under the floormat on the driver's side. Someone would find his vehicle there. Someone would tell him where she'd left it.

Phoebe tucked his T-shirt into the bag with his sneakers and shuddered, remembering. That was the last time she'd seen Lewis Hardin and the last time she'd ever wanted to see him.

Until this afternoon.

Of all places—to show up on the *Alberta Queen*. She wondered if he'd found his black-haired girl-friend; if he'd managed to carry out his pressing *other plans*.

She could just imagine what they were.

She set the bag with the sneakers and T-shirt on her bed and turned to stare out the window. There weren't many people about. Summer school was over. It was the quiet time between summer school and the start of the fall term. She could leave if she wanted. There was nothing really keeping her in the city between this reception today and the beginning of the school year. She'd planned to stay in town, catch up on some reading, do some shopping, go to a few plays.

But suddenly she was homesick. She wanted to see her mother and dad. Even Jill, who was in her last year of high school now and becoming more of a friend than the annoying kid sister she'd always been. And Renee, the youngest. It was her birthday soon. She'd be turning six, Nan and Harry Long-quist's last little one, coming more than ten years after Jill. And Trevor—would he be home? He was in his first year of veterinary college in Saskatoon.

Phoebe made up her mind suddenly. During the summer there weren't many students in the residence, so it wasn't as though she was leaving Lindy with a whole lot of extra work. And Lindy planned to go home, too, for a week. To Vegreville, where her family had a big hog-and-grain farm.

Phoebe changed, packed the suitcase Uncle Joe and Aunt Honor had given her for her high-school graduation, left a message for Boyd on his answering machine—she was glad he wasn't answering his phone—and wrote a note to her roommate. Then she grabbed the bag with Lewis's clothes and left the apartment.

The next week or so had taken on a whole new aspect. Midsummer. Foals and calves in the fields. Lazy sunny afternoons. Grasshoppers. Picnics. Fresh corn on the cob.

Mostly, though, it was the thought of going home to Swallowbank Farm. The thought of going home to Glory.

PHOEBE WAITED two days before bringing up the subject of the Hardins.

"Fine drying day, isn't it, honey?" Nan Longquist said with a sunny smile as she brought in a basket of clothes, fresh from the outdoor clothesline. "We've had a lovely month so far. I hope the weather holds for harvest."

Phoebe nodded. Her uncle Joe and her father were

out working on the big machines today, making sure everything would be ready when the grain was ripe. She was helping her mother fold laundry. Ironing— after sprinkling and rolling and folding into a plastic bag—would be tomorrow. Nan believed that air-drying clothes was superior to using the dryer, even though with her large family, that meant a lot of peg-ging out over the years. She still ironed pillowcases and tea towels, just as her own mother had before her. Phoebe thought it was a complete and total waste of time.

"Have you gone to Bearberry Hill lately, Mom? To the Hardins?" Phoebe glanced up from pairing socks.

"No." Her mother snapped out a tea towel and expertly dampened it and rolled it up. "Catherine told me she saw Mercy in town the other day. Look-ing like a total disaster, as usual. Needed a haircut something awful." Nan Longquist shook her head. "I don't know how those women manage, although I suppose that son of hers must send them money. When he's not in jail!" she added with a severe look and another shake of her head.

"Oh. I'm sure that was long ago, that jail busi-ness," Phoebe murmured, then stopped. She wasn't certain she wanted to pursue the subject. She knew her mother didn't think much of Lewis Hardin. Ever since his conviction for rustling years ago, he'd been persona non grata in the community. Rustling didn't go over in a farming and ranching community, particularly when the rustler was one of their own.

"I thought I'd drive out and say hello to them this afternoon."

"Oh?"

"Or tomorrow," Phoebe added hastily. "There's no rush."

"They'd like that, Phoebe," Nan said; handing her one end of a sheet to fold. "I've always thought the world of Mercy, keeping body and soul together, the way she has. Times have been tough, and having a no-good son is no help, that's for sure. And that Billy's never been much help. You know, as a girl, she was quite pretty and talented. Oh, yes, she had a lovely singing voice! I remember her well because she went to school with Aunt Dahlia." Aunt Dahlia was actually Nan Longquist's cousin.

"I don't know whatever happened to her. But it doesn't matter." Phoebe's mother frowned, her eyes on the folded sheet. "She's got a heart of gold, poor foolish thing, she really does. And where would Mercy be without her?"

Most people, Phoebe thought with a smile, had hearts of gold, according to her softhearted mother.

With the exception of that no-good Lewis Hardin, it seemed.

PHOEBE NOTICED the big, shiny, black Jeep Cherokee the minute she drove into the yard. A handful of dogs barked madly at her little ten-year-old Toyota, as usual. The Hardin dogs were well-known on the road that ran between Peskiko Creek and Glory, just at the edge of the property.

Mercy and Billy must have a visitor.

Oh, well, Phoebe thought, wondering why she'd felt compelled to come out herself and deliver Lewis's clothes when she could have given them to her mother or her aunt Catherine and they would have returned them eventually. *I won't stay long.*

She got out and stretched. Even though the big old house was ramshackle and needed paint, its porch sagging and four or five kinds of shingles on the roof, the property itself was lovely. There were big cottonwoods to the windward side and dozens of Norway maples and white birches that had been planted over the years. A tall, fragrant hedge of lilacs, past blooming now, separated the house from the large garden Billy and Mercy kept, with glorious displays of flowers and vegetables all summer long. They had irises to die for, her aunt Catherine always said. Phoebe could see that someone had been working a patch in the kitchen garden recently, turning over the rich black soil.

The old post-and-beam barn looked just the same as it had when she'd come here as a child with her mother—big, gray, weathered. Empty. She wondered if the makeshift room in the box stall was still there, with its pallet and homemade punching bag.

"Phoebe Longquist! Oh, my, let me get a look at you!" Mercedes Hardin limped to answer the door in response to Phoebe's light knock. Her badly cut iron-gray hair stood in a halo around her head and her pale blue eyes sparkled. Another dog barked from inside the kitchen.

Phoebe stepped forward to hug the old woman. "How are you, Mrs. Hardin? Mom said you were doing well, you and Billy." She gave Mercedes the plastic sack and a mesh bag of oranges she'd brought.

"What's this?" The old woman looked astonished. "Oranges? Clothes?"

"The oranges are just a little something for you and Billy. The other is some stuff that belongs to your son. A shirt and some shoes." She paused at the question in Mercy's eyes. "How did I get it?" Phoebe laughed somewhat nervously. "It's a long story. Just make sure he gets them back, will you?"

"Well, thank you, dear. You can tell him yourself—he's out on the back bluff working on his cabin. Come in first, though. Come in! Billy?" she called over her shoulder. "Put the kettle on, dear. It's Phoebe Longquist—Phoebe's come to visit us!" The older woman hobbled back into the kitchen, which was warm with the scent of fresh baking and cinnamon and wood smoke.

Phoebe followed her. *Lewis is here?* She felt a curious shiver run across her shoulders.

Phoebe nodded to Billy, who was famous in the district for her lack of sociability. The younger woman had put on the kettle at her mother's command and then skittered off to the rocking chair backed into a corner by the stove. There she sat and knitted and read all day, unless she was outside gardening. Phoebe had barely heard her speak five words in her life. Mercedes Hardin more than made up for her daughter's silence.

"A cabin?" Phoebe repeated. "Lewis is working on a cabin?"

Mercedes nodded vigorously. "Oh, yes! I don't know what's got into the boy. He's been cuttin' down trees back there and a-hammerin' and a-nailin' to beat the band. A home of his own, he calls it. Says it's time he had his own place." The old woman laughed, a high-pitched giggle, almost a frightening sound. "As if this isn't his own home, right here with us! As if Lewis didn't have enough to take care of in the little time he gets off!"

"Oh?" Phoebe ventured, accepting a cup of tea from the silent daughter. "Thank you," she whispered to Billy, who smiled shyly.

"Oh, yes!" Mercedes looked pleased. "He's quite the big shot on the oil rigs these day, you know. You haven't heard?" She seemed surprised, as though Phoebe would naturally have heard all about her son's exploits. "'Course, you're way up there in Edmonton and don't get the news. Oh, my, yes. There's all kinds wants to hire him away from the outfit where he works, but Lew is having none of it! No, sir. He likes where he is just fine, he tells me. He's stubborn. Why, only this morning someone called for him here, didn't they, Billy, trying to hire him away, and he said— Oh, would you like some more tea? There's plenty.'' Mercedes quickly changed the subject. Phoebe wondered why.

"He said—*what?*'' she asked plainly. Curiosity wasn't out of place here. Mercedes had asked her once when she was fifteen if she'd tried buttermilk on her freckles. And if that didn't work, she ought to try lemon juice, since many people swore by it.

"Oh, he hung up on him,'' Mercedes muttered, then bent to scoop up a whining cat that appeared out of nowhere. "You know our Lew!''

Our *rude* Lew, Phoebe thought. She looked expectantly at the old woman. *And?*

"Knows his own mind, he does. Can't no one tell him what to do if he don't want to do it. He's independent, no two ways about it.''

Phoebe supposed one could say that.

"Want Pretty for a while?'' Mercedes dumped the cat on her visitor's lap. Phoebe finished her tea, petted the animal for a few minutes, then stood. Pretty jumped onto a nearby chair. "I'd better be heading home.''

"Not without going out and saying hello to Lewis! He'd be wild if he knew you'd stopped in and never said a word. You go on back there on the bluff. It's not half a mile away. You'll hear the hammerin' and sawin', no doubt. Just take a few minutes, Phoebe, dear. Why, you two used to be real pals, weren't you?''

Phoebe smiled. Pals? She wouldn't have put it that way, but certainly, as Mercy knew, she was acquainted with Lewis Hardin. She slipped on her jacket and stepped onto the porch with a last wave at Billy, who offered a tremulous smile. ''Okay, I'll walk out and see what he's up to and say hello.''

''You're welcome to stay for supper, y'hear?'' Mercedes called through the screen door. ''Brunswick stew!'' The wire screen had been mended and patched with black thread. Phoebe glanced at her watch—it was just half-past three. Brunswick stew was generally made with chicken or rabbit these days, but the original was made with squirrel. She had no idea which version the Hardins preferred. Nor was she in the mood to find out.

''I'll be leaving after I say hello to Lewis. Thanks, anyway, for the supper invitation. Maybe another time.''

''All right, dear. You suit yourself. You know you're always welcome.''

Phoebe felt warm inside as she took the path that Mercy had indicated. It was the country way—hospitality. No matter what you had, how much or how little, you offered to share it to any neighbor or stranger who came by your door near mealtime.

Phoebe walked through the quiet copse of poplars and aspen that grew at the back of the farmyard. The house's location on a hill made it windy, but with all the trees around, the only effect was the constant soughing of leaves. It was very pleasant.

She heard the startup of a chain saw in the near distance. A cabin! Whatever for? she wondered.

Then she came around a bend and caught her breath. *Lewis!*

He was working in a clearing near the edge of the bluff. A cabin floor had been laid out and a partial stone chimney built at one end. The broad side of the cabin faced toward the view, a wide-open view to the north and west—miles of rangeland and, far beyond, the snowy peaks of the Canadian Rockies.

He didn't see her and, with the roar of the chain saw, the dogs didn't notice her, either. He looked magnificent. His shirt was off, his skin glistening with sweat. His work boots were dusty, his jeans well-worn. As she watched, he straddled a log that was lying supported at intervals with small chunks of wood and slowly and evenly began splitting it lengthwise. The chain bit and screamed and the wood chips flew. Methodically, he moved down the log. One of the dogs began to bark frantically and run back and forth, barking at him.

He grinned at the excited dog, revved the engine

once, then abruptly shut off the saw. The silence was deafening. The dog must have caught her scent then, for he turned and barked menacingly, front legs stiff.

Frowning, Lewis pivoted toward her, the chain saw still held easily in his hands, his shoulders bunched with muscle. ''Phoebe?''

CHAPTER FIVE

WAS HE DREAMING?

There she stood at the edge of the woods, watchful as a doe. He set down the chain saw and straightened, raising one hand in a slow gesture of welcome. She waved back.

This was no dream. Smiling, she moved toward him. One of the dogs rushed to forestall her and he called him back roughly.

"Here, Shep! Go lie down," he ordered.

"Hi!" She jammed her hands in the pockets of her windbreaker. "Your mom sent me out here. She said you were building a cabin."

"Yeah." Lewis stepped away from the log he'd just split for a beam and bent to retrieve his shirt from where he'd tossed it across the makeshift sawhorse. He walked toward her, intensely aware of her scrutiny of his upper body and the fact that his chest was covered with sawdust. He dusted himself off, including his face, and slung the shirt over his shoulder. "What brings you out here?"

"Believe it or not, I brought back your T-shirt and shoes. The ones you left on the boat?" She shaded her eyes from the afternoon sunshine. "I'm visiting my folks for a while before school starts. Ten days or so."

Her hair was alive with color, red and brown and hints of gold. Her freckles stood out like autumn leaves on a clear pond. She was gorgeous. She was the most beautiful woman he'd ever met. He'd always thought so, and now, seeing her all grown-up, he knew he'd been right. "They're up at the house."

"No kidding!" He shrugged on the shirt and left it hanging open. He needed a shower, first thing, to get rid of the sawdust. "I bought some new sneakers."

"Well, now you've got two pairs. It seemed a shame just to leave them there." She indicated his cabin with one hand. "Tell me what you're building here."

"Oh, it's just a small place. A retreat. Poplar, which don't make the best logs for a cabin. I'm going to have a hell of a lot of cracks to fill when they dry properly." He smiled. "I don't think you're supposed to build with green wood, but I didn't have time to wait."

"Why not?"

He hesitated, not sure if he should bring her into his world. They'd had a relationship, a kids' relationship, a long time ago. It wasn't something he wanted to develop now. Keep it straightforward... "I wanted a place of my own," he said simply.

"But…" Her eyes searched his. "Your mom tells me you're working up north somewhere. You don't even live around here. What do you need this for?"

She was still nosy and persistent as hell.

"Phoebe," he said, deciding to button his shirt, after all. "Everyone needs a place of their own. This is mine. Even if I only come here once or twice a year, it's mine."

She was silent. "I see." He could tell she didn't, not really.

"Come on, I'll show you what I've got planned." He felt like a kid again, full of enthusiasm. Ever since he'd struck on the idea of building a cabin during his time off this month, after the fiasco with Bethany, he'd felt different about himself. He realized he should have done something like this long ago.

"Okay, here's the front." He spanned the open side to the west and north. "Great view, huh?" The foothills and the mountains spread out before them like a distant carpet, a glorious painting.

She nodded. "Where will the door be?"

"Right here." He stepped forward and stood in the space he'd mentally designated for a door, holding his hands to mark the frame. "Windows on both sides. Like it so far?"

"Little panes of glass?"

"Sure. Why not?" He liked old-style windows you could open top and bottom.

"Yeah, why not?" she repeated with a grin.

He took four steps to one side, to the partly built stone fireplace. "Now this—this is the fireplace. I wasn't going to have one. They're big heat wasters, you probably know that—" she nodded "—but I figure they make up for it. I mean, could you see me seducing some willing young woman in front of an oil heater? Or a kitchen range?"

She glanced sharply at him and he thought her smile wavered, just a fraction. "No. A fireplace is definitely more romantic."

"I'm building it with river rocks, but I'm going to put a proper flue inside. I don't trust my masonry abilities and I don't want any draft problems. The river rocks will look right, though. Design-wise, I mean."

"Mmm." She stood so near him he could have reached out and pulled her into his arms. "You have anyone in mind for the big seduction scene?"

It was his turn to stare at her. "Nope. Why?"

"No reason," she said airily, turning away to walk the perimeter of the east side. "Just wondered where your black-haired friend fit in here, the one you were helping out at the boat last week."

Lewis laughed, feeling strangely pleased that she was so interested in Bethany. "That's history. Caught her fooling around with her assistant after I swam to shore."

"That *boy?*"

"Well, he's nineteen. I thought he was gay."

"Oh, Lewis! Just because he was working for a florist? Come on!"

Lewis grinned. "That's exactly what Bethany said. Said I was just one big cliché after another, that and a few other things not quite as complimentary…"

"Like what?" Phoebe seemed thoroughly amused.

"Oh, she called me an overmuscled macho roughneck with a hat size to match my boot size and more along those lines."

Phoebe's laughter rang out and Lewis's blood stilled. What if he kissed her now, took her in his arms and kissed her into silence. And then, more than silence…

"Didn't you care?" she asked softly, her eyes full of questions.

"Not really." He gave a negligent shrug. "The relationship was basically over, anyway. So, what do you think?" he said, clearing his throat and changing the subject. "Should I tack a porch on here on the front? Be a lot of extra work."

"Oh, yes! You need a porch. With a rocking chair and a homemade quilt hanging over the railing and a nice cat like Pretty sitting on the top steps, waiting for you to come home."

"Sounds good." Lewis wanted to add that he'd like to come home to a woman, too, a woman who'd have all the lamps lit and a pot of something good on the kitchen stove. But he was no fool. This conversation could carry them both away. He didn't know about Phoebe, but it wasn't a side trip he wanted to pursue.

He walked around his work site, picking up his tools and wiping them and stowing them under a tarp on the cabin floor. He was always careful with tools.

"You finished for the day?" she asked when she saw what he was doing. She'd dropped the topic of the porch when he hadn't elaborated on her silly suggestions.

"I think so. I want to see if Ma or Billy needs anything from town. I might drive in for a movie later, maybe check out some friends."

Her attitude changed. Cooled. He wondered if she was remembering the last time they'd spent together in town, at the Glory Hotel tavern. "Hey, listen. I never apologized for being such a creep after that auction a few years ago."

She laughed softly. "Oh, that's okay."

"No, it isn't." He stopped and turned to face her. "It was inexcusable. It was ungentlemanly. It was plain, downright outrageous behavior. I don't know what got into me."

"Whiskey?" she asked slyly.

He shook his head. "Whiskey, for sure. I don't drink like that anymore. Maybe a few beers now and then. I haven't touched the hard stuff in years. I want you to know I'm sorry about what happened. I should have gotten in touch with you right away—"

"I'm sure you had some explaining to do when your boss found you on his porch in the morning." She looked as though she wasn't going to hold the incident against him. He felt relief.

"I did." He shook his head ruefully. "Man, what a mess! His kid, Rosie, found me. Carolyn, his wife, reamed me out good, and Adam warned me next time it happened I was out of a job. I needed that job. I stayed sober."

Phoebe reached over and touched his forearm. It was an impulse; it had to be. Lewis looked straight into her eyes. They seemed more blue today than green. She smiled, her eyes intent, as though she'd suddenly realized—as he had—that there were plenty of unfinished things between them, no matter what they decided to talk about and not talk about since they'd met again so unexpectedly a week ago. She pulled her hand back. Her tone was gentle. "All is forgiven. Let's forget it now. Okay, Lewis?"

"Okay." They walked in silence for a few yards. Lewis realized they were automatically following an animal path down the hill, toward the wide-open range below. The path came out below the old orchard and, farther along, the barn. He had discovered it when he'd first surveyed his building site and figured it was the work of some wily coyote or fox, hopeful of making a raid on the henhouse if anyone ever forgot to shut the door at night.

Lewis was a step or so behind Phoebe on the narrow path. He studied the top of her head, her hair loose and tangled on her shoulders. He watched the way she walked, carefully but swiftly, stepping over the occasional branch or crevice in the uneven ground. He felt like a hunter behind her, shadowing her, mimicking her every move. It made the blood surge in his veins. There was something ancient and primitive about it. Elemental. Something very, very male. The excitement of seeing prey move away from you. The desire to overtake. The way a cheetah never chased a tame goat—but let the goat start to run…

Either hunter or protector. Which?

Protector, of course. Anything else was sheer fantasy, the kind of stuff you thought up when you had too much time on your hands. As they reached the beginning of the scrubby orchard, Phoebe stopped abruptly and turned. Lewis nearly collided with her.

"Hey!"

"Listen, remember when I saw you here? How old were you?" She didn't stop for an answer, just went on, gesturing toward the old tree trunk that still lay there in the turf, covered now with moss and lichen. "I was about fourteen, I think. I was so thrilled to meet you—an ex-convict! I remember wondering what my friends would think if they'd seen me—"

"A *convict*," he corrected ruefully. "Not ex. Don't forget, I was on the run. Laundry truck, wasn't it?"

"No," she said, laughing up at him. "That was the next time. When you hid behind the raspberries at the farm."

She swung around and began picking her way along, as before. Then she stopped again and this time Lewis did run into her. He grasped her shoulders lightly, felt her breath coming rapidly. "Phoebe, you've, uh…" He was lost, looking into her eyes as she turned. He wanted to tell her to quit stopping like that.

"I was so thrilled." Her eyes were dancing. "Imagine, fourteen! I thought you were terribly romantic, you know."

"You did?" Lewis swallowed. Never mind the past; he was lost in the present.

"Oh, yes! Like a pirate or something. A highwayman. You have no *idea* how boring my life was then." Again Phoebe swung away from him, seemingly unaware of their brief physical contact, and Lewis followed, heart hammering.

Holy cow. He had to be careful. She obviously regarded him as no more than a friend from the past. A childhood acquaintance, long forgotten.

They walked along the bottom of the orchard. By now, only one dog was with them; the other two had cut up toward the house through the orchard and under the fence. Lewis knew if they kept on this track, they'd end up at the barn. Her car would be parked at the house.

He presumed she'd leave as soon as they got there.

"Oh, hey! Here's the barn," she said. "Remember this? Remember me spying on you up in the rafters?"

He frowned. "You were?" He felt stupid; she obviously remembered a lot more than he did.

"Yes!" She actually clapped her hands. "I was up in the hayloft and you threw me a little wooden frog. I think you carved it yourself."

He nodded slowly. It had been years, but the wooden frog rang a bell. He used to whittle quite a bit, an old wood-carving turn he'd learned from Angus Tump, one of their neighbors. He'd helped Angus on his trapline one winter over the Christmas break and Angus had shown him how to carve.

"I've still got it!" Her eyes were wide, full of excitement and memory. "It's at home somewhere. I left it there when I went to college." She looked down. "You don't remember," she said quietly.

"I do," he lied. "Let's go in."

"You had a little room set up, in a stall. With a punching bag and a table and bed. I thought you lived there, like Robinson Crusoe or something. I think I read too many books!"

She followed him to the big door of the barn, which was partly open and sagging on its big overhead roller. They stepped inside, sending a rush of swallows off their nests and out through the holes in the roof and the broken windows.

"Here, wasn't it?" Phoebe rushed over to the first box stall on the right. Lewis followed and looked into the stall. It was filled with bales of timothy hay for the sheep.

"Oh, darn!"

She seemed so disappointed he wanted to laugh. He walked to the next stall. A limp feed sack hung on a beam, its burlap fabric full of holes and its stuffing long gone.

"Maybe here…" he ventured. She came over to stand beside him.

"Must have been," she agreed, and hurried inside. "Yes, here's the table." She pushed at the table under a million cobwebs, and it wobbled and one leg buckled. "Oops!" She giggled.

He walked in beside her and put one hand on the rickety table. "I'm a slightly better builder now than I was then."

"I hope so." She looked around. They both spotted the narrow wooden pallet he'd built against the wall, with its striped, mouse-eaten mattress. "Not much has changed," she said, craning her neck to look up. "See? That's where I spied on you." She pointed to the square hole above the manger, where feed would have been thrown down when the barn was in use for animals.

Lewis stepped next to her on the pretext of following her gaze. He just wanted to be close to her, to catch the occasional whiff of her scent, her hair, her skin.

"You know," she said softly, turning to him, "you were the first guy I ever kissed."

"I was?" Lewis smiled. Her eyes shone in the gloom of the barn. The swallows had returned to their nests high above and were twittering and squeaking.

"Yes." She stared down at her hands, turned them over, as though inspecting them, then took a deep breath. "I lied. I said I'd kissed lots of boys before, but I hadn't." She gave a shaky laugh. "It's so dumb! I dreamed about it for months—"

"Phoebe." He put his hands on her shoulders and gently drew her closer. He brought one hand under her chin and tipped up her face. Then, ever so deliberately, he lowered his mouth to hers. A flood of joy raced through his veins, freed at last. She was so sweet! She was so warm and loving. So caring. She was the first person who'd ever cared about him for who he was, not for what he could do or bring to the relationship. She'd seen through to the essential Lewis Hardin, where he lived, right through the tough facade he presented to the world.

He tightened his arms around her and felt her raise her own arms to twine around his neck. He pressed his body against hers boldly. She didn't shrink back. If anything, she was pliant and willing. As eager as he was.

As hot.

He moaned and backed her slowly up against the box-stall wall and pushed against her. She made excited little female sounds that shot through his entire body. He raised his head reluctantly. "Phoebe," he said hoarsely, "I never forgot you, either." He lifted his hand to trace the curve of her cheek. Her eyes clung to his. He was drowning in that sweet blue gaze. "I've never met a woman like you since. I—I know this isn't right, but damn it! I've wanted you since that day we kissed in the orchard. The very first time. You were too young then. So was I."

"I'm not too young now," she whispered. Lewis's ears rang. He'd never had a clearer invitation. With a muttered oath, he kissed her again, and this time he slid his hand under her jacket and T-shirt so he could caress her back, her side, tease himself with the brush of his thumb over the swell of her breast. She wasn't wearing a bra.

His libido—what was left of it that hadn't already caught fire—exploded. He wanted her like he'd never wanted a woman before. *Now!*

He brought his hand around to cup her breast. She took a quick breath. "Lewis! I'm...I'm scared."

"What are you scared of, honey?" he muttered, kissing her nose, her cheeks, her closed eyes. "You know I'd never hurt you."

"I know. It's just..." She pulled back a little and Lewis remembered where they were. Who they were.

What time of day it was. The season. The fact that his mother and Billy were up at the house, no doubt waiting for her to come for her car.

He cleared his throat and took a step backward. "Sorry." He held up his hands. "Phoebe, I—"

"Oh, Lewis! Don't apologize." She pushed her hair back from her face with both hands, looking distressed. "*Don't!* It's just that—oh, I don't know."

"We're not right together?" He was guessing. "This is a bad time? There's someone else?"

"No, that's not it," she said, searching his eyes. "Not at all."

"So, what is it?"

"I like you, I really like you, but..." Phoebe's face was red. "I don't know how to say this, Lewis, but I've never been with a man." She looked miserable. "There's been no one else, not...not that way."

He was shocked. What was she? Twenty-two, twenty-three? And still a virgin? And he'd been about to take her on the barn floor like some randy goat? Lewis stepped farther back and ran his hand through his hair. "Whoa! Man, I'm glad you told me that." He took a deep breath.

"Why?" she asked, sounding defiant. He glanced at her to see that her face was still very red. She was embarrassed. As if being a virgin at her age was something to be embarrassed about.

"Hell, Phoebe. I was ready to make love to you

right here, no questions asked. I thought you were ready, too.''

"I was." She bit her bottom lip, her brow furrowed. "But…what if I got pregnant?"

"Then I'd have to marry you," he said easily, smiling. She was so naive. What a question. Pregnancy could be prevented; she knew that. "I could think of worse consequences."

She laughed. "You idiot!"

He clasped her hand and raised it to his mouth. He kissed the palm gently. "I'm crazy about you, Phoebe. I always have been. I'd make love to you in a minute. I'd marry you in a minute. But I don't think that's what this is about, is it?" He met her gaze and held it for a few seconds. "This is about lust. It's about sex. Hot, cheap—" he held her eyes even though she colored as he spoke "—quick sex."

She nodded and took a deep shaky breath and pulled her hand from his. "I'd better go. I'd better get back to the house. They'll be wondering what happened to me."

"Okay." He smiled and took a step toward the open gate of the box stall. "Now, let's start this reel over again. How are you, Miss Longquist?" He gave her a mock bow. "Nice to see you. I understand you are up at the university on a big scholarship. You must be doing well."

"I am," she said lightly, entering into the spirit of things. "I'm finished my degree and I'm going into postgraduate studies this fall. Mom and Dad are very proud of me. They expect me to go far. I have excellent prospects. Friends. Even—'' her voice quavered ''—even *men* interested in me! I've got everything I ever dreamed of having. Well—'' her voice dropped and she became very solemn again ''—almost everything,'' she finished on a whisper, her eyes pleading with his.

''Goddamn it, Phoebe,'' he said on a growl, grabbing her with one hand and slamming the stall gate shut with the other. ''We've got unfinished business, you and I. It's time we damn well finished it!''

And he pulled her back into his arms.

CHAPTER SIX

LEWIS WALKED UP to the house to rummage in the glove compartment of his Jeep for some condoms. Damn it. Was he really prepared to accommodate any virgin who wanted to change her status? Much as that notion stuck in his craw sideways, at the same time he was incredibly turned on at the thought of making love with Phoebe. So turned on it was tough to walk. He hoped Ma and Billy stayed in the house. He didn't want either of them coming down to the barn for any reason. He'd have to set a dog on watch, just in case.

"Here, Shep!" he called to the dog he'd scolded back at his cabin site. Shep fell happily into line. Lewis decided to pinch a couple of quilts off the fence, too. Ma had hung half a dozen out to air. A roll in the hay was fine for a teenager, but he was a little past that stage. At the last minute, he picked up the hose and hosed himself off. He was still covered in sawdust and wood chips.

He shrugged his shirt back on. He couldn't believe what was happening. Well, it hadn't happened yet, had it? *Hold on, fella. Settle down.* He'd long ago learned not to count his chickens early. He'd been handed too many rotten eggs.

THE TWO WOMEN watched through the kitchen window as Lewis walked down the road.

"Looks like he's goin' to the barn," the older woman said. "He took two quilts."

"Barn?" Billy looked dazed.

"She's down there. The Longquist girl. I'd bet on it. Her car's still here." Mercy let the curtain go and it fell back into place, covering the multipaned window. "She's a nice girl, Billy. A nice girl for our Lewis." She grabbed up her walking stick and made her way painfully back to the range, where she lifted a lid over the firebox, stabbed around with the poker and then shoved in another chunk of firewood from the box nearby.

"We got to tell him, Billy. He's a grown man now. With a future we can be proud of, both of us. I know we can. He's settled. He's on the right track now."

"No!"

"He's got a right." The old woman's eyes were damp. She lifted the corner of her apron and wiped first her left eye, then her right. "I know it hurts, honey, it hurts me, too. But we got to tell him."

Silent tears ran down her daughter's face and she left the room, her expression frozen in pain and fear. The older woman shook her head sadly.

"Got to," she repeated, to no one but the snoozing Pretty and the ticking kitchen clock. "Got to tell him soon."

LEWIS DISCOVERED that Phoebe had spread out a bale of hay for a bed while he was gone. Nice touch.

"Quilts?" She was giggly, almost silly. No wonder, considering.

"Yeah. I nicked them off the fence. I hope Ma doesn't notice they're gone and start looking for them." He spread them both out on the hay. "You're sure you want this, Phoebe?"

"I do," she said softly.

"Take off your clothes," he ordered. He'd see just how committed she was. He had half an idea she'd get down to her underpants and socks and chicken out. He was prepared for the disappointment. This was her call, all the way.

"All right." Phoebe took off her windbreaker. Then she took off her sneakers and her socks. Then, defiantly watching him, she undid the snap on her jeans and pushed them down, stepping out of them gracefully. She was wearing white cotton underwear, nothing sexy about them—except that *she* was wearing them, which made them sexy as hell.

Lewis realized his breathing was tight and short. He realized she meant to go through with it, that he hadn't frightened her by producing the quilts and the condoms. *Holy cow.*

She reached up and took off her T-shirt, letting it land where it fell. Her breasts were high and round and white. Small. Perfect. Lewis swallowed, his throat suddenly dry.

Then she peeled off her panties with one smooth move and stood naked before him. Her cheeks were on fire.

Lewis felt cruel. He stepped forward and took her in his arms. "Oh, baby! I didn't know if you really meant it—"

"I did. I do," she whispered against his mouth as he kissed her. "Your turn."

"Me?"

"Fair is fair." She stood back and shivered. Lewis could see the gooseflesh go up her shoulders, tighten the buds of her breasts, make the hair on her arms stand up.

He was out of his clothes in three seconds flat, remembering at the last minute to get the condoms from his jeans pocket. He knew he must look ridiculous standing there, stark naked, with an erection that would do an elephant proud, digging through first one pocket, then the other looking for the elusive foil packets which he knew he'd put *somewhere,* trying to kick off the last leg of his jeans before he fell over.

If she giggled…

She did. She covered her mouth with her hand, like a schoolgirl.

Lewis felt himself wilt. He moved forward and took her in his arms. "No laughing! Listen, we're not going to do this standing up, so…"

He drew her down onto the quilts, wishing he'd kept one to cover them with. Somehow they were so…so bare.

Her skin was rough with gooseflesh. "I'm c-cold."

Lewis lifted her slightly and positioned her on one quilt. Then he pulled the other quilt free and covered them both with it. "Better?"

"Much." She was quiet for a few seconds. Her cheeks were still very red. Lewis understood that this was a lot more difficult for her than it was for him, even though he was definitely not finding it easy. He had lots of questions, but now was not the time to ask them. Now was the time to shut up and get down to business.

He kissed her mouth and when she clung to him, moaning softly, he knew this was really happening between them. *After all these years.* "Lie still, honey," he whispered, and began kissing her slowly and expertly. "Let me kiss you." Her mouth, her throat, her ears, working his way slowly to her breasts.

"You're gorgeous, Phoebe, you know that?" She shuddered as his mouth covered and teased one rosy nipple. She gripped his hair, as though to make him stay.

"I—I'm not!" she gasped. "I'm skinny and I have freckles."

"You have freckles all over. Everywhere." He kissed her shoulder. "I love freckles. You're gorgeous and sexy and I'm crazy about you. I always have been." He kissed her mouth deeply, feeling her tremors of arousal in response. She was eager for him, desperate for him. As turned on as he was.

He realized there wasn't going to be a whole lot of foreplay this first time. He reached down to position the condom, aware that she was hardly experienced enough to do it herself. Then, the instant he got it on, he went limp as a dishrag.

There's something so goddamn wrong about this!

"What's the matter?"

"Nothing." He kissed her again, praying that plain, old-fashioned politically incorrect lust would return. And pronto. "Er, why?"

"Then why don't you just, well, do it?"

"Damn it, Phoebe!" He rolled onto his side of the hay bed. "It's not that easy, you know!"

She was silent for a few moments. "I'm sorry," she said in a tiny voice. "I…I wouldn't know."

He sighed. "It's not your fault. I think it's this whole business of you being a virgin. It scares the heck out of me. I've never slept with a virgin before. It's not my…my style."

"I'm sorry," she said again, this time her voice even quieter. "Should I get dressed and go home?"

"No, damn it! Give me a minute." Lewis lay there for a few seconds staring up into the dusty rafters, then the foolishness of his situation struck him. He started to laugh. In a few seconds, she joined him. She squealed with laughter. He roared. The swallows far above complained loudly and left the barn in a muttered jumble of squeaks and whistles and a whoosh of wings.

"Oh, hell, Phoebe," he finally said, when he could get his breath.

"Yes...*hell,*" she said emphatically, still giggling.

He pulled her close and began to kiss her again. He'd give her satisfaction, at least, no matter how he had to do it. There was a certain small matter of his pride.

He began to stroke lightly between her thighs, reveling in the heat and moisture he found there. Then he stroked deeper. She was hot, all right. Her skin was silky, her kisses were sweet. He kissed her again and again, feeling his body harden in response. He hoped it wouldn't betray him now.

He felt her arch to meet the pressure of his fingers, her breath coming in short gasps, her grip on his hair tightening painfully. "Oh, baby," he whispered. "Let it happen. Let it happen."

She climaxed with a shudder and a loud wrenching moan, and Lewis exulted that he'd been able to give her this pleasure at least. Her gleaming eyes and moist, parted lips invited him to kiss her again. He did. His mouth still on hers, Lewis positioned himself over her and slipped inside her with one quick hard thrust. She cried out, surprised, and Lewis whispered his apologies into her mouth.

"Sorry, babe, sorry. I didn't mean to hurt you…"

"No, no," she whispered back. "This is what I want." She wrapped her legs around his, a wholly natural, instinctive gesture. "Honest."

He began to move ever so slowly inside her, worried sick that he'd hurt her. He needn't have worried. She writhed against him and cried out again, and this time he knew it was with pleasure, not pain. He was glad he'd waited. He groaned as he spilled himself into the condom. Aftershocks rumbled through his body, again and again. That had to be some kind of record—under a minute in his estimation. Certainly under two. He ought to be ashamed of himself. Well, damn it, he was overexcited.

Cautiously, he eased his weight to one side. "You okay, honey? Sorry, it was so…so fast."

She smiled. A big happy smile. Her face was damp with sweat, her hair stuck in strands to her face. "I'm great, Lewis. I'm wonderful. You're wonderful. Thank you for this. I wanted it so much. Ever since I saw you again. Was that fast? I thought it was just…just perfect!"

Lewis collapsed, his head next to hers on the bed of hay. The quilt had come off them both and he reached around and gently pulled it over her shoulders, to his chest. *Perfect.*

"I wanted it, too, baby." He smiled. He felt terrific. They were in one hell of a jam, but he'd never felt better. "I wanted you. You're special to me— you always have been. I think I've been half in love with you since you kissed me down there in the orchard."

"You kissed *me.* You made me kiss you," she said slyly. "Let's get it straight. I was shocked at the time, you know."

He contemplated that. And a lot of other things that had happened before and since. Then he sat up and reached for his shirt, which he'd thrown down. He rummaged in the pocket for his papers and tobacco, and began to slowly and methodically roll a cigarette. He inspected it, pinched off the stray ends of tobacco and lit one end. It was a ritual he enjoyed. The very occasional home-rolled smoke. The fragrant tobacco filled the cool air.

"You still smoke? I'm disappointed," she said.

Lewis regarded the small, twisted butt in his hand. "Oh, once in a while. I just smoke homemade." The truth was, he hardly smoked at all, maybe two or three a week. He offered her the cigarette, and she smiled and took a puff, then sat up, choking and coughing. He grinned and patted her on the back.

"Better lay off, honey."

He lay back, pulling her down to him, and she

nestled her head on his arm. He took a deep breath. "So, Phoebe. What's next?"

"What do you mean?"

"For us. Isn't this the beginning of something, not the end?" He shifted toward her and gazed seriously into her eyes. "I can't just turn you over to that…that professor guy. Not after this."

"I don't know," she whispered. Her face was solemn. "I haven't thought that far. My…" She looked down and colored and twisted a bit of hay between her fingers. "My parents aren't crazy about you, as you probably know. And I'm not really ready for a relationship. Not a *real* one."

Lewis laughed. "Hell, nobody in Glory's crazy about me. Tell them I've reformed. Tell them I'm a solid citizen now. Good job. Oil field. Loaded with dough. Prospects."

She smiled. "My parents have a bad idea of you from way back. Before." She glanced down, twisted a piece of straw on his chest. "You know how people are."

He felt an icy chill wash over his insides. *She meant it.* "Because I'm not religious?"

"Oh, it's not that at all! They're not like that. Dad never goes to church. It's just a big deal for Mom." Phoebe laid her hand on his arm. He stared at it, so soft and white, the back dusted with freckles against his dark tanned skin.

"From when I was in jail for rustling steers?"

"I guess so. And then when you broke out and got more time. Twice. They thought that was...well, irresponsible, I guess." She looked down again.

He laughed harshly. "Not good enough for their daughter, huh?" Small towns! They never changed.

"Something like that."

He took a draw on his cigarette and blew the smoke into the air, watching it drift up in the vast interior of the barn. "Oh, well." He shrugged. "How do you feel about it, Phoebe? What your parents think."

"I'm not happy," she said. "But there's not much I can do, is there? Besides—" she sat up and pushed the hair from her eyes "—I don't see that it matters all that much what people think. About whatever we decide. If we see each other or not."

"No." He thought for a moment. True, it had never mattered to him—before. "I suppose not. But you can't go sneaking around behind your parents' backs."

"Why not?" she said bluntly. "I want to see you and it's really none of their business. I'm all grown-up. Are you going to say anything to Mercedes and Billy?"

Lewis laughed. "No. Why would I?" He carefully doused his cigarette by squeezing it between thumb and forefinger. "Hell, maybe we're making too big a deal out of it. I mean, it's not as if we've decided to get married or anything. I mean, this sex thing—"

he waved his hand between her naked body and his "—it just happened. Right?" He looked at her and grinned. "It's all brand-new."

"Exactly." Phoebe had an odd expression on her face. A little embarrassed. Preoccupied. He wanted to know what she was thinking. Or thinking up, knowing her. "I'd better get dressed."

Leave sleeping dogs lie. Lewis threw off the quilt that covered them. "Me, too. I'd better get these back on the fence before Ma finds out. We can talk later, if you want."

She giggled. "Honestly, Lewis. You'd think we were still a couple of kids, the way you're acting!"

"Yeah." He smiled. She wasn't far wrong. "Ain't that the truth?"

TROUBLE WAS, he was tired of acting like a kid.

Did kids have the kind of responsibility he had at F&B Drilling for million-dollar oil-field jobs? Did kids get partnership offers from their employers? Headhunters making their lives crazy?

No.

That reminded Lewis. He'd been furious when he received the call from Wild Rose this morning at breakfast. He'd heard enough from that outfit. This wasn't the first offer he'd had from them, either. Next call he got, he was going to threaten someone.

How the hell had they tracked him down to Glory?

He had to hand it to whoever was on his case—they got full marks for persistence.

Today's was the third offer he'd had, right out of the blue. He'd had a call at Bethany's one weekend, from a woman, a secretary, he supposed. Then a call from the same woman on his cell phone when he was driving to Athabasca one Friday a month ago and now this. A guy. Name his price, come over to their side. Their drilling division was competition for F&B, but they were bigger. Wild Rose did more than drill. They were an oil company, too, with their own properties, and they drilled their own holes, both for exploration and for wells. He'd heard how secretive they were in a business that was legendary for its secrecy.

He didn't care. He got along fine with the F&B bosses, and that was good enough for him. Money wasn't everything. His company freelanced. They drilled for whoever would pay the bill, but lately they'd been doing a lot of work for Dextron Mines, one of Wild Rose's biggest rivals, or so he'd heard. Was that their game—looking for insider information from him? It would be a cold night in hell before he told them anything. That wasn't his side of the business, anyway.

He had another week before starting the next job, a short one, on an option southwest of Edmonton in the hills west of Rimby. At least he wouldn't be entirely out in the boonies, although if it was another tight hole, which meant the crew would have to live in trailers on the site. He could sneak out a few times, as he'd still have the assistant push he was training. He could go and see Phoebe in Edmonton. Get to know her a little better. Maybe even court her seriously.

Since their afternoon tryst in the barn three days ago, Lewis had done a lot of thinking. He wanted Phoebe. There was more between them than some old boy-girl thing from when they were teenagers. He could see developing a real relationship with her, maybe eventually marrying her and settling down one day. She was his kind of woman; he felt it in his bones. She'd always been his kind of woman.

Obviously, marriage—*if* it happened—wouldn't happen for a while.

Unfortunately, her parents were a problem. She was a good girl. She was used to doing what her parents wanted. And they saw him as a cattle thief, a rustler, a man with a criminal record. Worse, a small-town boy gone very, very bad. And she had a brilliant career ahead of her in her chosen field. Pond scum or some damn thing. But she could be married and still have a career, right? Lots of women did. Phoebe would never be happy with him and a couple of babies, the way some women would. She was too smart. Too brainy. Too determined to succeed in a tough academic field.

He liked a woman with brains, always had.

Still, reasonable or not, the idea of just forgetting about their liaison, letting her go back to her own world while he went back to his, didn't sit well. He couldn't forget her now. Not after seeing her again all these years later. Not after they'd made love.

Maybe he should go out of his way to try to win over her folks. Improve their opinion of him. Couldn't hurt. Ma had always been fond of Nan Longquist. That was a start. Lewis had never met Phoebe's dad, Harry. Maybe it was time he paid a visit to Swallowbank Farm.

And if he couldn't change their minds...ah, well, then, to hell with them!

It wasn't as though it was *them* he was sleeping with.

CHAPTER SEVEN

SWALLOWBANK FARM was east of Glory, toward Vulcan. Joe Gallant, Phoebe's uncle, farmed hay and grain there, and the farm supported both the Longquists and the Gallants. Joe had gotten married a few years earlier, to someone from Calgary Ma didn't know. All of Lewis's information came from Mercedes. He'd offered to bring her out to visit her friend Nan, but Mercy had declined. She'd sent a half a bushel of Jubilee corn as a gift because, as she said, "ours is always a week earlier than down there."

So he had a load of corn rattling around on the back seat of his Jeep.

It was a beautiful day. Hot, but not too hot. August could be great in this country. Dry, warm, rarely any rain. The fields were tall with barley and wheat as he headed east toward Vulcan. Farmers were taking off their second, even third crops of hay. He got gas at the little corner store at the intersection of the highway that led on to Vulcan and the north-south one that led to High River and Nanton. The gas kid told him exactly how to get to the Gallant farm.

Lewis rehearsed what he was going to say to

Phoebe's parents. He'd be charming. Offer Nan the corn, wish the father a good day and a good harvest. He knew Harry farmed with Joe Gallant. He'd inquire about the Longquist children. Compliment Nan Longquist on her roses, if she had any. Glance around, see if Phoebe was home. If she wasn't, he'd ask to be remembered to her. Then he'd take his leave. Too bad he didn't wear a cap—he could doff it.

"Real nice guy, that Hardin kid," he could hear Phoebe's dad remark to her mom when he left. "Just the kind I'd like to see our eldest daughter marry one day."

Yeah. Lewis grinned to himself. *In your dreams.*

A beat-up blue hatchback came toward him on the narrow road, and he pulled to the right to allow plenty of room. As the car passed, the driver hit the horn. Lewis looked in his rearview mirror. The hatchback was stopping. He slowed, then stopped, too. When he saw the other car begin to weave backward toward him, he put his vehicle in reverse. Must be someone who knew him.

"Hi!" It was Phoebe. She waved her hand out her window and smiled at him. "I'm just going to town to take in some mail for Mom and pick up some stuff at Sears. Where you heading?"

"I was going out to the farm to see you," Lewis lied. Of course, he really *did* want to see Phoebe. Seeing her parents was just a ruse to get out there.

She looked great, hair tied back with a green scarf. Sleeveless pink T-shirt.

She grinned and put her car in forward gear. "Well, why don't you follow me, big fella? I've got some time. I can show you a favorite place of mine." She winked.

If that didn't sound like an invitation, Lewis didn't know what did. A pickup approached on the narrow road and honked its horn once before swerving into the shallow ditch and passing Phoebe on the right side. She waved. "Trevor," she called, by way of explanation. "My brother. Going to work."

Lewis put the Jeep in motion, contemplating an oil-field U-turn on the gravel road, which was basically a hard left and then gunning it, a back-end slide on the gravel completing the 360-degree maneuver. He decided he didn't have the speed for it, plus, it would be unseemly, considering. Might look like showing off. So he just steered to the left, backed up, then pulled up behind Phoebe. She screeched off with a puff of dust. Lewis followed, his heart thudding. Lucky he'd stopped in town the day before yesterday and bought a new box of condoms.

She drove like a maniac. By the time he'd caught up with her after she'd turned onto a rough dirt track that went off to the right for half a mile or so, ending in a clump of trees, she was parked and already had her jeans and shoes off. She was taking off her T-shirt, laughing, when he parked.

Holy cow.

"How much time you got?" he asked out the Jeep window.

"About half an hour," she said, her voice muffled. Then she yanked her head free and she was stark, raving naked, the sun dappling her lean freckled body through the dense canopy of cottonwood leaves. Lewis glanced behind him. What if some damn farmer drove up? Whoever owned this road? It was the middle of the afternoon, for crying out loud.

With a roar of his engine, he reversed and parked so his vehicle blocked the access. At least if anyone drove up, they'd hear the engine and have a chance to get their clothes back on.

His pulse was hammering in his head when he got out of the Jeep.

She ran up and threw her arms around him, laughing. "Surprise!"

"You crazy woman," he growled, grinning broadly. "Hijacking a guy like this—"

"Quick! Take off your clothes," she said, unbuttoning his shirt as she spoke. Lewis threw his shirt into the Jeep then followed her into the shady interior of the copse. Then they were lying in the grass, both naked as magpies. Lewis dragged her into his arms and began nuzzling her face, her breasts, her shoulders. "You are one crazy, crazy woman," he muttered again.

"And you love it!" She giggled and tugged playfully at his hair.

"You're damn right I do. I love every bit of it."

This time, when they made love, Phoebe was a full partner, shy but willing. Eager. Lewis was overcome with emotion. The tenderness. The sweetness. The deep peace and satisfaction, the oneness he felt with her, making love under the clear blue sky. This woman was everything to him—*everything!* How could he possibly let her go?

When they finally decided to get dressed and carry on with their plans for the day, Lewis had lost all interest in visiting Swallowbank Farm. He could hardly go out there now, could he, and talk and joke with the Longquists, knowing that he'd just made love with their daughter.

Phoebe drove off on her errand to town, with a wave of her hand and several frenzied silent kisses. Lewis climbed in his Jeep and drove slowly and thoughtfully back to Bearberry Hill. Was this what their relationship was going to be like?

Just before the bridge that crossed the Horsethief River, he stopped and turned around. No, he had to go through with it. How many chances would he have to get on the good side of the Longquists? He wanted to keep seeing their daughter, regardless of what might be in Phoebe's mind right now. She'd said she wasn't ready for a serious relationship. Well, he was.

He'd never receive an engraved invitation from her folks. He'd better deliver Ma's corn. A wasted opportunity like this was…well, wasted.

A real shame.

SWALLOWBANK FARM was well tended, with solid fences and freshly painted outbuildings. The lawns were mowed and the hedges were clipped. What a contrast to his mother's place.

The Longquists lived in a two-story white clapboard house, with a big lilac hedge to the east and a garden to the south. The mailbox right in front of the graveled drive read H. Longquist, so Lewis knew he was at the right place. He didn't really remember the layout from the time he'd been there before. Besides, he'd had his mind on other things. The shingled chicken house out back with the rusty rooster wind vane looked familiar. He remembered waiting there for Phoebe, shivering and hungry.

She'd brought him a jacket and a quart of milk and a plate of home-cooked food. Then they'd talked and laughed and kissed until way past midnight. If a man could ever point to one single incident that had changed his life, Lewis knew he could point to that night.

He pulled up to the house and applied the brake slowly. No dust. No gravel flying. He got out and then opened the rear door and reached into the back for the box of corn. He rang the doorbell and waited, feeling like some kind of traveling salesman.

"Yes?" The attractive woman with streaks of gray through her dark hair must be Nan Longquist. Lewis hadn't seen her in years. She looked harassed. "Can I help you, young man?" She glanced at the box.

Young man.

"Hello, ma'am," Lewis said politely and nodded. "I brought some corn for your family, courtesy of Mercedes Hardin. She says yours comes on a little later than hers does—"

"Oh, heavens!" He received a big smile, and she held the door wider. "Do come in, won't you? We're having a little crisis here, and if you'd be so kind as to carry the corn in and—" Lewis followed her into the kitchen "—set it on the counter here, if you can find room. That Mercedes! She's so thoughtful." She turned toward him. "And who might you be, young man?"

"Lewis, ma'am. Lewis Hardin."

"Lewis!" Her smile disappeared and her tone became much cooler. "Lewis Hardin? Why, you were just a boy last time I saw you. That would be before you…before you—"

"Before I went to jail, ma'am," Lewis interrupted smoothly. He grinned. *May as well play it straight up.* "Well, I've paid my debt to society and I'm a solid citizen now, you'll be pleased to know."

Nan did not grin back. "Well, we'll have to see,

won't we? I know you were quite a disappointment to all of us at the time—a source of considerable grief to poor Mercy…er, Harry?''

Lewis looked around the kitchen. It was in disarray, with dishes stacked on one side of the sink and a pile of wet cloths on the other. The cupboard doors under the sink stood wide open, and Lewis could see a pool of water under the drain.

''Problems?''

''Oh, the plumbing in this old house! It's criminal. The whole place needs to be redone, but that takes money, doesn't it. Harry! Could you come in here a minute, dear?'' She turned to Lewis. ''I want you to meet my husband.'' Her eye held him with an eagle's glare. *Don't you dare leave without meeting my man and protector, you low-down criminal, you,* it said.

''Now what's wrong, Mother?'' came the impatient response from the direction of the hall. Lewis heard a faint, unusual creaky noise, then caught his breath as Harry Longquist wheeled into view. *He's in a wheelchair!* Phoebe had never mentioned it. Nor had Ma.

''Honestly, you can leave that football game for a few minutes, can't you? I want you to meet Mercedes Hardin's boy—Lewis!'' she said triumphantly. ''He used to…to work for the Blakes! You remember.'' She glanced from her husband to Lewis. Her cheeks were red. Lewis stepped forward and offered his hand.

"Sir."

Harry Longquist offered his reluctantly. "Humph. You the fellow rustled his boss's cattle a few years back? Out at the Rocking Bar S?"

Lewis dug deep for a smile. "The very same, sir. All rehabilitated. Left that kind of thing behind me. I'm in the oil fields now, tool-push."

"Well." Phoebe's father didn't seem much more enthusiastic than his wife about a famous local jail-bird standing in their kitchen. "That's a responsible job, I suppose," he grudgingly admitted. He turned away from Lewis. "Damn sink actin' up again, Nan? Just when the fourth quarter's startin', too."

"It's only leaking this time, hon," Nan said. "Just a seal, I'll bet." She managed a shaky laugh for their visitor. She addressed Lewis, with her hands clasped in front of her, over her apron. "Thanks for bringing the corn, Lewis. You be sure and thank your mother, now. It was, er, nice to meet you. I'm glad to hear you've turned over a new leaf. You tell Mercy I'll be up to see her one of these days real soon."

"Listen. I could give you a hand with that sink," Lewis said. The Longquists looked at each other, then at Lewis. Nan shook her head, her lips pressed firmly together.

Harry's face held some interest. "You done that sort of thing before, young man?"

"Sure have. I've fixed all kinds of things over at Ma's place. Still do, whenever I'm home."

"I don't know," Nan said doubtfully. "We couldn't impose...."

"For Pete's sake, woman, let the man help if he wants to! If Trevor was here, he'd do it. Or Jilly. You know what it's like for me, getting twisted up under there with my damn useless legs!" Harry wheeled himself over to a bureau at one side of the kitchen. He rummaged through the contents of a deep drawer. "Should have everything here, son. See if it's a washer that's needed this time. Or a seal, as usual."

Son. Things were looking up—at least with the old man.

Lewis rolled up his sleeves. He sorted expertly through the drawer as Harry watched him, pulling out a couple of likely-size seals and washers and a crescent wrench.

"Boy looks like he knows what he's doing, Nan," Harry announced to his wife, as though Lewis wasn't even in the room. Her face was very flushed. Lewis could tell she wasn't pleased at the turn of events. But it was heaven-sent for him, a chance to do something for Phoebe's parents. A favor. Something he could maybe build on. Because he had no intention of giving up on their daughter. Yesterday he'd thought that might be the best course of action, but this afternoon's experience in the farmer's field had changed his mind for good.

"What's the score, sir?" he asked casually as he walked back to the sink.

"Never mind that sir stuff—it's Harry," Phoebe's father growled. Another improvement, in Lewis's view. "Stampeders are up one field goal. They gotta win this game or they'll be out of the playoffs."

Lewis didn't figure this was the time to tell Phoebe's dad that he was an Edmonton Eskimos fan. The rivalry between the Calgary and Edmonton football teams was a long and fierce one. Lewis wedged himself under the sink and began to inspect the damage. Phoebe's mother was right. Looked like just a leaky seal. The old galvanized plumbing had obviously been patched many times.

"Water's off, is it?" He decided he'd better check, even though this was a drain.

"Oh, yes!"

Phoebe's mother watched carefully as he applied the wrench. As though he might jimmy it, maybe put a U-turn in it and give them the surprise of their lives next time someone used the sink. Five minutes, and he'd made the repair.

"I have some Goop out in the Jeep. That'd do the trick, finish off, here. You got some, Harry?" Lewis glanced at the man in the wheelchair. This was guy stuff. This was bonding. This was the best thing that could've happened. The corn was one thing—nice, neighborly behavior. Fixing plumbing was something else altogether.

"There should be some Goop in that drawer, I think," Harry said, frowning and wheeling himself back to the drawerful of mechanical gadgets and tools. "Yep, here it is. Not much left, but ought to get the job done. Damn old pipes!"

He maneuvered the wheelchair back to the sink and handed Lewis the tube of thick, viscous plumber's helper. Lewis retightened the pipe over the new seal he'd installed, then put plenty of Goop around the connection from the bottom. That would hold for a while.

He heard a roar from the crowd on the television in the living room and saw Harry gaze longingly toward the hallway. "You go ahead and watch your game, sir. I'll be finished here in a jiffy." The *sir* stuff was hard to drop.

"You like CFL? Why don't you watch the last quarter with me?"

That'd be pushing it. "No, thanks. Got to get back to town. Another time maybe."

Over my dead body, Nan's stiff expression seemed to say. She was busy carrying china from the kitchen table to the china cabinet in the corner. It appeared that she'd been washing the china when the sink had sprung a leak, judging by the number of plates and bowls and cups on the table.

Lewis extricated himself from beneath the sink and held up his hands. "Nice dishes," he said lamely. What else could a guy say?

"You think so?" Nan smiled almost cheerfully. "They belonged to my great-aunt. It's a lovely pattern, isn't it? Petit point. I had a big platter, too, but it got broken a few years ago." Nan gazed fondly at the dishes. He'd obviously said the right thing. "Oh! You can wash in the bathroom. I'll get you a clean towel." Nan hurried down the hall ahead of him. Her hospitable impulses outweighed her reservations about him, at least temporarily.

"Never mind a clean towel. I'd just get it all dirty," Lewis said, following her into the roomy bathroom. He saw pink bath gel on the windowsill, a pale yellow bathrobe hanging on the back of the door, noticed the faint scent of green apples in the air. Phoebe's stuff?

Lewis examined his face in the mirror over the sink. He winked at himself—*why, you charming son of a gun, you*—grinned, then paid attention to getting his hands clean.

This visit was a start. Not much more than that. But he was damn glad he hadn't thrown the corn into the river on the way back to Bearberry Hill.

Now if he could just get out of here before Phoebe returned. He didn't think he'd be able to hide his feelings if they were both in the same room together. Pretending to be polite when they'd just enjoyed each other's bodies to near distraction in a farmer's barley field down the road.

He might have made some gains today, but if either of her parents suspected for even a minute that something had already happened, they'd be wild. Their darling daughter and a…a jailbird? A criminal? A low-down, no-good rustler? If they realized how serious the something was that had already happened between them—twice now—he figured there'd be no more of that *son* stuff from Harry Longquist, either. In fact, he'd lay odds that Harry would turn out to be a pretty fair aim with a 16-gauge where his daughter's reputation and welfare were concerned, bad legs or no bad legs.

CHAPTER EIGHT

NEXT TIME they made love it was in the back of his Jeep, with the rear seat folded down, and the two of them squeezed into the cargo space, arms and legs jockeying for position. One thing about Phoebe—she wasn't shy. Not anymore.

Then two days later, she came out to Bearberry Hill with her mother to have tea with Ma and Billy, and under the pretense of wanting to see his cabin— nearly finished now—they strolled to the work site. They made love by the creek and afterward washed each other's flushed and fevered faces, laughing and splashing and staggering naked in the cold water while the dogs barked worriedly on the bank. Then they'd both gotten dressed and gone back to the house to have gingerbread cookies and tea. Phoebe kept meeting his eye and smiling. Lewis was in a fever, his mind whirling, his brain trying to follow the women's conversation while his body still hummed with their lovemaking.

Lewis had it bad. This had to be love. There was no doubt in his mind. The question of any kind of relationship had never come up again, not since their few words in the barn that first time.

He had to leave Glory soon, and so did she. This was just an unexpected liaison, as far as she was concerned. And he'd be back on the job in two days' time, which meant packing up here, checking in with his office in Calgary and getting to the site for some preliminary work before the rig was brought in. Phoebe was going back to the university the following Tuesday.

Two days. Two short summer days. That was all they had left. A week together was all they'd had in their entire lives. Man, what could happen in a week!

LEWIS BECAME AWARE of something tickling his nose. He brushed his hand across his face, but there was nothing on his face. A fly, maybe. He realized that the light was streaming through the window of the Trillium Motel end unit, although he knew he'd closed the curtains tightly the night before.

There it was again....

He opened his eyes. Phoebe was sitting cross-legged on the rumpled bed, her limpid sea-blue gaze inches from his face as she bent toward him. She was smiling. In her fingers was a short feather that must have escaped from one of their pillows, and it was that instrument that had been doing the damage.

"Wake up, sleepy!" She reached forward and tickled his nose again.

Lewis stared up at her. She was wearing nothing but earrings and a pair of socks. He recalled vaguely that she'd complained of cold feet the night before. How she could have been cold, any part of her, escaped him.

"I'm awake," he said. "Now." He pulled her down beside him and leaned over to kiss her.

"Yech!" she yelled. "Morning mouth! Last one in the bathroom is a rotten egg." She leapt off the queen-size bed and strolled seductively down the short hallway to the bathroom, glancing at him over her shoulder. Lewis watched her go. He'd use the bathroom in a minute. He wasn't quite awake yet and he wanted to think.

What was coming next?

Lewis had called Phoebe after the afternoon visit to the farm to try to explain his feelings and to say goodbye in his stupid awkward way. First thing he knew, they'd decided to spend a whole last day together. It was Phoebe's suggestion. When Lewis had met her at the motel in Lethbridge the previous afternoon, he didn't know what she'd told her parents. He hadn't said anything to Mercedes and Billy except that he'd be back the next day to pack up and leave for work. They hadn't asked. Ma and Billy were used to his coming and going as he liked. He'd been on his own, making his own decisions, since he was a boy of twelve and had been kicked out of school for a week. He'd spent it fishing with old Seth

Wilbee, the town tramp, and had never even told Mercedes he'd been suspended.

They'd checked in as Mr. and Mrs. Lewis Hardin—again, at Phoebe's suggestion—and had spent the rest of the afternoon in bed, alternating lovemaking with watching daytime television. Lewis particularly liked the way people on the soaps talked to themselves in empty rooms. Phoebe shushed him, rapt. She told him she'd been watching *Days* since she was a teenager and hardly got a chance to anymore.

Around seven, they'd gotten dressed to go out and had had a magical evening at an Italian restaurant near the river. Their first real date, Lewis reflected.

Conversation. Holding hands. Feeding each other bites of focaccia, as lovers do. Stealing kisses. Slow-dancing. Not even seeing the yawning waitress glancing at her watch at half-past nine, the chipped paint and the stale decor—mainly red-and-white-checked tablecloths and candles in wine bottles. The food was decent—he thought. He hardly knew what he'd ordered.

And then back to the motel...Lewis was almost glad he had to go to work the next day. Much more of this could wear a fellow out.

He heard the shower go on. She was obviously doing more than brushing her teeth. He got up and strode into the bathroom naked. Phoebe was humming in the shower. Some Metallica tune. He looked at himself in the mirror. He could use a shave, that was for sure. No time. He brushed his teeth, then stepped into the shower with Phoebe.

She wrapped her arms around him. "Good morning, Lewis," she said softly, holding up her face to be kissed. Her hair was wet and her face was shining with water. "I'm so happy, aren't you? This was *such* a good idea, wasn't it?"

"Your idea, hon." He kissed her thoroughly, feeling his body respond as always to the sight of her, the taste of her, the feel of her in his arms. "I'm happy, too. I wish this didn't have to end. Ever."

Her face clouded and she seemed about to say something, then changed her mind. She held out the motel's tiny bottle of complimentary shampoo. "Do my hair."

He took his time, soaping and rubbing her scalp slowly and thoroughly. He loved doing this for her. Then he helped her rinse, lifting the russet mass in his fingers, letting the water trickle through.

"Your turn," she said, emptying the bottle into her palm and reaching up to shampoo his hair. He submitted, bending down and closing his eyes to the sensuous pleasure of her fingers in his hair. He tried to ignore the way her body kept rubbing up against his as she massaged his scalp. He had a feeling it wasn't all accidental.

"We haven't made love in a shower," he said when she'd rinsed his hair and he finally opened his eyes. He pulled her close and growled, pushing his knee between her legs.

She laughed, her eyes alight with a gleam he was coming to know and appreciate. "Yet," she said, and raised her leg to his hip.

Twenty minutes later, they were drying off in the small bedroom. Phoebe's hair was damp and hung in crinkly ropes. This motel didn't supply hair dryers.

Lewis fastened his jeans. He watched as she stuffed things into her small, soft-sided bag.

"Let's go out for breakfast," he said, putting on his shirt. "I'm starving. There's an I-HOP down the street." He hated the finality of packing up and leaving so soon. He'd meant what he'd said—he didn't want this to end, ever.

"Sure, but I'd really like to check out, if you don't mind," she said, with a worried look. "This place is depressing. I don't want to come back here."

"Oh." He searched her expression. "I thought it was okay." He slowly buttoned his shirt. She seemed agitated and he wondered why. "You ready to go home?" It was still early. He'd hoped they could spend most of the day together. Neither of them had talked about tomorrow, when Lewis would have to leave Glory. The fact was, they never talked about the future. It was always like this—as though now was the only time they had or would ever have.

"No. I, uh…" She came over to him and stood in front of him. He put his hands on her waist. She was wearing shorts and sandals and a T-shirt. She looked about fifteen.

"What is it, hon?" He rocked back on his heels, pulling her gently with him. "What's bothering you?"

"I'd like to go for a drive. Can we? After breakfast? To the mountains?"

"Sure." He frowned. "That's not what's on your mind, though, Phoebe, is it."

She shook her head. "No."

"Well?"

She looked down for a few seconds, and when she looked back at him, Lewis caught his breath. Her eyes were huge, glowing, passionate....

"I want to get married, Lewis," she whispered. "Let's do it. Let's drive to Tamarack and get married."

THEY STOPPED at a jeweler's on the way to the I-HOP and bought two plain white-gold bands. Lewis preferred the yellow gold, but hers would have needed sizing and they didn't want to bother. Phoebe said she liked white gold better, anyway.

Then they had OJ, a stack of pancakes, maple syrup, ham and coffee, and marveled anew at their sudden decision. He was used to the idea now. Well, used to it might be overstating the case. He was still reeling.

"Marriage?" he'd said, stunned, half an hour before when she'd sprung it on him. *"Marriage?"*

"Why not?" she'd responded quickly, her eyes searching his, vulnerable, hopeful.

"Oh, baby," he'd said, not quite trusting his voice. He'd managed a shaky laugh. "I thought you'd never ask!"

It was nearly ten o'clock now. Lewis asked the young waitress for the location of the nearest provincial office where they could pick up a marriage license. She didn't know.

"You two gettin' married?" she'd asked, her eyes darting from one to the other. "Cool! More coffee? I'll ask Dodie—she'll know. That's so cool!"

The older waitress directed them to a brick building on Nelson Street. They arrived just after it opened and produced their identification and filled out the forms. It turned out to be pretty easy to get married in Alberta, if you had proper ID, showed up together for the license and were residents of the province.

Tamarack had only one marriage commissioner, so Lewis phoned, on the clerk's advice, to make an appointment for that afternoon. The marriage commissioner's answering machine told him she was out of town until the following Monday.

"Darn!" Phoebe said. "I wanted to get married in Tamarack."

"Why?" he asked, grinning. He hadn't stopped

grinning, he realized, since she'd announced she wanted to get married. "What's with Tamarack?" Tamarack was a little mining and ranching town nestled at the foot of the Rockies, about an hour and a half drive from Glory.

"Oh, I don't know. I just always liked the sound of the place. Hannah's from there—you know, one of the librarians?" Lewis knew Phoebe had volunteered at the town library when she'd been in high school. He'd never met Hannah. The library was not a place where he'd spent much time.

THEY MADE an appointment with a Lethbridge marriage commissioner for two o'clock that afternoon. That meant nearly three hours to kill. They went to the park along the river, and Phoebe spread out the blanket that Lewis kept in the back of his Jeep, Lewis went back into town to find a food store and a wine store to buy some supplies for a picnic. They hadn't had breakfast all that long ago, but he was starving again.

They ate salami sandwiches and surreptitiously drank reisling from paper cups—it was illegal to drink in a public place in Alberta—and talked. Then Phoebe propped herself on her elbows and began to read the book she'd brought with her—she needed something to focus on, to settle her nerves. Lewis lay down beside her and stared at the blue, blue sky.

"You're sure about this, Phoebe?" he asked once.

"Absolutely," she answered swiftly. She looked at him. "Are you?"

He nodded. "Yes. I love you, babe. I'd do anything for you. *Anything.* But you've got to admit, we're pretty different. And this has all happened kind of fast. I'm a high-school dropout. You're a brain. I'm a detail guy and you're a big-picture gal."

She elbowed him playfully. "Get off it! How about this? I'm broke and you're loaded. Did you ever think I might have ulterior motives?"

Lewis considered that. "True," he said, and she elbowed him again. "Ouch! I just wanted to make sure it's what you really want, that's all."

Phoebe felt her eyes fill with tears. "I adore you, Lewis. I love you." He hooked an arm around her neck and pulled her down for a quick kiss. "I've loved you, I think, since I was ten years old," she said, tracing the outline of his mouth with her forefinger. It was true; she'd been in love with him since she was a child, in the deep, intense way that only a child could love. She'd lost him for years and now she'd found him again. She'd dreamed of being Lewis's woman since she was a girl with knobby knees and pigtails. She wasn't letting him go now. She wasn't letting him go back to Edmonton and decide maybe he didn't like freckles all that much, after all, and find some other woman. Besides, she was tired of always being the good girl in her family,

JUDITH BOWEN 135

always doing what her parents expected of her. She was tired of always having to be sensible.

But how to explain this sudden urgency? The sudden, overwhelming desire she'd felt this morning, watching him sleep, to be his, really his. Truly his. In the most sacred, profound way. *Marriage.* "I know this seems kind of crazy, but doing it this way cuts out a lot of trouble. You know what I mean?"

"Uh-huh. Your folks."

Phoebe glanced away, at an old couple strolling on the riverside path. "Them. And everyone else. My relatives. People at school. They don't know you the way I do. They don't know what a wonderful, kind person you are. My folks just see that dumb rustling thing, from years ago." She met his gaze again. "I know they'll get over it eventually, but they'd bring up all kinds of complications. They'd think we should get married in a church. All that fuss. Weddings are just too…too stupid, anyway! *Being* married is what counts."

"Is it?" He turned on one side to study her. "You know I'll do anything you want, Phoebe, even sneak off like this and marry you. But we can't hide forever. There's still going to be trouble. Maybe more. Running off could make it worse in the eyes of your folks. You thought of that?"

She stared at him for a full minute. Surely he didn't mean it! Surely he wanted this as much as she did! "Lewis Hardin. Do you *really* care what they think? What anybody thinks?"

"No," he said, and she knew that was a fact. He'd never cared what other people thought of him. She had to admit that had always been part of his appeal. "But I don't want to make extra trouble for you, Phoebe. Or for me. They'll be my in-laws, don't forget."

"So, they don't have to know, do they? Not right away. I'll be settled in Edmonton, at school. I can't give up my job at the residence without notice, anyway. I need the money, even if I do have a rich husband." She smiled at him as she thought about their situation. "You'll be living out…out in some bunkhouse somewhere in the middle of nowhere. We can't live together right now, so why tell anyone at all? For a while?"

She bit her lip suddenly, thinking. All her life she'd entertained herself by daydreaming. It was fun. She was a famous bareback rider, in a circus. She was a scholarship winner who'd take the university by storm—that part had come true. She was a deep-sea diver. She was a pirate's lady. It was all part of the rich imagination that she knew she had and treasured as one of her real talents—as long as she didn't let it get the best of her. "It'll be a secret for a while. Ours!"

He lay back on his crossed arms and smiled.

"Okay. I'm not crazy about the secrecy angle, but we'll have to work it out later, I guess."

He shut his eyes and his breathing slowed. Amazing! He was asleep. This must be what shift work did to a person. Catching forty winks whenever you could.

She gazed at him, loving every bristle in his two-day beard. He needed a shave desperately. Loving every laugh line, every wrinkle, every freckle. Hey, he had a few, too.

This was an adventure, the kind of adventure she'd only dreamed of before. But then, her relationship with Lewis had been an adventure ever since she'd first crawled into the hayloft to spy on him. Marriage wasn't supposed to be an adventure, though, was it? It was a sacred vow. A commitment. She could see her aunt Catherine lecturing her on the duties of matrimony.

He loved her and she loved him. That was all that really mattered. Like he'd said, they'd work out the details later. Somehow.

Phoebe tried to pay attention to her book. She woke him after an hour and they packed up and drove to the marriage commissioner's, a real-estate broker in a small office next to a bakery.

Half an hour later, they were back in the August sunshine, husband and wife.

CHAPTER NINE

BART TANGUAY, the president of Wild Rose Oil, was accustomed to success. When he said jump, people asked, "How high?" Or else they just shut up and jumped.

Lewis Hardin was proving to be more difficult than he'd expected. That, Tanguay decided, was his mistake, right from the beginning, thinking he'd be a pushover. He had to admit, with an element of reluctant admiration, the kid had balls.

But Lewis Hardin was no kid anymore; he was twenty-seven.

That florist girl's place had been a challenge. His secretary had placed the call. The cell phone was easy. Then, there was Glory. Why hadn't he thought of that earlier? It made sense that Lewis would head home once in a while.

Three offers so far, but Hardin wasn't biting. He'd even had the goddamn nerve to hang up on him. Nobody hung up on Bart Tanguay. *Nobody.*

Tanguay swung his leather executive knee-tilter away from the window on the seventeenth floor of the Leduc Tower and reached for his phone. He had a couple of more cards to play. And, of course, there was always the trump card. He didn't think he'd ever have to play that one, not for a long, long time, but if he had to…

Tanguay would do anything that was necessary to guarantee his success, both personal and corporate. He hadn't clawed his way up from basement to boardroom to let a small-town loser like Lewis Hardin get in the way of his company plans. He'd made up his mind that he wanted Hardin aboard Wild Rose, and the guy was a fool to think he could keep saying no. All it took was the right hook. That was Tanguay's job, to find it.

As if Hardin wasn't made out of the same flesh and blood as every other man was…

Nope. There were several ways to skin a cat, and Bart Tanguay hadn't even started on Hardin yet.

"Florrie? Call my wife, will you? Tell her I'm not going to be home tonight. Yeah, yeah, I know about the dinner party, she can handle it herself—and listen, get me Fred Billings's private number. Yeah, Billings from F&B Drilling. He needs a sponsor to get into the Devonian Club. I'm thinking maybe I can do him a favor."

"I MISS THAT BOY." Mercy stood at the wood-burning kitchen range and stirred the big enamel pot of peach jam. There was a perfectly good electric stove in the Hardin kitchen, but they rarely used it.

Should have today; it was a scorcher both inside and out.

"I was getting used to having him around here, weren't you? He helps out and he's a good eater, always has been. I like that. It's a pleasure cooking for a good eater." She smiled. "Not like you and me."

Mercy had picked up a forty-pound crate of bruised peaches from the man who came around with a van at this time of year selling Okanagan fruit, and was putting it up before she lost it. The box had cost her five dollars. The man had been planning to throw it away. Even though Lewis sent money regularly now, thriftiness was a lifelong habit. And old habits died hard.

"Oh, yes. I miss him." Billy looked up from where she was sitting at the kitchen table, cutting pictures out of magazines. Billy liked making picture collages on different themes. She'd glue the cutout pictures onto cardboard and brush varnish over them. They had examples of Billy's artwork hanging on just about every vertical surface, including the chicken house. "But it's just as well, Ma, isn't it?" she went on in her soft voice. "It's just as well he's gone away again." She returned to her careful snipping.

Mercy glanced sharply at her daughter. Billy liked to pretend. She'd always been the weak one. Weak and tender. Premature, an eight-month baby, and touch-and-go with her in the first few years. Billy had caught everything going—whooping cough, croup, chicken pox, measles, mumps, ear infections, you name it. Not like Lewis, who'd been a strong, lusty infant right from the start. Mercy wondered sometimes if all the sickness had affected her daughter's mind. But there was nothing wrong with Billy's mind. She was just shy. *A tender soul.* Shy and fearful.

And no wonder.

Mercy gave the simmering pot another stir, then set down the big wooden spoon and limped over to the sink to rinse her jelly glasses. They were artistic, both she and her daughter. They had temperaments. Billy with her gardening and her pictures, Mercy with her quilts and her fancy work. All those old clothes people kept bringing her had sure been a blessing for her quilting. She sold them for money, too.

There wasn't a knitting pattern Mercy Hardin couldn't study and pick out for herself. Women in the district often stopped by to get her advice. Even Granny Longquist, who thought she was quite the knitter, had sent her daughter-in-law Nan with a few samples of knitted lace for Mercy to puzzle over.

"He'll be getting married soon enough," Mercy said, rattling the jelly glasses in the bottom of the roaster that she used to scald them in. She cradled the roaster against her hip and reached for her stick.

"We'll need new dresses. We'll be goin' to a wedding any time now. Won't that be fun?"

Billy let out a soft cry, like a wounded bird.

"Yep." Mercy watched at her daughter and set her mouth in a firm line. "That Longquist girl, if I'm not mistaken. He's got a good job, and he's handsome, just like Grandpa Hardin was. Oh, my, old Mr. Hardin was a fine-lookin' man! You wouldn't remember him, of course. Girls have always been partial to our Lewis, you know that. If it isn't Nan's girl who reels him in, it'll be someone else, sure enough."

She hobbled back to the stove and set the roasterful of jelly glasses over the fire, then poured in hot water from the steaming kettle that sat at the back of the range. "Lewis is a man. He'll be starting a family of his own soon. He's got a right to know, Billy, no matter what. He's a man now. The past is the past and time moves on, you know it does, Billy."

As always, when Mercy brought up the subject, Billy removed herself from the conversation. She left the room now, leaving her papers fluttering on the table in a sudden breeze. Mercy walked over and closed the kitchen window, which had been open to let in some air. It was hot as Hades with that stove going.

She sighed. She was just sixty-three, but sometimes she felt like an old, old woman. She picked up her wooden spoon again and began to stir the bubbling cauldron of jam. You had to watch peach; it scorched awful easy.

MARRIED!

The first week back at university, Phoebe hardly believed her own thoughts when she looked in the bathroom mirror in the mornings and said to herself, *You're married now. Lewis Hardin is your husband.* There was no outward evidence; she wore her ring on a chain around her neck, under her shirt.

It was almost as if nothing had happened.

The first part of the semester was a busy time for her and Lindy. Students were settling in and there was always a lot of hand-holding with the first-year girls, many of whom had never lived away from home before.

Then there was the usual flurry of getting her own program of studies under way. She had books to buy, lab supplies to organize, interviews with her adviser and other people in the department about her research project. In addition to her own studies, she was expected to hold tutorials with first-year science students and had agreed the previous year—before she'd known she'd have a rich husband!—to help one of the science professors with his marking. That was one obligation she'd try to palm off on another graduate student who needed the income.

Lewis phoned twice in the first week. Once from his car when he was on the road somewhere. The second time, he said he was coming to Edmonton the following week to see her, and she panicked.

"You *can't* come and see me!" she exclaimed, glad that Lindy had gone downstairs to run some errands. They only had one phone and there was very little privacy in the tiny apartment. Besides, she hadn't even discussed her new situation with her roommate yet.

"Why not? I'm going to be in town, anyway." He sounded hurt and Phoebe felt a flood of love for him. How could she have done such a stupid thing as to get him tangled up in this secret-marriage business? They'd gone ahead and done everything backward. Sometimes her sense of drama got her into predicaments. Maybe this was one.

"I...I just don't think it would be a good idea," she said, hedging. "I haven't told my roommate anything about us, and I think I'll have to, don't you? I haven't thought up a good story yet. Don't worry, she can keep a secret."

There was a long silence at Lewis's end, as though he didn't approve of the secrecy at all. She *knew* he didn't; he was just humoring her. "All right. I'll call you later, when I'm in town. Friday. Maybe you'll have changed your mind."

"Okay," Phoebe said, relieved—and kicking herself for feeling that way. Yet at the same time she wished, childishly, that Lewis had insisted.

"You having second thoughts, honey?" Lewis's voice was calm.

"Of course not! I...I just have to figure things out here, and right now it's so busy—"

"I'll take you out for dinner, babe. We'll go somewhere nice. And then we'll get a hotel room and I'll take your clothes off and seduce your beautiful freckled body all over again," he murmured, and Phoebe felt the tiny hairs on her arms and shoulders stand on end. Man, he knew how to do it to her!

"Okay," she murmured breathlessly, afraid Lindy would be back any moment. "Okay, I'll see what I can do. Call me on Friday, then."

Now what? There was no way she was telling Lindy anything until she'd thought it all through. Every detail. She needed a story and then she needed to stick to it. Somehow, telling her roommate she'd gone off and gotten married and hadn't told anyone yet just seemed too...straightforward.

By Friday, Phoebe had decided she was overreacting. She'd tell Lindy she was seeing Lewis, period. Dating. Why not? After all, it wasn't as though he'd be in town that often. Then she could logically move on to being engaged and by the time she and Lewis were ready to tell everyone the truth shortly after that, well, Lindy, at least, would be used to it. Lindy was not a romantic person. She'd think being secretly married was just plain stupid, and Phoebe couldn't count on her not blowing the whole thing next time her mother or dad called and Lindy answered. Her roommate could be too honest for her own good—or Phoebe's good, anyway.

And if Phoebe said she was seeing a guy from out of town, that would make it easier to put off her other callers. She hadn't had a terrifically active social life the previous year, but Boyd Paterson was interested in her as more than a colleague, she knew that. And she'd dated a couple of engineering students, as well, neither of whom had called since the summer.

Boyd called, though. In fact, he wanted to take her out to dinner and a movie the same night Lewis was going to be in town. He said he couldn't wait to tell her about his field work over the summer. Lake sediment. Phoebe turned him down.

She still hadn't said anything to Lindy.

Friday evening, when the buzzer she'd both longed for and dreaded sounded from the first floor, Phoebe took a deep breath and hit the buzzer to let Lewis in. She fumbled with her shoes as she slipped them on and ran damp palms down the on-sale little black dress she'd decided to wear again. It was her best dress. *Lookin' good, Pheeb,* she mentally told herself after a quick once-over in the mirror behind the bathroom door. *Basic black and freckles go together so well.*

A sharp rap at the apartment door told her Lewis was there. *Her husband!* She opened it.

"Lewis!"

He took one stride inside and pulled her into his arms. His kiss was possessive. Possessive and thorough and very, very masterful. Oh, it felt so *good* to be back in his arms!

"I've waited too damn long for this, Phoebe," he growled in her ear and she shivered.

"Me, too," she whispered. Then he released her and stepped back.

"Where's the roommate?" His dark eyes swept around the tiny apartment. "You sleep over there?" he asked, not waiting for her reply and pointing to the tiny alcove on the right that formed Phoebe's private space. Lindy's was on the left, with the folding doors closed. He didn't miss a thing.

She nodded. "Lindy's out. She had to go over to her aunt's. Do something for her. She lives in Strathcona—her aunt, that is," Phoebe explained, babbling, closing the doors to her own sleeping alcove. She'd been relieved when Lindy had received a phone call an hour ago and suddenly gone out.

Lewis's gaze returned to her, and Phoebe wondered at the muscle she saw moving in his jaw. "You've told her about us." It wasn't a question.

"N-not exactly."

He stared at her for a few seconds. He was wearing a charcoal-gray sports jacket, black slacks, a black turtleneck—and a wedding ring. He looked dark and dangerous, like one of the romantic heroes she used to read about. Dangerous and wonderful. "Okay, where's your coat? Let's get out of here. I've got reservations for seven.''

''Where are we going?'' Phoebe felt terrible. He was clearly disappointed that she hadn't told Lindy yet. She'd had a week to come up with something. Why hadn't she? She just couldn't seem to settle on what exactly she was going to tell her roommate. *I'm married, but don't tell anybody. I'm sort of married. I'm getting married.*

''The Macdonald. I've reserved a table by the fire in the Harvest Room.'' He sent her a slow smile that did jiggly things to her insides. ''With a surprise for dessert.''

''A surprise? Let me just whip into the bathroom for a minute before we go,'' Phoebe said, scuttling to the bathroom where she frantically searched for her wedding band in the zipper pocket of her purse, found it and slipped it onto the third finger of her left hand. Had Lewis noticed she wasn't wearing it? Well, he had to know she could hardly wear a wedding ring if she was keeping their marriage a secret. He was wearing *his* ring. Did this mean he was telling people? His bosses? His co-workers?

Of course, Phoebe knew no one in the oil industry. Nor did her parents, as far as she was aware. So, it wasn't as if her secret would get back to them, which was the main reason she'd wanted to keep everything quiet for now. As long as Lewis didn't tell Billy and Mercy that he was married, it should be okay. She had to prepare her parents for the news. Break them in to the idea that the man she loved was not the terrible person, the criminal, they thought he was. Maybe by Christmas…

Lewis had cleaned out his Jeep. There was no longer even a hint of the mud and dust of the oil field. The exterior was polished and shiny black; the chrome gleamed. An orange hard hat on the back seat, sitting on top of a few magazines and some unopened mail, was the only sign of his occupation.

The sun was low in the sky as they crossed the North Saskatchewan River on the Fifth Street Bridge. The river valley was alive with the vibrant yellows and golds of poplars and aspens. Joggers and cyclists in brightly colored clothing lined the walks and paths that stretched for miles in both directions from the parliament buildings. Edmontonians were proud of their river heritage, and the city fathers had wisely preserved the entire valley for the enjoyment of everyone.

The Macdonald Hotel, built early in the last century and recently refurbished to reflect its age and grandeur, had a sentinel position on the north side, overlooking the North Saskatchewan. The hotel had been built to accommodate the many businessmen and important travelers coming to the brash new city by train early in the last century.

The Harvest Room was a premiere dining spot in the city. Phoebe had never been there. As for the hotel itself, she'd only been in the lobby once, when she was meeting her aunt Honor, who'd been in Edmonton on legal business for the firm she worked with in Glory.

The maître d'hotel escorted them to their table with a smile. Phoebe couldn't help noticing the admiring looks her husband received from other women. She felt a rush of completely female energy. *He's mine,* she thought fiercely. *Mine.*

"Wow!" Phoebe whispered to Lewis, taking in the fabulous view outside the huge windows of the beautifully decorated room.

"Some advantages to marrying for money, huh?" He grinned at her and took her hands across the table. He bent his head and studied their hands, one tanned and one freckled, both wearing plain white-gold bands. Phoebe felt tears gather in her throat. This was so beautiful. This was so wonderful. This was so... *exciting.*

He bent toward her and she leaned forward to meet him in a soft kiss. "I love you, Phoebe," he said, squeezing her hands gently. "With all my heart and soul. Let's have a bottle of champagne and we'll drink to no regrets."

CHAPTER TEN

THE NEW YORK STRIP was superb—the best Phoebe had ever had. The dessert, a sticky date pudding with whiskey sauce, was delicious. Even the coffee was good, and Phoebe was very particular about her coffee.

She felt a bit tipsy after the champagne. She and Lewis had talked about everything—his job, their relatives, her school year, even the weather. Lewis wanted to take her on a ski holiday at Thanksgiving, to Jasper Park Lodge, if there was enough snow in the mountains by then. She'd never skiied, but she was eager to try. This was new, being able to do things and go places she couldn't have afforded in the past. Now, as Lewis's wife, it was part of her lifestyle, too.

"What about your cabin?" she asked, refusing a second cup of coffee from the attentive waiter.

Lewis glanced sharply at her. "Down at Ma's? I'm going to finish it. Maybe next time I go there. I'd always figured it for just a little hideaway. A bachelor place. I'd better start working on something else now that I'm a married man." He grinned at her suddenly. "Unless you'd like to raise five kids there."

They both laughed at the idea. It was preposterous, of course. But where *would* they set up married life…eventually? Phoebe realized she didn't know any more about Lewis's hopes and dreams now than she had as a fifteen-year-old. Kids? Yes, Lewis would probably want children. They'd never talked about children, how many or if they'd even have any. Phoebe felt a chill grip her heart as it occurred to her that she'd never really considered the subject before, not even as a dreamy teenager.

Lewis's deep voice interrupted her thoughts. "Ready for my surprise, Phoebe?"

"Surprise? I thought it was dessert?"

"Better than dessert. Come with me, my love." He bowed gallantly, and she giggled and rose to allow him to escort her from the dining room. He took their coats at the coat check and helped her into hers.

"A ruse," he said mysteriously, winking at her.

"Ruse?"

"Yeah, the coat." They walked into the hotel lobby. "Okay, close your eyes, Phoebe. I've got to take you somewhere for the surprise and I don't want you to see where we're going."

"Lewis!" Phoebe looked at him, delighted with the game. "What are you up to?"

"Shh. Never mind, woman," he said with a jaunty smile. "Just follow instructions."

"Okay!" she said, and cheerfully shut her eyes tight. She didn't even peek, even though she knew very well they were getting into the hotel elevator. She let Lewis take her arm and cover her eyes with his other hand as they walked down a long carpeted hallway.

"Keep them closed!" She heard him fumbling with a key and sensed a door swinging open.

"Just another minute, honey. This won't hurt a bit, I promise." And with that he swept her up into his arms and took a step forward. Phoebe's eyes flew open as she flung her arms around Lewis's neck.

"Ooooh!"

They were in a large, beautifully appointed room overlooking the river. There were flowers everywhere—pink roses—an ice bucket with ice and a bottle of champagne. An open box of Belgian chocolates sat on the bedside table, along with a box of condoms. *A box!* On the other side, draped invitingly across the pillow was the most beautiful pale-apricot peignoir set Phoebe had ever seen. It was lacy and see-through, and the robe had satin trim. Gorgeous.

"Like it?" Lewis was grinning broadly. He shut the door and locked it. Phoebe noticed he'd put the Do Not Disturb sign on the outer doorknob. "That was my big moment, I hope you realize. Carrying my bride across the threshold, so to speak."

"Oh, Lewis!" Phoebe was nearly in tears. "It's wonderful! I...I don't know what to say."

"I thought we should have a real honeymoon in a nice hotel, even if it's just one night," he said. "Better than my studio suite over on Ninety-Eighth. I figured this would appeal to you."

He walked over to the champagne bucket and removed the bottle, wiping it with the cloth provided. "I think I can handle this by myself. Why don't you, uh—" his dark eyes looked her over from head to toe and back again, slowly and deliberately "—get into zomething more comfortable while I pop zee cork." His French accent was atrocious.

Phoebe felt like a virgin all over again, shyly changing in the bathroom. She hung her black dress on the hook behind the bathroom door and pulled on the nearly invisible short nightie, then the robe. She fluffed her hair. Her eyes were bright; she couldn't stop smiling. She had to admit she'd never looked better. A tube of toothpaste and two brand-new toothbrushes, one blue, one pink, rested on the vanity. She unwrapped the pink one and brushed her teeth. What a man. He'd thought of everything!

Lewis had taken off his jacket and poured the champagne. His appreciation when she emerged was plain to see. He adored her. Phoebe blushed. She felt like a schoolgirl. She'd worried so long about her homely freckles and her lean, athletic build. Now she'd met a man—the man she'd always secretly loved—who thought she was just perfect the way she was. And it wasn't as though she was the only lover he'd known, as he was for her. Life was full of miracles.

"Here you go, honey," he said, handing her a champagne flute. He held his glass high.

"No regrets?"

Why did he always put it that way? "No regrets," she said, raising her own glass. They both drank deeply of the bubbly liquid.

He walked over to the entertainment center and flicked a couple of switches. Soft music filled the room—"Unchained Melody." Phoebe shivered. Now, *that* was a romantic tune.

"Now," Lewis said with a wicked smile, "I think we should dance."

THEY DANCED for a while and then Lewis produced a jeweler's box from his pocket.

"For you, darling," he said, his voice warm and his eyes glowing. He took the ring finger of her left hand and slid on an emerald ring. Square-cut and green, flashing with a small diamond on each side in a platinum-and-white-gold setting. "An engagement ring. Kind of backward, but there it is."

"Oh, Lewis." Phoebe was stunned. Tears ran down her cheeks. "It's…it's gorgeous."

He kissed her and when he spoke, his voice was rough. "Just like my bride."

They danced again and then they made love. Lewis was a marvelous dancer. And a marvelous lover.

Later they ordered cheesecake from room service and talked. That was when she found out that Lewis had been saving money for a few years and eventually wanted to start a ranch of his own in southern Alberta. They'd joked about his being rich, but it turned out he really did have a lot of money saved and in investments, waiting for the day when he could either build up the Hardin homestead or buy himself a new place.

She told him about her research project for her master's degree. He didn't seem all that interested, and when she chided him gently, he replied, "Sorry, honey. I just can't get that worked up about algae and bugs and all that scientific stuff. I'll leave that to you."

The next morning, the phone rang while they were making love and Lewis reached over and flicked the mute button. Half an hour later, it blinked, indicating another call, and Lewis answered it. Phoebe listened to the conversation from her position beside him, her head resting on his shoulder. She turned and twisted her left hand, admiring the way the light caught the emerald and diamonds in her ring. It was exquisite. Her new husband had impeccable taste.

They were covered only with a cotton sheet. The peignoir set had long since disappeared.

It sounded as though the caller was someone from the rig site.

"Problems?" she asked, stretching languidly. It was broad daylight—nearly noon—and pretty soon she'd have to get up and shower and get dressed and go back to the residence. How was she going to explain the ring to Lindy? Should she come right out and say she was engaged and keep the wedding band hidden? That would certainly be jumping ahead with the story.

"A few." He was frowning, apparently deep in thought. "Nothing I can't take care of from here, though."

"On a Saturday?"

He glanced at her, preoccupied. "Saturday's just like any other day of the week on this job, honey. That's something you'll have to get used to."

"Oh, well," she said lightly, "it's not as though we can live together, anyway."

He shot her a sharp look, then flung back the sheet and stood beside the bed, magnificently naked. He was lean and muscular with broad shoulders and a narrow waist. There wasn't an ounce of excess flesh on his body. His muscles were hard, defined. His hands were rough with calluses, the hands of a workingman. She'd felt his strength when he'd whisked her off her feet the evening before, picking her up as though she was a featherweight, which she knew very well she was not. She'd sensed his strength, held in tight control, when they made love. He made her feel precious and delicate. Loved.

"Mind if I take a shower first?" He reached down and cupped her left breast with his hand. "Or maybe I should—"

She turned away from him and squealed. "No way! I couldn't!"

"You could."

"Take your shower."

He grinned. "Okay. If you insist." He stalked naked into the bathroom and a few minutes later Phoebe heard the shower go on.

She lay in bed for a while. She needed to think.

Lewis wanted to be a rancher.

This news had come as a shock to her. Sometimes she thought she'd spent her whole life trying to escape the farm. Why had she worked as hard as she had at school if it wasn't to win a scholarship so she could get a decent education and get out of the small-town world her parents lived in?

And kids. He'd mentioned kids. They'd never discussed kids. Now that she thought about it, she didn't know how to react. Sure, she adored children, and couldn't think of anything she'd love more than to feel Lewis's baby growing inside her—but when? She had a career to prepare for and then to pursue. How could she fit children into that? And she was still young. She hadn't planned to marry until she was maybe thirty or so.

But here she was, twenty-three and secretly married to the romantic highwayman of her teenage dreams. A bad boy with a prison record and an eagle tattoo on his shoulder. An oil-rig worker. A guy who didn't know the difference—and didn't care—between algae and amoeba.

Three weeks ago, she'd been a virgin. Now she was a sex maniac. She *loved* making love with Lewis. Even this secret night in the hotel—it was a fantasy dream come true. He was the perfect man for her, because they shared the same crazy imagination.

Was that *really* true? Phoebe thought so hard her brain ached. Something was wrong with this picture, but she wasn't sure what. Maybe it was the secrecy, although she didn't see how she could change that for a while. And, really, it made sense for right now, didn't it? *Especially* now.

Maybe it was the romantic-fantasy angle, the fact that they met the way they did, in restaurants and in hotel rooms. He wanted to take her skiing, stay in an expensive ski resort. He bought her glamorous jewelry, even though, technically, the emerald took the place of an engagement ring, which most girls got. Every girl who got married, anyway. None of it was the stuff of ordinary life. Certainly not ordinary married life.

Yet they *were* married. They were husband and wife. She'd promised to stay with him, to love, honor and cherish him forever. She'd meant every word of her vows.

At the time.

"What about Howard? Can he take over?" Lewis had stalked out of the bathroom, still naked, with his cell phone clapped to his ear. He didn't even glance toward the bed where she lay, thinking about getting up. She was a little hurt. Couldn't he even look at her?

"Where the hell's Saunderson? He should be there, damn it!" Lewis pulled open the heavy curtain that blocked the sun, and light spilled into the room. "Uh-huh. Well, maybe you can give him a call. I'll be back as soon as I can." Luckily they had a river view, or people out walking their dogs would have had quite an eyeful. Lewis didn't show the slightest embarrassment. He was perfectly at ease, whether wearing jeans and a hard hat or naked as a jaybird.

She sat up. He still hadn't glanced her way. She had a riveting view of his back, his buttocks, the long, strong length of his legs. He ran his free hand through his damp hair as she watched, setting it on end. He was totally involved in his conversation, staring out the window.

The way she was when she was doing lab work. Total concentration.

Still, the woman in her would have liked a leer or two.

"Okay, okay." He sounded impatient—finally.

"Let me get back to you. I have, uh, one or two little things to clear up here." Now he did turn and glance at her, offering a quick distracted smile.

She arched a brow. Oh. So she was one of the little things he had to clear up. She could take a hint. Phoebe got out of bed, stretched briefly, then went into the bathroom. She locked the door. It made a satisfying *thunk*.

Her feelings weren't seriously hurt, but she didn't want him coming in apologizing. *If* he'd even noticed she was annoyed.

She realized to her dismay that she was looking for reasons to quarrel with him. She wasn't ordinarily a difficult person, but something in Lewis had brought out a horrible bitchy edge in her she barely recognized. She wanted to *blame* him for something. Why? *Why?*

It wasn't right. Or fair. They were perfect together. He loved her. He adored her. He'd married her, hadn't he? An hour after she'd asked him! She loved being with him. She loved talking to him. She loved sex with him.

Sex. That was it.

She wasn't in love with Lewis Hardin. She was in *lust* with him. She'd married him because she was a well-brought-up girl, an eldest daughter, who'd always done what was expected of her. She'd married him so she wouldn't feel guilty about their affair. She was a good Catholic girl. She wasn't supposed to have affairs.

But that was what it should have been—an affair. Sex outside of marriage was wrong, or so she'd been taught. She'd married him to get around it! Phoebe felt scared. Could that possibly be true?

She didn't want to be a rancher's wife. She didn't want to raise five kids in the sticks somewhere. She wanted to *be* somebody. She was brainy and bookish and energetic; she wanted to *do* something with her ife. Something exciting.

Well, she'd done something, hadn't she? She'd married Lewis Hardin less than two weeks after she'd lost her virginity to him. She hadn't had the experience or sense to realize what these feelings really were. *Sex.* So much for brains! She'd saved herself for him all those years, like some silly romantic girl who'd read too many love stories.

Now she had him.

She had the chili-pepper hots for him, and now, like it or not, she'd have to learn to live with the whole enchilada. And he was not a guy you could *manage,* like Boyd.

Marriage. It wasn't something you did just for the heck of it on a sunny August afternoon.

Her aunt Catherine would have told her so—if she'd ever thought to ask.

CHAPTER ELEVEN

LEWIS STARED at the bathroom door. He'd heard the click. Funny, he hadn't taken Phoebe for the melodramatic type.

He'd been trying to pay attention to what Charlie was telling him over the background noise out at the rig site. They'd had some mechanical screwups, which was par for the course, and the waterman hadn't shown up. He had a substance-abuse problem, but he'd been in detox and Lewis had wanted to give him a second chance. Maybe it was time to pull the pin; you couldn't be too much of a bleeding heart in this business and Saunderson knew it. He'd had his chances.

The job of bringing water trucks to the site was critical. The crew needed water to prepare the drilling mud, which lubricated the pipe underground as they drilled. Lewis knew someone he might be able to hire on short notice. He quickly dialed Marv Sloboda, a waterman he'd worked with on another job up north. Luckily he was home and said, sure, he'd go out to the rig that afternoon if he could get a ride. His truck was in the shop. Lewis said he'd pick him up at two.

Then he stood for a moment, frowning at the closed bathroom door, wondering if he should rattle the doorknob and get Phoebe to let him in so he could try to explain. He didn't have that much experience with placating women. She didn't realize that his job was 110 percent with him. Even if they'd been having an honest-to-goodness honeymoon, he'd have had to be available to his bosses and crew.

Not many women understood that kind of devotion to duty, judging by the numbers of divorced and single guys in the business. Was Phoebe going to turn out to be one of those women?

He was just about to go to the bathroom and beg her to let him in when his phone buzzed again.

Goddamn it—now what?

"Hardin here," he answered tersely.

"Lewis Hardin?"

He didn't recognize the voice. "That's right."

"Bart Tanguay. We haven't spoken before—"

"How the hell did you get my number?" Lewis asked angrily. It was one thing to be bothered in his hotel room by co-workers, but it was another to have every Tom, Dick and Harry calling him up.

There was a brief pause and Lewis nearly hung up. "Never mind that, Hardin. I want you to come work for me. Name your price."

"What are you talking about?" Lewis scowled into the phone, feeling his temperature rise. "And who the *hell* are you?"

"Wild Rose. We know how good you are, Hardin. We want you on our side. We're a big company. Money, titles, perks—you name it, it's yours."

"Well, listen here, Tanguay. I don't care if you're a goddamn oil sheik from the Middle East, I want you and your people to leave me alone. I'm tired of hearing about Wild Rose. I'm staying right where I am. And if I was thinking of leaving my job, you'd be the last outfit I'd call."

"Why's that?" The man sounded amused.

"Because you're a pain in the butt, that's why. Can't you take no for an answer?"

"Be reasonable, Hardin. We could do business. I can make it worth your while—"

Lewis clicked off the tiny phone. It wasn't nearly as satisfying as slamming down a receiver the old-fashioned way. What the hell was so attractive about *him?* Why wouldn't they leave him alone? The phone rang again.

"Yes?" Lewis was ready to chew nails.

"Let's talk." Goddamn Tanguay.

"There's nothing to talk about. When are you guys going to give it a rest?" Lewis glared out the window again. It was a beautiful fall day. Indian summer. The kind that couldn't last.

"When we meet."

"Okay." Lewis made up his mind. He would meet him—once. Get it over with. Make his point loud and clear. In person. "Where?"

"Calgary. My office. Leduc Tower."

"And you won't call me again?"

The man laughed. "I won't have to. You'll be working for me."

"Like hell! I won't see you at all unless I've got your word that you lay off and quit harassing me."

"Sure, sure. Although I wouldn't call offering a man the chance of a lifetime harassing him."

"I'll decide that. Okay." Lewis picked up his watch, which he'd left on the bedside table. He checked a date, did some figuring. "The last week in October."

There was a long pause. "Not before then?" It was just mid-September.

"Nope. I'm busy. Last week next month or nothing."

"All right. Until then…" Tanguay hung up. Lewis cursed the tiny phone in his hand. Hanging up was *his* prerogative.

Phoebe looked pale when she came out of the shower. Lewis was dressed by then. He didn't want to seem too eager to leave, but he had this problem at the site, and he had to solve it. Now. Time wasted was profit down the drain. No profit, no crew bonuses.

"You okay, honey?" Lewis walked toward her and touched her cheek gently with the back of his hand. Poor kid, she hadn't had much sleep last night. He hadn't slept, either, but he felt like a million bucks. Terrific. They'd needed this, he and Phoebe. A whole night. So far, their time together had been a few hours snatched here and there, in hay fields, in the back seats of utility vehicles. In cheap motels. It was ridiculous.

And it was no way to start married life. The sooner he could talk her out of that dumb idea of not telling anyone about their marriage, the better. He wanted to settle things, maybe buy a house here in the city. She could live there and go to school, and he could be with her whenever he had time off. Her parents would come around eventually; they had to.

"I'm fine," she said softly. Her eyes had dark smudges under them. "Just tired, that's all. I can sleep when I get home." Her smile was thin.

Lewis frowned as he watched her dress. Something was wrong. But, damn it, he didn't have time to find out what it was. He had to meet Sloboda in less than an hour.

"You want to have lunch somewhere?" He caught himself hoping she'd say no. "Look, I'm sorry about the phone calls. It's just the way it is in this business. Things screw up, they've got to be fixed right away."

"I know." She turned so he could zip the back of her dress. She lifted her arms to raise her hair from her shoulders. He dropped a kiss on the side of her neck. "I'm just tired, Lewis. Honest."

She bent to retrieve the peignoir set from the floor,

where it had landed sometime during the night. He'd paid plenty for the delicate garment in an upscale lingerie shop, but it was worth every penny. She was a goddess in it, with her coloring. And the emerald…perfect. A goddess in gold and green.

"Here." He took it from her and folded it carefully if a little clumsily and put it in the hotel's white plastic laundry sack. "You want to take the roses, too?"

She hesitated, then he saw the old mischief return to her eyes. That was a relief. "Sure. I'll tell my roommate I have a secret admirer!"

MERCEDES HARDIN made her way slowly from the kitchen garden to the house. The doctor had said they could do something for that hip of hers now, some kind of newfangled reconstructive surgery, but Mercy was reluctant. Who would take care of Billy while she was gone? What if she came out a worse cripple than she already was? There were no guarantees. No, she was too old for that nonsense. She'd make do with her stick.

The gardening was almost finished for the year. A few more rows of spuds, the late Kennebecs, to dig. And there was the usual cleanup and composting, but Billy generally did the heavier work. She was younger. Mercy looked after the putting up and preserving. This year she'd made twenty-two quarts of beet pickles from the Detroit reds and two ten-gallon

crocks of sauerkraut from the new Danish ball cab-
bages Billy had planted. They'd never eat all that
over the winter, but they could give some away to
folks who could use it. And preserves made good
Christmas gifts for her neighbors.

Squirreling away food for the winter was one of
the truly satisfying parts of country living, in Mercy's
view. She didn't know how people in the city stood
it, having to go to the store every time they needed
anything. If it wasn't in the Hardin cupboard or pan-
try or root cellar, she and Billy did without. Life was
simpler that way.

Took less money, too. Truth was, they had too
much money now, her and Billy. Why, there was
over three thousand dollars in that calico sack she
kept under her bed! It was a worry. What if there
was a fire? Mercy had never trusted banks, except to
handle the checks Lewis sent her. She paid all her
bills in cash, always had.

She'd told Lewis he should quit sending money,
but he never listened. Thought they should buy themselves some extras, now that they could. Maybe a
new truck. But what was the point? The old one still
worked just fine, if you knew how to baby it along.
Waste not, want not. Extras? They had everything
they needed. What more could a person want?

Mercy gripped the porch railing with her hand and,
using the stick in her other hand, laboriously clambered up the steps. *Lewis.* He was on her mind these

days. Billy had slipped into one of her spells, and Mercy was quite sure it was her own fault for bringing up the boy's name so often. She wanted her daughter to get used to the idea that Lewis would be getting married soon. He'd be moving out of their lives, leaving them and starting his own family somewhere. He'd be closer to his wife's family once he was married; that was only natural. He'd stop visiting. That was the way men were. People said you didn't lose a son when he married but you gained a daughter. Mercedes thought it was more the other way around.

Of course, Billy didn't like such talk. Anything that upset her world was a torture to her. A ewe that had a black lamb when Billy thought she'd have a white one upset her. One or two duck's eggs that didn't hatch out in a clutch made her weep. She was fragile, hated any kind of change. Liked things to go on just as they were.

Mercy entered the dim kitchen and snapped on an overhead light. There! Lewis thought they shouldn't worry about money so much, ought to spend a little. Well, there you go—it was only a bit gloomy in the kitchen, she could still see, but she was using up electricity, anyway. He ought to be pleased!

She ran the kettle full of fresh water at the sink. It was time for a cup of tea. Where was that girl, anyway? Girl? She was forty-two years old! Billy had come up to the house from the garden a while back for some scissors and hadn't returned.

The phone rang. Mercy began to make her way toward it, but after it rang twice more, it stopped.

"Dang nuisance!" They'd only had the phone installed five years ago. Lewis had insisted. Said they needed a phone, all alone and way out of town. But she wasn't alone—she had Billy. And they'd always managed just fine without any of those contraptions. She'd only gone along with the idea to humor him. She figured he liked worrying about them the way he did; it made him feel better. Men were like that. So she let him.

The phone rang again. This time Mercy picked it up. "Yes?"

"Is this the Hardins'?" A man's voice, unfamiliar to her.

"It is."

"Mercedes Hardin?"

"Yes." Mercy frowned. "Who is it?"

"It's Bart. Bart Tanguay."

Mercy felt for the chair she knew was behind her. Her mind went blank, and her heart stopped for a few seconds. At least it felt as if it had. She put her free hand on her chest and sat down heavily.

"Why…what do you want? What are you doing phoning here?" Anger swelled in her lungs as she caught her breath.

"I want to know if you've told him. If he knows anything."

Mercy sat silently for a full half minute. "No, no, we've never said a word—"

"Good," the man interrupted. "Keep it that way. It's better for all concerned."

And then he hung up. Mercy listened to the buzz of the dial tone for a while and then she hung up, too. The kettle's whistle had started to warble, prior to a full-throated shrill. She started to get up, but she just didn't have the strength.

When Billy came into the kitchen a few minutes later, presumably to see why the kettle was making such a racket, Mercy was weeping. She couldn't stop. She hadn't wept for years, not since Lewis was born.

Billy took one look at her mother and burst into tears, too.

What a pair they were, Mercy thought, wiping at her streaming eyes with her apron. What a pair. She *had* to get up. Somebody had to get that damn kettle!

LEWIS WAS WORRIED. He hadn't heard from Phoebe all week. It could be that she hadn't been able to reach him at the site—that made sense—but she could have left a message.

It was this whole stupid secret-marriage business. He should never have agreed to it. They'd done everything wrong. Backward. Making love like a couple of rabbits ever since they got back together, then that crazy wedding in Lethbridge, right out of the blue. He'd jumped at the chance because he wanted to keep her. He might have proposed marriage himself when he felt the time was right. Maybe after he'd tried to win her parents over. Or after they'd dated a while longer. Or after he believed she was really in love with him.

But it happened the way it happened. Now he had to make sure it worked out. And he intended to, only it was hard when you were on a twenty-four-hour-a-day job, working 150 miles from where your wife lived. Lived in a crummy student residence, for crying out loud, with a roommate who didn't even know she was married!

One day he was going to show up and surprise the hell out of that roommate.

As for the marriage? He just wanted to hurry up and start acting like a married man. He had no regrets—except about the secrecy. He wasn't so sure about Phoebe.

"Hey, Hardin!"

Lewis swung around. It was Fred Billings, one of the F&B partners. He dropped in at the site from time to time.

"Fred!" The two men shook hands. Fred was a head shorter than Lewis and carried about twenty pounds more on his stocky frame. His thinning crown was covered by a ball cap, pushed back on his head. The two men had seen a lot of CFL games together. They were good friends, even though Fred was ten years older than Lewis and an Argos fan.

"How's it going?"

"Fine," Lewis said, falling into step beside him. "Now that we've got Sloboda on the job, we're okay."

"Saunderson?"

Lewis caught the other man's sharp glance. "Had to let him go." He shook his head and looked down at the rough ground they were covering.

"Tough, eh?"

"Yeah." Lewis didn't tell him that he'd told Saunderson he'd give him another chance if he went back into detox and stayed with it this time.

"Kids?"

"Yeah. Three. Teenagers. His wife works at the hospital in Drayton Valley."

"Uh-huh." Lewis could tell his boss didn't have his mind on the issue or the work site, even though his keen blue eyes darted here and there, not missing a thing. He already knew who was on the site, how many pickups were in the parking lot, what the energy bill was on this job, how much it cost to feed the crew breakfast on any given day. Details were his business, just as they were for Lewis.

The two men stopped at the edge of the drill platform. They were hitting 3,000 meters this shift. The job was going well. Core samples already looked good. Lewis knew a little from experience, although he was no geologist.

"You ever heard of Bart Tanguay?" Billings yelled over the noise of the machinery.

Lewis was shocked. "Yeah," he yelled back. What the hell was *this* about?

"He's been leaning on me. CEO of Wild Rose. Says he wants to talk to you."

Lewis gestured Billings back to where the noise was a little less, over by the bunkhouse trailers. "He's been calling. He called me last weekend," he admitted. "What's he want, d'you know?"

"Wants you to work for him." Billings looked edgy. Evasive.

"So he says." Lewis waited. What exactly was Billings getting at?

"What do you figure, Lewis? Might be a good chance. Tanguay's turned Wild Rose into quite a company. You could be consulting engineer." The consulting engineer was the oil company's representative on a site, the top dog. The tool-push worked for the drilling company.

"I'm happy right where I am," Lewis returned. "Unless you're thinking of getting rid of me—"

"Hell, no!" The other man laughed, looking relieved. "I'm glad to hear that. You know what we think of you, Boxer and me." Boxer Williams was the other partner in F&B Drilling. "I, uh, I told him I'd talk to you about it. You know I hate surprises.

Thought I'd feel you out on this one before you pulled the pin on me.''

Lewis smiled. Nobody liked surprises in this business. Billings offered him a chew of tobacco from his small can, which he refused. He thought about what Billings had said. This Tanguay was playing hard. Very hard. From a couple of angles. Exactly what his game was, though, remained a mystery. Maybe he'd better drive down to Calgary before the end of next month. Nah, he couldn't spare the time.

The attention of both men was caught by a young roustabout who'd come out onto the step of the trailer that housed the administration office of the drill site. "Yo! Lew!''

Lewis raised a hand in acknowledgment.

"Charlie says phone's for you!''

"Look, Fred, you sticking around? I'll just take this call and maybe we can grab a coffee over in the cookshack.''

"Never mind, Lew. I've got to be on my way. Just thought I'd drop in, is all. See which way the wind was blowing.''

The two men shook hands and Billings headed back toward the parking area. Lewis hesitated a moment, then strode into the office.

"Hardin,'' he said bluntly, taking the receiver from the desktop. The roustabout had left and Charlie, the assistant push, was nowhere in sight. Probably in the can.

"Lewis?"

"Phoebe! I've been trying to call you, honey. Where are you?"

"I'm at the residence." Her voice sounded very small and faraway.

"Something wrong?" A cold fist grabbed Lewis's heart. *Please, God, let it be all right...*

"Lewis, I need to talk to you. I've been thinking about everything and...and I don't think this was such a good idea, after all. Getting married. You know? I...I think we should try and get out of it somehow."

CHAPTER TWELVE

LEWIS'S BLOOD ran cold. "What are you talking about, Phoebe?"

"Us. I really think we need to talk about this." She spoke quietly, nervously. "I…I'm just not comfortable with it anymore…"

"*It?* That's our marriage you're talking about!"

"I know. It just doesn't feel right, Lewis. I can't get used to—"

"It's the secrecy crap, isn't it? Whose idea was it to keep the goddamn thing secret?" Lewis was furious. He'd tried to prepare her for the reality. He'd asked her again and again how she felt about their marriage. Then landing this on him? When he'd been trying to call her for days? Where the hell did she get off?

"Mine. My idea." There was an ominous silence. Maybe he'd come on too strong. He knew he was running scared. He had to do this right. His whole world was cracking.

"Let's talk about this, Phoebe. Rationally, like two adults. The fact is, we're married. Legal and proper.

We can't just jump over a broomstick or something and it's all over.''

"I realize that. But I thought maybe we could, you know—''

"Maybe, nothing! There's no way we can just change our minds, like a couple of ten-year-olds playing house. You know that.''

"I do. I do know it's all legal and everything.'' She sounded on the verge of tears. He felt like a first-class jerk. This was the woman he loved....

"Listen, honey. Okay, let's back up here. What brought this on? Why the cold feet all of a sudden? Is it your parents? Something at school—''

"It's just everything, Lewis. Everything! My folks, school, everything. I feel like we…we rushed into this marriage.'' He rolled his eyes skyward, aware suddenly of how tightly he gripped the phone. *Whose idea was this again?* "I don't think I was really ready—''

"We're good together,'' he interrupted. He was pleading. He hated the sound of his own voice. "You know that.'' Hadn't he expected something like this right from the start? The last month had been too good. Too perfect. He wasn't used to things in his life being perfect. "It's not the marriage, Phoebe. Believe me. We were meant to be together, I know we were. It's not you and me. It's this goddamn secrecy—''

"Don't take the Lord's name in vain!''

"All right." He held back his temper, barely. He'd forgotten her family was religious. She was on edge; a woman—a virgin—who'd hopped into bed with him the way she had couldn't really be all that upset about the odd curse word. "All right. It's this don't-tell-anybody stuff, isn't it? It's dumb, that's what it is. We should've come out with our situation immediately. It's not like we're a couple of kids, you know. We're both legally adults. We want to get married, we get married! We elope. Whatever. Nobody can stop us."

"I know. It's not just my folks. They might come around, anyway. It's...it's..." She paused. "It's everything! I don't know what to *do* anymore, Lewis. I think...I think I just got carried away. I was in love with the *idea* of marrying you. And physically... well, I was just swept away physically. You know— sex?" *That makes two of us,* he thought. *At least we're on the same wavelength there.* "That's not love, is it?" she whispered.

"It could be. I love you," he said seriously. "That's all there is to it for me. I love you and, yes, we have good sex. That's a bonus." He heard his assistant coming back. "Can we meet to talk about this? Can I come to town this weekend, maybe tomorrow if I can get away?"

"No, I don't think that would be a good idea, Lewis. We need to think about it separately. If we're together, we'll just end up…end up in bed or something.''

Yeah, he thought, *exactly where I do most of my best thinking.* ''Okay, honey,'' he said, drawing on every reserve of patience and understanding he could muster—when what he really wanted to do was go out and smash something. ''Okay. I'll call you tomorrow. We'll decide what to do then. All right?''

''Okay. And, Lewis…''

''Yeah?''

''I really do care about you, you know. More than anyone! It's just that…that's not the basis for marriage, is it?'' She sounded like she was trying to convince herself.

''It is for me, babe. We'll talk about it later, huh?''

Phoebe said goodbye and after he was sure she'd hung up, he slammed down the phone and cursed savagely. Charlie Fipke, the assistant push, darted a glance at him.

''Trouble, boss?''

''Woman trouble,'' Lewis replied shortly. Charlie nodded sagely.

'Nuff said.

PHOEBE LONGQUIST was the best thing that had ever happened to him. He remembered grabbing her ankle through the long grass by the fence back when he'd deked out of jail for the second time and hitchhiked out to her uncle's farm. She'd giggled; they'd necked in the grass. He was crazy, and he knew it. Every time he went AWOL, he got another year or eighteen months tacked onto his sentence.

Phoebe had shown him there was another way. When she'd asked him if he didn't want to make something of himself, he'd realized for the first time that, yes, he *did* want to make something of his life. He wanted to prove something to himself. And to all the people, like her parents, that thought he was a lump of cow dung because he'd been in jail a time or two.

It wasn't like he'd been mugging old ladies. He'd been stealing steers so he could put bread on the table for Ma and Billy. And stealing the odd car? Hell, that was kid stuff! Sure, he had his wages, which he could use to provide for his family, and he did hand over money regularly. Sure, he knew it was wrong to steal. But, hell, he'd been eighteen years old, working for minimum wage. The rustling had seemed like a good idea at the time—steal a few cows and get a decent stake together. He'd fallen in with a couple other lowlifes, and all of a sudden it was possible. Anything was possible. They'd even talked themselves into believing that Cal Blake wouldn't miss a steer or two.

But of course they'd been caught and he'd been sent to jail. With his various hijinks in jail, plus two escapes, two years had turned into three and a half by the time he left with a jailhouse education and a high-school diploma. Star graduate of Her Majesty's Crowbar High. He'd been bored enough turning out license plates and sanding picnic tables that math class had seemed a pretty good alternative.

Then, shortly after he got out, he'd headed for the rigs, where they didn't inquire too closely about a man's past just so long as he put in a hard day's work. He'd shown he could hold down a responsible job and save money. He had a car paid for, investments, money in the bank. Plans, big plans, for a ranch of his own someday. He took care of Ma and Billy. He was ready to settle down and start his own family. Be a solid citizen. He was married, damn it!

Now the truth had come back to haunt him. *He wasn't good enough. He'd never be good enough. He was a Hardin from Bearberry Hill. A loser. An ex-con. No dad, a simple-minded sister, raised by a crippled old woman. He'd never amount to anything.*

Lewis walked back to his trailer in a daze. He heard someone call him, turned and dealt with the query, but five minutes later couldn't recall who had spoken to him or what he'd requested.

Phoebe wanted out. She said she'd made a big mistake marrying him. Lewis felt like driving to the nearest town and getting drunk. He hadn't been roaring drunk since the night Phoebe had dumped him at the ranch where he worked, back that first summer he'd been released from jail. He'd discovered there was no pleasure in it anymore. No forgetting in the bottom of a bottle of rye.

And there was no way he could go out and get drunk now. He had responsibilities. A crew relying on him. Bosses who depended on him to get the job done. He'd worked hard to get where he was today, and he wasn't going to throw it away.

He shut the door of the small trailer he called home while he was on the job. He picked up the phone and told Charlie he wasn't taking any calls for the rest of the day, unless it was a certifiable emergency. There had to be blood or smoke involved.

Then he lay down on his bed and crossed his arms under his head and stared at the fly-specked ceiling.

He'd been in love with Phoebe most of his life, when it came right down to it. He wasn't about to let her go now. Not on some whim of hers. Not without a fight.

But what did that mean? A woman wanted out, you couldn't just say no. Lewis pondered his dilemma for hours, until the light faded and the camp settled down into the half-night of flares and spotlights and the clank and throbbing of big machinery. Generators hummed, night and day. There was never any peace or quiet on a drill site.

His mind registered a shift change. New sounds. The off-duty crew coming back to their trailers, cleaning up for supper, some laughs and a few hands of poker before hitting the bunks.

Was he going to do the honorable thing and let her go, as she'd requested? Take the gentlemanly route? No damn way. Everything in his being resisted that option. She'd married him. That had to mean something.

Was he going to tell the world about their marriage, over her objections? He could, but no, he wasn't going to do that, either. That was a one-way trip to serious marital discord, more serious even than her request that they call off the marriage. At least now, they had a chance. *He* had a chance. If he blew the whistle, told her folks, for instance, she'd never forgive him. Never.

There had to be another way.

Lewis stared into the darkness a long, long time before he made his decision. She was right—they'd married too fast. They'd never had a proper courtship, never really gotten to know each other or had any kind of engagement. They'd hopped in the sack within hours of getting back together. Hours! They'd done everything completely wrong.

So, he was going to court her properly. The way a lady should be courted. No sex. Flowers, chocolates, the works.

And this secrecy was a big, big mistake. The only solution he could see, now that they'd started off all wrong, was to bring her parents around himself. He couldn't count on her doing it anymore. Ease them into the idea. Fixing their kitchen sink that day was a beginning. It was time he made a few more moves on the home front again. Bring the old man some football tickets. Ingratiate himself with Nan. Hell, he'd bring her flowers. Play ball with the kids— whatever it took, Lewis was prepared to do.

No matter how modern and forthright Phoebe considered herself, she was young—just twenty-three. And she was the eldest daughter of a tightly knit, loving family. She'd always been a good girl. She was expected to do the right things—and she'd done them. Until now. She'd gone to church, stayed a virgin, minded her manners, studied hard to win a scholarship, and she'd made her family very proud of her.

Until now. Marrying Lewis Hardin was definitely not the right thing to do, and Phoebe had finally figured that out. She was scared. She'd followed her heart, but her brain had caught up finally and put the brakes on.

He'd have to change her mind. One way or another, he had to turn this around. Give Phoebe the opportunity to realize that she really was in love with him. Show her folks that he was the kind of son-in-law they'd always hoped to have. Maybe they'd end up begging him to marry their eldest daughter!

Then he could say, "Guess what? I already did."

Yeah. In your dreams, Hardin. In your dreams.

THE BUZZER WENT just as Phoebe was rushing madly, getting ready to go out for her evening tutorial. Since she'd summoned the courage—or was it cowardice?—to call Lewis, she'd been in a daze. If only she could be sure she was doing the right thing!

"Lindy, can you get that?" she called to her roommate. Lindy was reading a magazine in their small living room, and she had a habit of not paying attention to the phone or the doorbell when she was reading. Lindy moved pretty much according to her own personal planetary alignment, Phoebe had discovered over the two years she'd roomed with her.

"Sure!" A few minutes later Lindy called out, "It's a delivery. You expecting anything?"

"No." Phoebe got down on her knees and looked under her bed. Where was that lab coat? She was going to throw it in the washing machine in the laundry downstairs before she rushed off to her class. She needed the coat tomorrow, and Professor Mavis would scold her if it wasn't spotlessly clean. Mavis Pritchard was the iron-willed spinster who taught plant science.

Aha! Phoebe pulled the lab coat out from under the bed where she'd obviously kicked it in a cleaning frenzy earlier this week. It was wrapped around her favorite pair of sneakers, which had gone missing, too.

"Wow! A secret admirer. I wish I had one." Lindy came to the door of Phoebe's small bedroom alcove with a florist's box in her arms. She'd opened the envelope and read the attached card.

"Who's it for?" Phoebe asked, stunned. *For her?*

"You. 'To my darling Phoebe, from your secret admirer,'" Lindy read. She grinned and thrust the box at her. "Here! See for yourself."

The box was filled with two dozen beautiful long-stemmed red roses. Phoebe felt tears prickle behind her eyes. She couldn't speak. She buried her nose in the flowers. Not much fragrance, but they looked stunning. *Lewis!*

"Who's the secret admirer?" Lindy asked with a quizzical expression. "Same one you got all those roses from last week?"

The pink roses she'd brought back from the Macdonald Hotel hadn't lasted long. Phoebe had reluctantly thrown them out a few days before. "I guess so," she said shakily. Then she laughed. "Secret admirer! Isn't that just like in the movies?" She wished she hadn't said that. She'd already gotten herself—and Lewis—into far too much trouble with her stupid romantic notions.

Lindy returned to her upholstered chair and her magazine without further comment, and Phoebe quickly clipped the ends of the rose stems and thrust them into tepid water. She'd arrange them when she came home later. Lewis had sent such lovely flowers.

And after she'd broken the news to him three days ago that she wanted out of their marriage. It had taken every scrap of nerve she had to call him and tell him what she'd decided. But she *had* to tell him; she just couldn't let him go on thinking she had no regrets when she did.

Her hands had been trembling when she hung up. She'd stared at them, then placed her icy-cold fingers over her hot cheeks. Had she done the right thing? How could she know?

She still felt sick inside. She'd agonized over it for a week. Ever since the idea had struck her in the hotel that maybe she was in *lust* with Lewis, not in love.

Whatever that was.

But he was right. They were married. Being married was a lot more complicated than just planning to get married. And he was right about another thing—it had been her idea.

But it wasn't too late to do something about it. No one knew they were married. Just the legal people at the province's Vital Statistics Department and a couple of people at a real-estate office in Lethbridge.

She didn't want to be a rancher's wife. She didn't want to raise five children—or however many he had in mind—on some backwoods cow station in the middle of nowhere, hanging out diapers and making bologna sandwiches and scrubbing out lunch buckets. She liked living in the city. She liked city things. Sure, she wanted children someday, maybe one or two. But she was only twenty-three so that wouldn't be for years and years!

Maybe she'd fallen for Lewis physically—and who wouldn't have?—but she had a brain, didn't she? She was smart enough to realize it was just physical. Just sex. She could get over it. Unfortunately she'd been swept away by the sheer romanticism of their quick hot affair, and the secret marriage had seemed like the next step. Her crazy imagination had gotten her into trouble before, mostly of a minor type, but this time there were consequences. She was actually married. And she'd involved another person in one of her harebrained schemes. But people could get unmarried. They just had to agree about it, that was all.

She didn't think Lewis was in agreement. He hadn't taken the news well. And these flowers were not the gesture of a man who'd given up on their marriage. Or on her.

She sighed. She had no time to think about that now. She had to get to class. She gathered up her stuff and went to the door.

"Bye! I'll be back about ten. If I get any calls, just take a message, okay?" She shut the door firmly. It didn't look as though Lindy had even heard her. Lindy never took messages, anyway. She rarely even answered the phone. That was what they had an answering machine for, she always said.

"BETHANY?" PHONE TO HIS EAR, Lewis leaned back on the desktop in his site office. It was rainy out, fairly unusual for an Alberta fall. Nice for a change, though. "How's it going?"

Bethany was her usual chatty, sociable self. She filled him in on what had been happening with her business since the riverboat contract, with her love life since Lewis had caught her and Reg in the back room, and with her new diet before she asked how things were going with him.

"Fine, fine," he lied. "Listen, Beth, I want you to do me a couple of favors. Yeah. First of all, I want to place a standing weekly order for two dozen of your finest roses. What's that?" He grinned. "Yes, I've got a lady in my life and it's serious. You can do that?" He gave her the address and a message for the weekly card. She congratulated him on his romance—that was one thing about Bethany. Easy come, easy go.

"And one other thing. You ever heard of some kind of old-fashioned china that looks like it's got stitching in patterns all over it? Dishes. Yeah, that's it—petit point. I want you to track some of it down for me. No, it's not for the lady in question." He wasn't going to tell her it was for the lady's mother. After all, Bethany probably thought he was already pretty far gone with his standing order for roses. If she knew he had plans to romance Phoebe's mother, too, she'd think he'd fallen over the deep end.

As he had.

Lewis hung up the phone and crossed his arms. So far, so good. He had a plan. And he intended to carry it out, step by step. He was a detail man, and he was going to pay attention to every single detail. This was one time when the means more than justified the end.

And the means were going to give a lot of people pleasure, too. Who could possibly have a problem with that?

He had one more call to make.

"Ticketmaster? Yes, I want to check on some tickets to the next Stampeders game in Calgary. Yeah, good seats, right on the fifty-yard line. Three."

Might as well invite the brother along. He had a whole family to win over.

CHAPTER THIRTEEN

THE CUSTOMER AT THE end of the bar wasn't an old guy, no more than fifty or fifty-five, by the look of him. Well fed, well barbered, well tailored. Big square diamond on his pinkie. Wedding ring. Rolex. Lodge pin in his lapel. The barman had seen the type many times.

"Another one, sir?" It was nearly closing time. Table in the far corner was getting ready to leave. Which just left this guy.

The customer pushed his glass forward. "No. Call me a taxi. I'm too goddamn drunk to drive home."

No doubt about *that,* the barman thought, relieved. He turned to the wall phone.

"A cab will be along in ten minutes, sir," he said, picking up the man's empty glass, then swabbing at the place in front of the customer with his spotless cloth.

"Here—take my car keys, too," the man growled, and reached into his pants pocket. "Save me from changing my mind."

The bartender dropped the keys into a locked drawer. It wasn't uncommon for clients to leave their keys with him, then take a cab back to the International to get their cars the next day.

"Ah, hell. Bring me another one," he said suddenly.

"Your cab?" The barman hesitated.

"Why the hell should he care as long as I pay him enough?" The customer sounded belligerent. "Isn't that the way it goes? High card takes the table? Money talks?" The barman slid another single malt over, followed by a bowl of pretzels. *The customer was always right.* Even when he was wrong.

"Problems, sir?" Sometimes they liked to talk about whatever was bothering them. In his time, he figured he'd heard just about everything. Not that he was all that interested in hearing what this character had to say. It was late and he wanted to close up.

"Problems?" The man raised his head and glared at him. "Hell, no. I don't *have* problems, sonny, I solve them. Or else I create 'em!"

"I see, sir," the barman responded with a polite smile, polishing the wineglasses that had just come out of the bar mini-washer.

Nine times out of ten, he guessed guys overindulged because of some kind of woman trouble. This one wore a wedding ring, but that didn't rule out anything. After that, it was business trouble. Guys getting themselves in too deep too fast. The whole city was full of high-flyers and wannabes.

"If you want the truth," the customer said

abruptly, "I got family troubles. Wife's mad. Wants to go on a cruise and I won't take her. I got too much work, story of my life." He frowned into his glass and continued, "Work. I didn't get where I am today taking goddamn cruises all over hell's—"

"Kids?"

"Nope. No kids," he said quietly, then he stared at the bartender. "Not that it's any of your goddamn business."

"You're right, sir. None of my business. Say, that taxi's here."

The man stood up and practically fell.

"You want some help, sir?" Looked as if his customer was drunker than he'd thought. The cabdriver, standing just inside the door that led to the street, stepped forward to lend a hand.

"Help? Ha!" The man swung around clumsily and shook his fist in the barman's face. "That's a good one. Nobody helps *me,* y'un'erstand? Nobody!"

He lurched toward the door. The barman noticed that when the cabbie tried to take his arm, he cursed and shook him off, too.

Some jokers! After quickly wiping and polishing the spot on his bar where the businessman had sat, the barman put the empty glass into the dishwasher. That was it for glassware. He flicked a switch to start the machine. Another long, boring Friday night. He wondered if Marlene, the new waitress in the piano bar, had already left for the evening. Maybe he'd go up and find out.

HEY, A GUY COULD get used to this, ferrying a wheelchair around. They got to park right at the entrance by the elevators, and he and Trevor and Harry had some of the best seats going, on the aisle, right at the fifty-yard line. The stadium was sold out. The Stampeders might go all the way to the Grey Cup this year, and the fans were jubilant.

"Beer?" Lewis asked Harry once they got settled, with a quick glance at Harry's son. He wasn't sure how old Trevor was. A little younger than Phoebe. Legal drinking age, for sure, which in Alberta was eighteen.

"That'd be fine," Harry rasped, with a short nod at Lewis. "Thanks, Lew."

"No beer for me," Trevor said. He was studying the crowd, which was full of wild and crazy fans with cowboy hats and painted faces, the usual fan scene at a playoff game.

Lew. He was Lew now. Lewis made his way back to the inner stadium, where the concession was. He'd pick up a big Pepsi and a couple of hot dogs, too. Kids were always hungry.

Things were going pretty well, considering. He'd called the Longquist farmhouse a week ago to invite Phoebe's dad and brother—or mother, he was equal opportunity here—to the game. Harry'd been out and

Nan had taken his message very coolly. No, she had no interest in football personally, she'd said, but thank you, anyway. Yes, Trevor would be home the weekend of the game, she said. She sounded very skeptical, but she'd obviously passed on the message, because the next evening he had a call from Harry, accepting the invitation with thanks on behalf of Trevor and himself. Next time, he'd added gruffly, the tickets were on him.

At least he was thinking in terms of a next time, Lewis reflected, loading the two beers, the Pepsi and the four hot dogs onto a cardboard tray. That was progress.

Lewis had picked the Longquists up at their farmhouse—again, at his insistence—and they'd driven together to McMann Stadium in Calgary's northwest, near the university, where the Stampeders were playing the B.C. Lions. This way, when he drove them home later, he'd have a chance to say a few words to Phoebe's mother. Keep his hand in there. She was definitely the nut to crack, he realized. It didn't take Trevor or Harry long to figure out that getting midfield tickets for a sold-out game was a good thing, but Nan wasn't so sure. Lewis figured she was wondering why all the sudden attention.

Just like a woman. Couldn't accept things at face value, like a man.

And Phoebe. She was something else! He didn't know how long he'd be able to keep up this hands-off, don't-touch courtship thing. She'd called him and thanked him for the roses, the first delivery, which he'd used as a chance to make a date to see her. He'd taken her for dinner at The Last Chance, a misnamed upscale eatery in the Old Strathcona area, along the lines of chèvre and hearts of palm. Not his favorite type of cuisine, but Phoebe was delighted. At the end of the evening, he'd kissed her until their juices were running every which way—he couldn't help himself—and then left her to cool off herself at the dormitory door. It had taken real willpower. No mention of a hot night in a hotel or his studio apartment. No quick feels in the hallway, no gropes in the Jeep, all that fun stuff they'd shared before. She'd warned him on the phone that she didn't want to see him if they were just going to hop into bed together, so he was taking her at her word. She wanted to talk breakup.

He wanted to talk love and marriage. Courtship, that was the thing. Even though he couldn't believe how stupid this hands-off business was, considering they'd been married for nearly a month and a half already. He'd taken a long, cold shower when he got back to his studio. Courtship was damn hard on a guy's hormones.

Still, he was sticking to his game plan. It was a good one and he intended to win with it. He'd be back on the job for six days after this tonight, and then he was driving to Edmonton to see Phoebe again.

The game was under way when Lewis returned to his seat. Harry was leaning forward, hands gripping his chair. His eyes, when Lewis handed him the beer and dog, were fierce.

"Second down and they got their ten yards already!" he said. "Lions can't stop 'em now!" It was just the beginning of the first quarter. Lewis grinned and edged past Harry. He handed the Pepsi and two hot dogs to Trevor, sitting beside him. "Your dad likes his football," he said with a wink.

"Oh, yeah," Trevor shot back with a skyward glance. He took the two dogs and the drink with thanks, and Lewis noticed he'd downed both hot dogs within five minutes. No problem.

Lewis settled down to enjoy the game. Just like he'd remembered, a kid was always hungry.

HE WAS ACCOMPANYING Phoebe to a musical production at the Citadel. Her suggestion. He knew he was going to die before the evening was over, but for Phoebe, it was worth it. He'd put in two twenty-four-hour shifts during the week before their outing, so he was beat to start with, not to mention what a couple of hours of wailing and carrying on would do to him. It was *The Mikado*. Phoebe had assured him the music was energetic and lively. "You'll enjoy it," she'd said.

He was burning the candle at both ends, with his trips south to the football game, to see Ma and Billy and do a little work on the cabin, then back again for a full week's work. By rights, he shouldn't be leaving the rig site at all. He was just lucky he could count on Charlie, his second-in-command. And Fred Billings wasn't going to give him any grief, he was so darn pleased Lewis wasn't leaving the company for a better offer elsewhere.

Now, when he should be catching up on his sleep, he was driving to Edmonton again, to go out on a date. With his wife! And there'd be no mutually satisfying physical payback at the end of the evening, either. Just another in what was starting to feel like an endless series of cold showers.

How the hell had he ended up in such a ridiculous situation?

Speaking of which, he had to remember to call Bethany while he was in town, see if she'd located any of that china Nan Lonquist was partial to—it had turned out to be a pattern that no one stocked anymore. He'd told Bethany to track some down, anyway, in an antique shop if necessary, spare no expense.

And he was changing the flower order. He'd realized that a couple of dozen roses every week was too much of a good thing. A place could look like a morgue in no time. Now Phoebe would receive a different arrangment every week; Bethany was to use her imagination.

Lewis checked into his studio apartment to take a shower and change. He was glad he'd kept the apartment for the time being. As soon as he got things ironed out with Phoebe, he intended to look around. Buy a condo, maybe, or a small house near the university. They could be a real married couple. With a cat or dog and a matched set of dishes in the cupboard. A lawn mower, if they bought a house. A wine cellar, instead of a beer fridge. A sound system and lots of CDs and a place to keep them.

Happy days, Lewis muttered cynically as he chose a shirt to wear for the evening performance at the Citadel. Oh, happy days, indeed.

He was a little early to pick up Phoebe. The roommate answered the intercom and invited him up. High time, Lewis thought with approval. He was finally going to meet the roommate.

"Hi! You must be the secret admirer." A short, dark-haired young woman answered the door. She had an impish smile. "I'm Lindy."

"Yeah, that'd be me," Lewis said with a grin. "Lewis Hardin. How are you?" He shook the roommate's hand. He glanced toward Phoebe's alcove. "She ready?"

"Just about." The roommate looked around their tiny living room. Lewis realized he'd been right: a person could get too many roses. "You want to sit down for a minute?"

He was just contemplating the invitation when Phoebe came into the room. She was perfectly made up and her hair was beautiful. Lewis noted that she was wearing the same black dress she'd worn when he'd taken her out to the Macdonald Hotel. She could use some new clothes. Pearls, at least, to wear with that dress. He'd love to take her shopping, buy her everything her heart desired. But his instincts told him he'd better keep his offers to himself for the time being. Phoebe was a woman of principle. Poor but proud. Like all her family.

"You look wonderful, Phoebe," he murmured, kissing her hand and winking so that the roommate couldn't see.

Phoebe blushed furiously. "You're early," she began accusingly, then quickly added, "I'm ready, though. Shall we go?"

Lindy wished them a good time and reminded Phoebe that she was going over to her aunt's place for the night.

Phoebe was very quiet. Lewis reached over and held her hand once they were inside the Jeep. "You okay, honey?"

"Fine, Lewis." She turned to him. Man, she looked gorgeous! "I'm just doing a lot of thinking these days, that's all."

"Me, too, babe," Lewis said with a smile. He was

pretty sure the thinking he was doing was entirely different from the thinking *she* was doing. ''Me, too.''

They were early for the performance, and Lewis fidgeted in the seat he'd been assigned. He wanted to stretch out his legs, which was impossible. The orchestra tuned up for an excruciatingly long time, and then, finally, the lights went down.

At last, Lewis thought, sticking his legs as far under the seat in front as he could and crossing his arms. At least now he could close his eyes and no one would notice.

A sideways glance showed him that Phoebe was rapt. Great—he'd married someone with a taste for highbrow culture. His idea of a good time was a ball game or a fishing trip or a ride into the back country on a good horse.

Still, what did they say? Opposites attract? They might be opposites in some ways, he reflected, which was probably what worried Phoebe, but they were alike in the ways that counted.

A bunch of dancers dressed up in Japanese-style kimonos came mincing onto the stage to the sound of a lot of scratchy Oriental music, and Lewis yawned. Oops! He caught himself just in time. He didn't think Phoebe had noticed.

He leaned a little, toward her and propped an elbow on the chair arm, then rested his chin on his palm. Maybe she'd think he was being contemplative, meditating, carried away by the glorious music. He'd seen pictures of a famous statue—guy with chin in hand, thinking or whatever. It was a classy pose.

Lewis stifled another yawn, and that was about all he remembered until Phoebe poked him in the ribs.

"W-WHA'?" HE SAT UP straight. "Is it halftime already?"

"Halftime?" She giggled. "It's intermission, you lout! Enjoying the performance, Lewis?"

"Oh, yes! Definitely." He tried to sound spirited. People were getting up and leaving. Two matrons in pearls and perms sat chatting quietly behind them, their minks nestled on their chairs. Time to go? He noticed that many people were leaving scarves and jackets on the seats. Intermission, she'd said. He wondered if they had hot dogs.

"It was great, Phoebe. Terrific."

"You sure you can tell?" she teased. "You were fast asleep!" Her eyes were dancing. He hadn't seen his wife so lively-looking and happy in a long time. Whatever he'd done must have been okay.

"Asleep? No way!" He shook his head, then added, genuinely surprised, "Was I?"

"You sure were."

"Was I, uh…" He shot a glance at the elderly ladies, then whispered, "Snoring?"

"No." She smiled.

"Drooling?"

"No, thank heavens! You were just peacefully snoozing."

He put his arm around her and pulled her close. "I'm sorry, babe. It's not like it's, you know, a football game or something really exciting. I find it kind of hard to keep track of what's going on."

She leaned across and kissed him. "You're forgiven. Let's go get a drink. Coffee for you!"

She hadn't kissed him like that, on her own initiative and with real affection, since she'd suggested they part two weeks ago. Was she having second thoughts? Lewis could only hope—pray—that she was.

The second half of the performance wasn't nearly as painful as the first, Lewis discovered. He actually found himself enjoying some of the music.

Roommate or not, Lewis couldn't do much more than kiss Phoebe good-night when he took her home. She hinted that something more might be welcome, like maybe a tumble in her little alcove bed, but he wasn't even tempted.

"Phoebe, hon—you know what we agreed."

She nodded and stood on tiptoe to kiss him again. She was deliberately trying to seduce him. "I know. But maybe, just this once—"

"No way. We've got serious thinking to do, you and me. And you know how sex can interfere with that," he said, reminding her of her own words.

She sighed. "I suppose you're right. When will I see you again?"

"Soon." He kissed her, regretting that he was so damn tired or he might be tempted to make love with her, as he'd been tempted so many times before. He wasn't made of steel. But no, that would be making a serious mistake. He had a game plan and he was sticking to it.

Lewis got back in his Jeep, yawning. Damn, he was tired! But Phoebe had been like her old self tonight. She'd been giggly and responsive and affectionate. Loving.

Was it *The Mikado?* Maybe. That was a new twist on seduction. But whatever it took, he'd do it. If highbrow productions like this cheered her up, he'd gladly snore through another chunk of Gilbert and Sullivan, even a symphony or two, if necessary.

Even a full-scale opera? Well, *almost* whatever it took. He had to draw the line somewhere.

CHAPTER FOURTEEN

MA AND BILLY generally cooked their Thanksgiving turkey on the Sunday, but Lewis had convinced them to switch to the day following, as many families did. Ma said it was all the same to her, and Billy, although she lived by routine, tended to measure it by days or weeks, not annual events. Unlike the American celebration, Canada's Thanksgiving was a floating harvest holiday the second Monday in October.

Lewis was banking on the Longquists being among the majority who cooked their Thanksgiving turkey on Sunday, particularly as they had children who'd likely be coming home for the three-day holiday weekend and who would need time on Monday to get back home for work or school on Tuesday.

He had a present for Nan Longquist—a humongous turkey platter in her beloved china pattern. Depending on how she took the gift—he didn't entirely trust that she'd be thrilled to bits—he had a teapot he was keeping in reserve. If she liked the platter, he'd produce the teapot. If she continued to regard him as something the cat dragged into her kitchen from the compost pile, platter or no platter, he'd hold on to it. Maybe Ma could use another teapot.

If that was the case, he'd have to think of a new tactic to use on Phoebe's mother. China diplomacy, so to speak, might not be the ticket. Flowers? She'd be too suspicious. He was pretty sure Harry and Trevor were onside. He hadn't met the rest of the family, but Thanksgiving seemed like the perfect time to rectify that situation. And, without a doubt, Phoebe would be there. Man, he couldn't wait. She'd been positively loving toward him lately, as if she just couldn't help herself, which was a good sign. A very good sign.

The neatly graveled lanes and parking areas of Swallowbank Farm were filled with cars and pickups. Lewis felt a moment's trepidation as he pulled in. After all, he wasn't family, at least not to the Longquists' knowledge. And, although he knew he was reasonably competent socially, he wasn't comfortable in a crowd of mainly strangers.

But then, he thought, braking beside a red four-by-four, who was? And he was motivated, no question.

Plus, this was a perfect setup for carrying out the next stage of his plan to stay married to Phoebe.

Lewis pulled the carefully wrapped platter out of the back of his vehicle. Now that he looked at it, all done up in pink and mauve ribbon and shiny paper featuring lilac sprays—Bethany's choice—he wished he hadn't let her do it. This looked like too big a deal. Some tissue paper and a plain paper bag would have suited him fine.

A dog got up and wagged its tail as he approached. He bent to pat the grizzled head. "Nice boy," he murmured. The dog licked his hand. Some watchdog. Lewis took a deep breath and rapped smartly at the door. It would be a wonder if anyone noticed. He could hear children crying and women calling and a television blaring inside. He was about to rap again, when the door opened and a young woman who looked remarkably like Phoebe, only with fewer freckles and darker hair, opened the door.

"Yes?" Her eyes were round and blue. She was very pretty. A smaller girl, dressed in a brown, wide-skirted dress and white stockings, peeked from behind.

The older girl had to be Jillian. "Er, hello. Is your mother in?"

"Sure." The girl stepped aside, the little one scuttling behind her as she moved. "Come on in. I'll get her."

Get wasn't exactly the operative verb as the older girl—who Lewis had decided was Phoebe's middle sister, Jill—turned and yelled into the noisy kitchen. "Mom! Mom! Somebody's here!"

Lewis was pleasantly assaulted by the succulent scents of roasting turkey and pumpkin pie. He waited politely while the two girls went into the kitchen, the older one impatient at the lack of a response. *"Mom?"*

"Who is it, Jilly? Oh, just a minute, then…"

Nan Longquist came into sight, wiping her hands on her apron, her cheeks very red and her dark hair, streaked with gray and what looked suspiciously like flour, tucked up in a loose, flyaway roll. "Oh! It's *you!*"

Lewis could have hoped for a better reception. "It's me, all right. I thought I'd stop by and wish you all a very happy Thanksgiving—" He stopped, not quite sure where to go from there.

"Who is it, Mother?" Harry wheeled into sight. "Well, come on in, boy, don't just stand there! Come in, come in!"

Harry shook his hand vigorously. Lewis was holding the gift tightly in his other hand. "What's this?" Harry had spotted the package.

"This?" Lewis looked at the large flat parcel as though he, too, wondered what it was doing in his hand. "Oh, it's just a little gift. For Nan."

"Did you hear that, Mother?" Harry cried. "The young fellow has brought you a present. Well, well." Nan *did* look a little pleased, despite herself.

"For me?" she asked, actually smiling. Phoebe had always said her mother was a tenderhearted woman who couldn't bear conflict of any kind. Maybe she really was.

"For you," Lewis said with a smile and a slight bow. He handed her the package.

"How do you like that?" Harry boomed. "Come on in, Lew. There's people I want you to meet. Jilly, get our friend a beer out of the fridge. Hurry now."

Lewis found himself propelled through the kitchen, filled with at least four or five women—none of them Phoebe—and several children, and into the living room, where the television was on. The big game between the Hamilton Tiger-Cats and the Toronto Argonauts was being watched by maybe a dozen men and boys. A long table—or tables, it looked like—was set up under snowy linen cloths and began in the dining room and stretched right into the living room, where the television set was. A motley collection of chairs surrounded the tables, and Lewis spotted quite a collection of the china bequeathed by the great-aunt. It looked like Nan Longquist had planned for at least twenty people at dinner!

"This here's my brother-in-law, Joe—" Lewis shook the hand of a good-looking man in his late thirties, obviously a farmer by his tan and callused grip "—and that's Ben over there, our oldest boy—" Lewis nodded at the vaguely familiar young man "—and, of course, you know Trevor, and this is our new neighbor Jack Gamble and his wife, Hannah. Hannah likes her football." There was a big guffaw of laughter from the men, and the young woman Harry had pointed out blushed prettily.

Harry winked at Lewis. "They just got married, those two. You can't hardly pry them apart. And over here's Jesse Winslow—he's just blowing through the district and stopped in for a visit. And back there in the corner is Tim, the young fella Joe hires on every summer to help us with haying. And, oh heck, there's more." Harry threw up his hands. "You'll meet 'em all sooner or later."

The buzz of voices and the announcer's excited monologue from the television made Lewis's head spin. He'd never remember all these names or faces. Someone thrust a cold can of beer into his hand. That, at least, was welcome.

"Pull up a chair, son."

"Oh, I can't stay, Harry," Lewis began to protest. *Son.* He liked the sound of that. The beer tasted good, too. "I just dropped by…"

"Well, you'll stay to dinner," Harry pronounced. "There's always room for one more in this house. And Mother promised she wouldn't serve until the game's over, and this game looks like it's going into overtime!"

"It better not, Harry Longquist," his wife called from the doorway. "That turkey will be done to a crisp if it's a minute more than half-past. And you promised to carve!"

Nan continued into the room, carrying the wrapped gift. "Lewis!" She beamed at him. He realized, with shock, that she'd decided once and for all to forgive him and his criminal past. Maybe she'd realized he wasn't such a bad guy, after all. Maybe she'd decided Thanksgiving was a good time to forgive and forget, especially if he was thoughtful enough to bring her gifts and take her men out to football games. Lewis felt a warm rush of pleasure. Who knew, truly, the mysterious ways of a woman?

"What a lovely surprise, stopping by today." He basked in every friendly word. "We haven't had a *bit* of trouble since you fixed that sink, not a bit. Of course you'll stay to dinner. And what in the world is this?" She set the package down on the dining-room table, after Jillian had cleared a space for it, and began untying the ribbon carefully, surrounded by a cluster of women who had followed her in from the kitchen.

"Oh, just break it, Mom!" Jill pleaded. "It's only ribbon!"

"And ruin it? Never mind, it'll just take a minute to untie the knot properly, and then Renee can wind it up for me and we can use it again." Lewis could tell Nan was excited. He was glad he'd brought her the platter—and he felt guilty, remembering that he'd had ulterior motives.

Where the heck was Phoebe, anyway? He'd expected to find her here.

"And the paper! My goodness, that's a pretty pattern. Did you choose it yourself?" She looked expectantly at Lewis. There was a groan from the men as the Argos fumbled the ball on the fifteen-yard line.

"No, no," Lewis murmured. "I had a, er, friend pick it out." Was it going to take her *forever* to open the gift? He was getting embarrassed at all the attention. Then he realized that this was something enjoyable to her—just as it was with Ma. Gifts were so special, so unexpected to these women, that the pleasure of receiving and opening them had to be drawn-out. Enjoyed. Made to last.

"Oh! My heavens—*Lewis!*" Nan had seen what was in the parcel and she was staring at him, her face wreathed in smiles, her cheeks redder than ever. "A huge platter in Great-aunt Sal's petit point." There was a soft collective *ahhh* from the women. "And I never *had* a platter big enough for turkey with this set. Not even the one I broke!"

To Lewis's astonishment, Nan flew at him, threw her arms around him and gave him a resounding kiss on the cheek. "You shouldn't have! Thank you so much for remembering! A lot of men would never have remembered my pattern." She then began animatedly telling the women about Lewis's coming to visit them in late August and fixing the sink and no wonder her friend Mercy was so proud of Lewis and how wonderful he'd turned out after that...that little spot of trouble way back when he was too young to know any better—why, any young fellow got into trouble from time to time!—and, to think that a fine

young man with so much on his mind and such an
important *responsible* position in the oil business
would think of *her* and remember Great-aunt Sal's
china!

There was no question. The platter was a big hit.
And Lewis Hardin was staying for dinner.

STILL NO PHOEBE.

By the time the game wrapped up, the Argos win-
ning 22-14, the house was in a fine state of disorder.
Lewis felt overwhelmed, and he stepped off to one
side, in a corner, out of the way. His experience with
family life, no matter how weird, had never had this
element of rambunctiousness to it. Excitement.
Verve. Discord. Five people talking at once. Three
tasks being carried out in kitchen and dining room
at the same time. Someone—Nan, presumably—giving instructions, making sure everything went as it
was supposed to.

Finally, Nan called the company to order. "Now
Dad will sit at the end here and carve the bird and
I'll sit at the other end, and the rest of you just take
whatever seat you can. We'll leave a place for
Phoebe. Darn that girl—she was supposed to be here
by now!"

Lewis felt a moment's alarm. Had something happened to her? He felt chills run down his spine. All
of a sudden, the day felt different. The heat and hu-
midity in the house and the smells of cooking, pleas-

ant until now, were unbearable. He wanted action. Fresh, cold air. To leave, to go find his wife, wherever she was, to make sure she was all right. Safe.

Then, just as they were about to sit down, a shout went up from the kitchen, from Jilly, who had been delegated to carry in the bowls of vegetables. ''Pheeb's here!''

For a few seconds, Lewis felt relief melt his bones.

Phoebe came into the room, but it was a moment before she spotted him. Her eyes froze in amazement. He grinned foolishly and waved his empty beer can. She talked to various people around her, but Lewis knew that her attention was completely on him. She wore the usual jeans and a crisp white blouse this time, not a T-shirt, but she looked…different. Radiant. Happy. Serene. Settled. With a shock, he saw that she was wearing the emerald. Not the wedding band, but the ring they'd laughingly termed their engagement ring. No one seemed to have noticed yet, in the general excitement of the prodigal daughter returning to the fold.

''Phoebe, honey!'' Her father called to her from his position at the head of the table. He was in his wheelchair, waiting for the turkey to be brought out. Ben had been delegated to carry in the bird on the brand-new platter. ''Come over here, baby. There's someone I want you to meet.''

Lewis realized to his shock that Harry meant him.

How were they going to play this? He'd have to take his cues from Phoebe.

Phoebe bent down and kissed her father, then stood by his chair, smiling broadly. "Yes, Dad?"

"Phoebe, I want to you to meet my good buddy, Lewis Hardin. Lewis stopped by, and Mother and I invited him to share our Thanksgiving dinner with us. Lewis, this is my Phoebe, our oldest girl—"

Lewis was prepared to stick out his hand in a formal welcome, depending on what Phoebe did. Never in his life had he been so unsure of what to do next.

Phoebe's eyes met his and he knew instantly that everything was all right. No matter what happened— *everything was all right.* Phoebe slid into his arms and raised her face to his and whispered, "I've changed my mind. Kiss me, Lewis."

He did, wrapping his arms around her and holding her tight. He kissed her as he'd never kissed her before. He heard a din erupt around them, but neither paid any attention. Finally, with a soft kiss on the nose, Lewis released her. Phoebe grabbed his hand and they turned to face the crowd.

"Holy cow, Lew!" Trevor blurted. "I guess you do know my sister. What the heck's goin' on?"

"We've met," Lewis admitted with a smile, not sure how far Phoebe wanted to take this. "As a matter of fact, we've been, er, seeing each other up in Edmonton."

"Dating?" screeched little Renee. She jumped up and down. "You mean dating? Oh, boy!"

"And we have some big news for all of you," Phoebe said. "Some really big, really happy news." There was a tiny tremor in her voice. She held up their linked hands for all to see the emerald and diamonds glittering on her third finger. "We're engaged. We're going to be married at Christmas!"

Again? Lewis squeezed her hand silently. Sure, he'd marry her again. Christmas. New Year's. Valentine's Day. Hell, he'd marry her a dozen times if she wanted. He had to hand it to her; it was a creative solution to the secrecy situation—just get married again.

Nan, who'd returned with Ben carrying the turkey from the kitchen, had missed the big kiss but arrived in time to hear the news. She clapped both of her hands to her red cheeks, her eyes huge. "Oooooh!"

As her aunt Catherine recounted the story later, you could have leveled the entire company with a single feather.

Lewis had a few things to take care of before he told Ma and Billy. He knew how Billy hated surprises. He wanted to make sure everything was in place—their plans, the date, the location, the guest list—before they presented them with the news.

Plus, he had to work. The following week Lewis was finishing up the job west of Rimbey and then he planned to take a couple of weeks off. He wanted to get his cabin finished—he hated leaving ends untied—and he wanted to look at some real estate. If he narrowed down the options to half a dozen places by the weekend, he and Phoebe could go and look at houses and decide. They could be in their own place by Christmas, lock, stock and barrel.

And he was tired. He needed a rest. Lately there'd been far too much excitement and not enough sleep in his life.

There was also that business of meeting with the fellow from Wild Rose. He'd have preferred to forget the whole thing. He had no interest whatsoever in what this Tanguay character had to say. But he'd promised to meet with him the last week of October. He'd given his word.

It all seemed to be working out perfectly. He had three tickets for the final game in the CFL Western Conference for himself and Harry and Trevor. That was on the Thursday. He'd see if he could meet with Tanguay earlier in the day, go to the game that evening, then scoot up to Edmonton to meet Phoebe and do some serious house-hunting. He was looking forward to spending some time with her, making some plans. Since the big surprise announcement at Thanksgiving, he'd barely seen her. Too much to do at work, not only finishing the drilling but winding up the site and getting ready to move out the rig.

He called Wild Rose. Yes, Thursday would be fine. Two o'clock? Perfect.

CHAPTER FIFTEEN

LEWIS STEPPED into the glass-and-bronze elevator and pressed the button for the seventeenth floor. He did not have a good feeling about this meeting.

But if it got Tanguay, whoever he was, off his back, it was worthwhile. Besides, Lewis was in Calgary, anyway, for the game. He'd booked his time off, as planned. He deserved it; he'd brought the job in early and under budget. There was always real satisfaction in that. Now Harry and Trevor were working hard on converting him from the Edmonton Eskimos to the Calgary football team. The Eskies were already eliminated. Tonight the Stamps were up against the Saskatchewan Rough Riders for the western championship.

The Wild Rose offices were swank. Rich brown carpet, lots of brass and copper and a nice relief map of Alberta on one wall, with tiny blinking lights scattered here and there. Wild Rose properties? Lewis had no idea.

The receptionist, a young black woman in steel-rimmed glasses, looked him over carefully when he entered. "Mr. Hardin?"

She'd obviously been expecting him. Lewis resisted the impulse to glance at his watch. He knew damn well he wasn't late. He nodded and, at her invitation, took a seat in one of the deep leather club chairs in the outer office. No expense spared. Either Wild Rose really had serious money, or they wanted visitors to think they did. Probably the former.

Lewis had asked a few questions. Yes, they were a tough outfit to work for, but they paid their bills on time. Yes, they were doing a lot of drilling in central Alberta, mostly their own properties. No, no one had seen this Tanguay character. Lewis was particularly curious about that.

He picked up a newspaper, glanced through it, then set it down. Business stuff. *FP Magazine, Globe and Mail, Oil World, Wall Street Journal.* He could use a sports magazine. Even golf in a pinch.

He felt restless suddenly, as though he was waiting in the principal's office. Then he smiled and relaxed. Hell, wasn't that what this Tanguay wanted, making him cool his heels out here like a kid? Put him off balance? Lewis had half a mind to get up and walk out. It wasn't as though he was going to do business with Wild Rose, anyway, no matter what Fred Billings had said. And now that things were working out with Phoebe and her family, he had other interests, other concerns.

Five minutes later, the receptionist took a call, then

stood and looked over her high banquette. "Mr. Hardin? Mr. Tanguay will see you now."

Will see you now. As if the guy considered himself royalty or something. What was with this SOB? Lewis followed her down a plushly carpeted hallway, past several closed doors to double doors at the end. Bird's-eye maple. Very nice.

He took a deep breath as she opened the door and gestured for him to enter. He couldn't shake the bad feeling he had about this whole thing.

Lewis stepped inside and the receptionist closed the door silently behind him. He was facing a bank of windows, floor to ceiling, and a huge desk with a man seated behind it. Lewis got the instant impression that the man wasn't going to stand to greet him; wasn't going to offer his hand. He also got the impression that the man behind the desk knew damn well Lewis had no intention of shaking his hand. This was not what you'd call a friendly meeting. Maybe not even a cordial one.

"Lewis Hardin?"

Lewis nodded briefly and took a few more steps, taking in the whole room in a lightning-quick glance. He jammed his hands in his jacket pockets, just in case the message wasn't clear. He was dressed for success—black jeans and his black leather jacket. He needed a haircut, too.

"Bart Tanguay," the other man said, and cleared his throat. Almost as though he was nervous. Lewis looked at him, surprised, and nodded again. Tanguay was pale beneath a golf-course tan, in the grip of some strong emotion. His hands were out of sight beneath the desk. Lewis frowned. *What was going on?*

"You wanted to see me?" Lewis thought he might as well get straight to the point. He didn't plan to stay long.

"Yes. Sit down." Tanguay, a rather overfed handsome man with penetrating dark eyes and black hair streaked with gray, had regained some composure and gestured carelessly toward the cowhide sofa and two chairs that stood grouped in front of his desk, surrounding a low coffee table with some kind of native sculpture on its polished surface. Lewis considered standing, then realized there was no point in being too difficult. After all, he held the cards in this game.

Whatever the game was.

He sat down on the sofa and stretched his legs out in front of him.

Tanguay chuckled, and Lewis shot him a cool look. "What's so funny?"

"You. You don't want to be here, but you're too damn curious to stay away."

Lewis shrugged. He'd ignore that. "Maybe you could tell me what you're after. You wanted this meeting."

"I did." Tanguay paused and sorted through some cards on his desktop. Lewis waited impatiently.

The oilman cleared his throat again. "Where would you like me to begin?"

Lewis snorted. "Begin! I'm only interested in why you've been on my case. Say what you've got to say and then I'll be leaving."

The man smiled and steepled his hands together, fingertips touching. "I've been following your work, Hardin. You're good. You know what I want. I want you to come and work for us. I can give you considerable responsibility and the remuneration that goes with it. I can double what you're earning at F&B."

He glanced toward Lewis.

Lewis frowned, pretended to think for a few seconds. "Not interested. Anything else?"

For a split second, Lewis thought the man behind the desk had lost his composure; then he seemed to collect himself. "Why aren't you interested?" he asked evenly.

"Just not. Maybe I could ask you the same question—what's so damn special about me? Tool-pushes are a dime a dozen."

"Not ones like you."

"Oh, I'm flattered," Lewis drawled insolently. He started to get up. "If that's all you have to say, I've got a ball game to catch—"

"It's not."

Tanguay paused and looked down, then looked directly at Lewis. "I understand you have a serious girlfriend."

How the hell did he know? Well, it was no secret. The secret was that he was already married; only he and Phoebe knew that. "That's right."

"I understand she's on a full scholarship from Cross-Canada. It'll be coming up for renewal soon. I'm on the board. I could make things difficult for—"

Lewis leapt to his feet. He took two steps toward the desk and grabbed the edge of it and leaned over, his face directly in Tanguay's. "Are you *threatening* me? This is between you and me. You say another word about the woman I love and I'd be happy to use your three-piece to polish these windows—with your sorry carcass still inside. To *hell* with your goddamn scholarship! I can support my own wife!"

Tanguay had been startled by Lewis's violent approach. Startled but not frightened. If anything, he looked slightly pleased. He leaned back in his chair and clasped his hands behind his head. "Sit down, Hardin."

"*Understand?* My personal life is hands-off!"

"Is it?" Tanguay made a careless gesture, but Lewis knew that he wasn't nearly as unruffled as he appeared to be. "The fact is, I know more about you than you do about yourself."

Lewis stared at him. "Now what kind of stupid comment is *that* to make?"

"Never mind. Listen to me. Here's my situation. I am fifty-two years old and I have no family. My first wife and I are divorced, no children, and my second wife has never had kids, either. She doesn't want any now. I want someone to share in this company with me, someone to groom—someone who could possibly take over one day. I've got my mind set on you."

Lewis sat back down, stunned. *What was he talking about?*

"Me?" he managed. It was almost a croak.

"Yes, you. I've been watching you for a long time. Years, in fact. You're just the kind of man I need. Someone young, capable, from outside the company. Someone who knows drilling and field-work. Then there's the other side of it, someone with the smarts to see an opportunity when it knocks."

"That's where you've got me figured wrong, Tan-guay. I'm happy where I am. I like F&B. I'm making the kind of money I want to make. I've got the kind of deal I want with my bosses."

"They can't offer you ownership—"

"They already have," Lewis shot back. "And I've turned them down, too. You big boys just don't get it, do you? Up here in your glass-and-brass towers? Money isn't everything. You can't buy everybody. Get it? You can't buy *me.*"

"That hasn't been my experience in business," Tanguay said softly. "Or with people in general."

He studied Lewis for a long time, then added in a low, harsh tone, "Pretty talk for someone who came from nothing and nobody. Pretty talk for someone who spent his best years in jail because he stole cattle from his boss."

"Kids make mistakes. I've done my time, fair and square. I've never pretended otherwise. You've got nothing on me. Say what you've got to say, and get it over with!" Lewis was sitting up straight now, on the edge of the sofa, staring at the man behind the desk. *How did he know about Lewis's background, where he came from?*

"All right. Remember those envelopes that used to come now and then, Lewis? Money? Cash money?"

Lewis felt a cold chill run down his spine. A vein throbbed painfully in his neck. This—all of it—felt wrong. Bad. Evil.

"Just in time, eh? In time for some new school clothes? In time for paying the taxes? In time for buying seeds for the garden? Eh? You remember?"

Lewis just watched him. He couldn't speak.

"I was hoping it wouldn't come to this, Lewis. I was hoping to break you in to the idea gradually. Maybe wait a couple of years to tell you. But you're so goddamned unreasonable I've got to take the gloves off now. I'm sorry, boy. I really am."

"What the hell kind of game are you playing?"

"It's no game. I wish it was," Tanguay replied

calmly. "This is the way it is. This is life, Hardin. *Life*. I've made my share of mistakes. We all have. Sometimes what seems like a mistake, though, can turn out to be the best thing that ever happened. Like you."

The bastard was talking in riddles.

"Sometimes we bargain with God. We hope that the mistakes we make won't come back to haunt us. But they always do." Tanguay laughed and then paused, toyed with something on his desk. Lewis said nothing. He was too rattled to speak. Something was wrong here—terribly wrong. This was not the talk of a man who was just out to poach a top hand from a competitor. This was not business-as-usual in the oil patch.

"Do you understand me, Lewis?"

"No, I don't. I don't have a clue what you're talking about," Lewis said bluntly. Nor did he care. All he wanted was some fresh air. To leave. Tanguay gave him the creeps. He'd wasted enough time up here on the seventeenth floor—

"Who's your father, Lewis? Have you ever wondered?"

Lewis stared at him. He knew he'd gone pale under his own tan. *His father?!*

"You don't know, do you? Well, I can tell you who your father is." He paused. "I am. I'm your father."

"Like hell you are!" Lewis was on his feet again,

gripping the edge of the desk. He actually shook the massive piece of furniture his rage was so sudden and overwhelming.

"Your name should be Tanguay, like mine," he went on, seemingly unperturbed by Lewis's violence. "By rights, it should be. Of course, that's not the way it worked out, but—"

"Bullshit! You're crazy. You're…you're a madman." Lewis didn't know which horrified him more, the information that this man might be his biological father or the knowledge that…that he and Ma…

He couldn't even finish the thought. It sickened him. This man and…and poor old stumpy-legged Ma? Of course, that was a long time ago, and she wouldn't have been crippled yet…

He shook the desk again. "You *bastard!*"

"Why is that so hard for you to believe, Lewis?" Tanguay looked haunted, a man in real pain. As though he hadn't expected his news to produce this reaction. As though he'd thought maybe Lewis would be pleased. "You're my son. My only child. I can't let you go. I left the money because I felt I had to do something…"

"Do something! You bastard. You ruined her life. Both their lives. You left her holding the can while you took off and…and had your own life. Married another woman—two women! You—"

"I was pleased to hear I'd had a son," Tanguay went on, apparently unaware that Lewis had shouted at him. "You can believe that or not, as you like. Of course, I couldn't get involved. There was no way I could get mixed up on a permanent basis with your mother. No way. I had big plans for myself, and they did not include her or a child. Not at that time in my life. It was a mistake. Then later…" Tanguay shrugged.

To Lewis's amazement, he reached into a drawer and drew out a checkbook. "Well, who knew how things would turn out? That my wife—my fiancée at the time—wouldn't give me a son. Either wife," he said slowly.

Tanguay was nuts. Completely nuts. He began writing something, very deliberately. Oddly, Lewis noted the pen, big, fat and gold-capped. A fountain pen. Probably cost more than his entire monthly car payment.

He saw red. "You mean you were…you were engaged to someone while you screwed around with my mother? Messed up her life? You were two-timing her, both of them…."

Lewis covered his face with his hands and turned away. He took a deep breath. He had to get hold of himself. To think he could hate a man like he hated Tanguay right now. A man who claimed to be his *father*.

He whirled around. Tanguay stepped out from behind his desk and handed Lewis a slip of paper. Lewis took it automatically. He looked down. It was a check made out to W. Hardin for fifty thousand dollars. What...?

"What's this?" he asked hoarsely. "What's this— *a goddamn check?*"

"You're right. You say I ruined her life. Maybe. I left money now and again, but that wasn't enough, was it? And then I stopped sending it when you were about ten. I lost interest, I guess you could say. This ought to clear my debt with her. Five thousand dollars per year for, say, ten years. It's only fair. I don't know how much cash I left in the mailbox over the years. Quite a few thousand. I never kept track."

"You think you can buy me? Buy *her?*" He ripped the check in two, then in half again and flung the pieces in Tanguay's face.

"Nice gesture. But stupid." Tanguay held out another slip of paper. Lewis could see at a glance that it was a duplicate of the first. He'd guessed that Lewis would refuse the check. "Don't be so quick to rip up someone else's money. Do you really feel you can speak for her?"

"For Ma? For my mother? For the woman you knocked up and left? You fool, you haven't even made it out right." Lewis held the check in front of Tanguay's face "It's *M,* not *W.*"

"What are you talking about?" It was Tanguay's turn to look surprised. "*M* for what?"

"Mercedes!"

Tanguay's expression of scorn mixed with pity

scorched Lewis's heart. "You're the fool. Mercedes Hardin is not your mother. Billy is."

BILLY. LEWIS HAD always known that Billy was short for Wilhelmina, an old-fashioned name that had run through Mercy's family. He left the building, stepped out into the late-October sunshine. Cars honked as he walked across the street to the parking lot on the other side.

Billy—his mother! It couldn't be. He'd never had the slightest hint. She was his sister, that was what he'd always thought. What he'd been told. Ma and Billy, they'd both raised him. Two women. Why would he ever have questioned it?

Lewis had a sudden urge to hide. To go to ground like an injured fox. No way could he go to a football game tonight with Harry and Trevor. No way could he see Phoebe tomorrow, shop for houses on the weekend, as they'd planned.

He needed to be alone. He needed to think this through. Not only the raw facts that Tanguay had shot at him, but the fact—if it was fact, and it had to be, how else could he have known everything?— that Tanguay was his father. A father who suddenly wanted to claim him. After twenty-seven years. Why? Because he'd never had any legitimate children.

And a mother...

Dear God, Lewis thought frantically, a fragile,

half-broken mother, a child-woman whose stability of mind had always been questionable. How old could she have been? Fifteen? Sixteen? Had she ever been whole? Had Tanguay done this to her, turned her into the fearful, slow-witted creature she was today? If he had, the bastard should be made to pay!

Lewis located his Jeep in the parking lot and fumbled as he inserted his key in the lock. His hand was shaking. He felt icy cold, even in his jacket. It wasn't a cold day for late October. He'd never been in such bad shape before. Ever. Not even when he'd been convicted of rustling and sentenced to two years less a day in Fort Saskatchewan. He'd served three and a half years in total, paid his debt to society.

He had a criminal record.

As Tanguay had reminded him. Was there anything he didn't know? How long had he been tracking him? Spying on him? It made Lewis shudder.

A half-witted mother and a criminal record. And a megalomaniac bastard for a father. He'd been raised in a web of lies. He'd been abandoned by his own mother, for reasons only she knew. His father had tried to erase his existence from his life, except for the occasional envelope full of guilt money, stuffed in a mailbox.

Now, now when Tanguay wanted a successor, an heir, when he couldn't get a son any other way, he was willing to come out into the open. Why? Because he could use Lewis. Because he was willing to risk admitting paternity so he could use Lewis in his own company, to fulfill his own stupid dynastic dreams. But was he really so willing? Lewis realized that if Tanguay could have secured his cooperation any other way, tempted him through money or status or threatened him through blackmail, he'd have done it. And then, would he ever have told him that he was really his father?

Probably not. He was too ashamed of the connection. Big-shot Calgary oilman and white trash from Bearberry Hill? What would they say about *that* in the Devonian Club?

Lewis noticed that his vision was blurry, and he cursed and blinked away the tears. Crying? He'd never cried in his life!

He cleared his throat. First things first. He dialed the farm on his car phone. "Harry? Yeah, listen. I can't make it tonight. Do you think Joe might like to go with you and Trevor? Fine. Good. Go ahead and use the three tickets. I'll leave them at the gate for you. Another time, eh?" He hung up. Harry hadn't even asked why. He'd just accepted that if Lewis had changed his mind, he'd changed his mind. No questions.

It was going to be a lot harder dealing with Phoebe.

CHAPTER SIXTEEN

PHOEBE SWITCHED the wipers to their fastest speed and peered through the rain smearing the windshield. The day had started off overcast and now, midafternoon, the drizzle had turned into a downpour. Her little blue Toyota was coughing in second gear from time to time, as usual. At least the wipers worked. She just hoped the car would make it home to Glory. Lewis had said he'd buy her a new car, and she had just about made her mind up to accept his offer.

Lewis. She was skipping her Friday-afternoon organic-chemistry class tomorrow to drive to Glory today. She had to find Lewis and talk to him. She was going crazy not knowing.

She shoulder-checked and pulled over into the right-hand lane to make the turn onto 109 Street south, leading to the Calgary Trail, which would take her, via Highway 2, to Calgary in two and a half hours. She should be in Glory by suppertime. She still hadn't made up her mind if she should go to her parents' house and look for Lewis tomorrow or go straight to Bearberry Hill, where she suspected he was—thanks to Mercy's hemming and hawing and general inability to tell a good lie—and find him this evening. She wanted desperately to see him, and yet at the same time she was afraid. Why was he so determined not to see *her?* If there was bad news, she was in no hurry to hear it. On the other hand, it was better to get this over with, bad news or not.

She decided to leave her decision to the weather. If it got any nastier—the rain could turn to sleet or snow at this time of year, early November—she'd stay out at her parents' tonight. It would be nearly dark by the time she got to Swallowbank Farm as it was.

What she had *not* done was call off the wedding plans. No matter what Lewis said. Yes, it was true she'd tried to get out of the marriage herself, back in September, but that was before she'd realized she *was* in love with Lewis. That it wasn't merely lust. That somewhere along the way, she'd realized she should listen to her heart and not just her head. Once she'd figured that out, once she'd given herself permission to love Lewis, she'd fallen in love with him all over again.

She could still see him at Thanksgiving, the conniver, grinning at her and playing footsies with her under the table. Of course she was in love with him. What had she been thinking? She'd known right then, over the roast turkey and dressing, what an idiot she'd been to get cold feet at all. Lewis Hardin was the man for her. There'd never been any other man

and there never would be. She'd gone out to Bearberry Hill first that day—to tell him her new idea
about the engagement and that she'd stay married to
him, if he was still willing after all her foolishness—
but he hadn't been at Mercy's. That had made her
late for her parents' Thanksgiving dinner. And there
he'd been, smiling at her across the room, through
the incredible confusion that was a Longquist family
gathering, waiting for her.

She wasn't changing her mind again. They were
married and they were staying married. If they decided not to bother with the silliness of this sham
engagement and another wedding ceremony, fine.
They were still married. They could have a little
party to celebrate. And they'd simply tell her parents
and uncles and aunts and her roommate and her professors—not that *they'd* care—and everyone else, the
whole world. And the whole world could just live
with it.

Phoebe was through being cautious. Being careful.
Being a good girl. Did good girls go off and marry
guys, ex-cons, they'd been in love with since childhood and not tell anybody? No, they did not. And
she'd already done that, so she definitely wasn't a
good girl, anyway.

Skipping class wasn't something good girls did,
either. Not good girls on full scholarships. But
Phoebe hadn't been able to keep her mind on her
studies since she'd received the message on her ma-

chine last Thursday afternoon saying their get-together on the weekend was off. And then he'd dropped the bombshell that he'd thought things over and decided they should call off the wedding, after all, and the marriage, too, because something had come up—something big—that he couldn't talk about. Something that had changed the whole situation, he'd said.

What could that something be? Was he in trouble with the law again? Surely not! Phoebe was frightened. Another woman? Bethany, the little black-haired witch? Or some blond bombshell? That was her worst fear. No, her worst fear was that Lewis decided that their so-called marriage was a farce and had always been a farce. That he was not in love with Phoebe Longquist, and the biggest mistake he'd ever made was accepting her shotgun offer last August. He wanted out.

Never mind, a tiny voice nagged at her conscience, *isn't that exactly what you told him a month and a half ago? You wanted out?*

And did he buy it? Did he say, "Okay, Phoebe, we'll get a quickie divorce, I won't stand in your way"? No, he did not. He'd decided to fight for her. To court her, to court her parents, even her brothers and sisters. Win them all over.

Which was exactly what he'd done. Pieces of that ghastly family china—Phoebe always hoped Jilly would want it someday—for her mom, football tickets for her dad and Trevor. He had her parents, especially her dad, totally wound around his little finger. They'd kill her now if she didn't marry Lewis Hardin next month!

Phoebe chewed her lower lip until it was sore. This was all her own fault again. She shouldn't have burst into the Thanksgiving dinner the way she had and flashed the ring around and announced that she and Lewis were engaged. That must have been a shocker for him. She should have talked it over with Lewis first. A second wedding ceremony was another of her crazy ideas—a solution to the secrecy angle of the first wedding. She should have consulted him before going public. Well, she'd tried, hadn't she? That was why she'd been late getting to the farm.

Thinking about it all, turning the facts this way and that, gave her a giant headache by the time she drove into Calgary and took the exit for the Deerfoot Trail south. She stopped for gas and then went into the Circle K for a package of chocolate-covered peanuts and some licorice twists and a giant coffee, extra cream and sugar, to go. Lewis liked cherry licorice twists. It would be something silly to give him. An offering. Just in case he was angry at her for springing the engagement.

The coffee was pretty bad, but it was loaded with caffeine and that was what Phoebe wanted. She ate the peanuts and turned her radio on full-blast to a country station. Shania Twain bellowing into the car, which was cold, since the heater wasn't working properly, about being a woman, oh, man. Oh, please! Phoebe shut off the radio.

At least the weather was letting up. The rain had stopped as she drove through Calgary and here, just south of the city, it was clear. Ice, that was the next worry. Clear meant cold at this time of year, and this late in the day, after rain, cold meant icy patches to watch for.

Phoebe's imagination ran away with her for a few moments, but by the time she saw the whole Longquist clan weeping and wringing their hands and Lewis rushing to the Crowfoot General, where she was lying in a hospital bed after her accident, looking beautiful even though her leg was in traction and she had six broken ribs…she got hold of herself.

Whoa. Enough of that.

Think! Where could Lewis have gone? She remembered the first time she'd seen him, boxing at that old feed bag filled with straw in the barn. A scrawny fifteen-year-old trying to build up his muscles. The knife and candle and a few crusts of bread on the makeshift table. The bed, where he'd obviously slept from time to time.

He'd made himself a home in the barn. His cabin! *He's probably holed up in that log cabin he built.* It wasn't very big; he might have had a chance to finish it since the summer.

She knew she was right. She knew it in her heart.

And if she was wrong, why, she'd just get back in her car and drive home to Swallowbank Farm. Except that Swallowbank Farm wasn't home any longer. Home was wherever Lewis was.

WHEN SHE GOT to Bearberry Hill, it was pouring rain again and dark. Luckily, she had a flashlight in her glove compartment.

She parked in the rutted lane that led to the old overgrown cemetery adjoining the church, which stood on the other side of the road from the Hardin place, about a hundred yards from their drive. It was creepy but she didn't want to park at the Hardins'. She wasn't prepared to talk to Mercy or to answer any questions. This way, if she was wrong and Lewis *wasn't* at his cabin, she could just go back to the car and head to her parents' place, with no one any the wiser.

The wind had come up and was lashing the rain in all directions. Phoebe could feel ice in it. It was a cold night, darn cold. Phoebe pulled her hood over her head and snugged it to cover her hair. She only had canvas sneakers on, which would be ruined walking through this mud and wet, but that couldn't be helped. She hadn't thought to bring boots; of course, if she'd gone to the farm first, she could have taken a pair. There was always an assortment of rubber boots of all sizes littering the Longquists' mudroom.

But she'd come this far, and she wasn't going back for boots. She wasn't sure yet what she intended to say to Lewis when she found him. If she found him. She just knew she had to see him.

He was her husband, damn it. Signed, sealed and delivered. She loved him, and she wasn't going to give him up, no matter what. He couldn't do this to her—phone her like that, call off their marriage and then disappear into thin air.

She remembered the path that meandered from below the barn around the hill, coming out near Lewis's cabin. The cabin itself was about half a mile from his mother's house, as she recalled. The other, easier, way was to cut right through the farmyard, but she didn't want to risk the dogs barking and Mercy or Billy coming out to investigate.

She was probably going on a fool's errand, anyway! When she'd seen the cabin last, Lewis had just framed the roof. There were no doors or windows. No shingles. Maybe she was deluding herself in thinking he might have had time to finish it.

"Ouch!" Phoebe swore as a branch slapped her face. She couldn't see much with this pathetic discount-table flashlight she'd bought somewhere. Why was she always buying things on sale? The batteries were weak and, of course—like every flashlight—if you pointed it where you were going, you couldn't see what you were stepping on.

Still, she could make out the path, and that was

something. Her feet were soaked. Five more minutes or so, and she'd climb the hill again, to where the cabin was perched. Suddenly she could smell wood smoke and she stopped, her head up and her nose in the air like a pointer dog. Heavenly! There was nothing like the smell of a poplar fire burning on a cold night. It spoke of home and bacon frying and wool socks drying by the fire. Toast and cheese and hot chocolate. Warming reddened hands at the flames.

Of course, Mercy and Billy had a woodstove. It could be smoke from their kitchen fire.

Phoebe forged ahead. As she'd predicted, the path took a turn to the right and began to climb. She dropped her flashlight once, swore, then found it and wiped it on her jeans. Luckily it still worked.

The wind twisted and groaned, as if uncertain which way to blow. She shivered, wet to the skin. Then suddenly, Phoebe broke through the screen of trees and there, just to the east, was the cabin. Yes, it had a roof now. Galvanized tin? There was smoke coming out of the chimney—she wanted to shout! And, yes, there were windows and a door, and a dim light gleaming in the window.

Home!

Phoebe stumbled on and heard the faint bark of a dog from inside the cabin. A figure darkened the window, peering out into the storm.

"Lewis!" She called and waved her arms, but the wind picked up his name and tossed it away. She felt giddy, felt like laughing. At the same time, she was weak, shaking with exhaustion. And relief. He was here, in his cabin, as she'd so desperately hoped.

She approached the small building and now he must have been able to see her, because the clouds scudded away from the moon for an instant. He left the window, and a few seconds later the door was flung open and a dog darted out to circle and growl, then wag its tail and sniff at her knees.

"Phoebe?"

"Oh, Lewis!" She threw herself into his arms, not caring that she was wet and he was dry, that she was cold and he was warm. That the door was wide open, letting in the wind and rain.

Not caring about anything at all except that she'd found him now, was in his arms where she longed to be—*where she belonged*—and she was never letting him get away from her again.

THE CABIN WAS surprisingly cozy. Lewis threw another couple of logs on the blazing fire in the stone fireplace. There was a small range in the corner by the tiny table and two folding chairs that passed for a kitchen. Shelves above the table held plastic dishes and various cans and boxes of goods. Phoebe recognized a brand of pancake mix and another of evaporated milk. The place was neat and tidy, if sparsely furnished. There were no curtains on the windows.

"Okay, honey." Lewis came over to her and sat

down beside her on the bed, where he'd dumped her unceremoniously a few minutes earlier, after kissing her and nearly hugging her to death. He reached for her sweatshirt, and she obediently raised her arms so he could pull it off. "Let's get you out of this wet stuff and then you can tell me how you found me." Lewis's last words were muffled.

"You mean how I tracked you down?"

"Whatever." He grinned and knelt to untie and remove her sodden shoes and socks. He rubbed her feet briskly between his warm palms. It felt heavenly. Suddenly, looking down at Lewis's dark head as he ministered to her cold feet, Phoebe was overwhelmed with emotion.

"Oh, Lewis!" she said, and couldn't resist touching him. She buried her hands deeply in his hair as he glanced up, surprised. She'd noticed right away, even when he'd pulled her into the cabin and into his arms, that he seemed sad. He had a subdued, serious expression she'd never seen before. *What had gone wrong? What had gone so terribly wrong?*

"What is it, babe?" Lewis's smile was the same. The look in his eyes was the same. Adoring, loving…vulnerable.

"Why did you call me like that?" she said. "Last week. Left that message? I was so worried. I didn't know what had happened. Then you just…disappeared!"

Lewis sighed and got up to retrieve a blanket from

a pile stacked on small pine dresser at the foot of the bed. Phoebe noticed one of Mercy's faded quilts on the pile, plus another one folded over the end of the plain pine bed. Everything looked new, including the large Turkish-style rug, as though he'd made one trip to a household-furnishings store and purchased everything he needed.

"How about a cup of hot chocolate?" he asked. He apparently wasn't going to answer her questions. He tucked the blanket around her shoulders and under her thighs. "I'd take that damp sweater off you, too, but I don't think I'd be able to restrain myself, and I don't think that's what you want..." His voice was raw.

Phoebe grabbed his sleeve and pushed the blanket away. "Take off my sweater, Lewis," she urged hoarsely, her eyes searching his. "Take it off! That's *exactly* what I want. Didn't you...didn't you tell me you planned to seduce someone right in front of this very fireplace? When I first came out here to visit you?" Her eyes pleaded with him. "Well, here I am! You can seduce your *wife*, Lewis!"

His eyes darkened and he reached for the hem of her sweater. She wriggled out of it and then she was almost nude, clad only in her panties. The emerald ring, with its mate, the plain white-gold wedding band, hung on a gold chain around her neck. Lewis touched it. Phoebe looked down, his hand so large and strong, delicately touching the plain band dangling between her breasts.

"We're married, but for how long, Phoebe?" His voice was anguished. *"For how long?"*

Feverishly, she began to unbutton his shirt. "Forever, Lewis. Forever! I'm not letting you say no. I'm not calling off anything we've planned. I don't care what it is you've got on your mind, nothing can come between us. Nothing! I love you, don't you understand that?" she cried. "We're married and we're staying married!"

"Oh, baby," Lewis groaned, and helped her finish taking off his clothes. He held back the duvet and she scooted under it to the far side of the bed, against the rough log wall. He slipped in beside her and hauled her into his arms, his body warm against hers. The sheets were cool and scratchy. Brand-new. She lifted one knee, arched against his body. *Warm, secure, home again....*

He began to kiss her, with a passion she'd nearly forgotten. It had been so long! How long? Over a month? Since she'd decided on her own that she wanted out of the marriage. Since then, Lewis had courted her like some crystal-perfect, don't-touch virgin, had fanned her desire for him without satisfying it until she was nearly ablaze. No wonder she couldn't keep her mind on her studies.

"Hold on, baby, hold on," he panted, grabbing

her wrist as she reached for him. "Stop for a minute."

"What is it, Lewis?" She stared at him, one arm still wrapped around his neck, unwilling to let him go even for an instant.

"I don't have any condoms out here."

"You weren't expecting any ladies to seduce?" She grinned.

"Not exactly," he replied hoarsely. A question entered his eyes, a hopeful gleam. "You wouldn't be on the Pill, by any chance, would you?"

"No." Phoebe laughed and reached up to kiss him again. "Never mind, we're married, remember? We can do this. We're allowed."

"But, what if…you know, what if there's, er, results?"

"You mean a baby?"

"Of course I mean a baby, damn it!"

"It's not a good time for that, but if it happens, it happens. We'll just deal with it. We're allowed to have babies. Married people have babies sometimes. We're *supposed* to have babies. Not five, though. Maybe one or two."

"I see. So, I can stay home and look after them—"

"Them!"

"Him or her. Just one to start, right?"

"Mm." She nibbled at his chin. "Right."

"Uh-huh. I can stay home and look after our son

or daughter while you go out and slay pond-scum dragons in the name of science?'' The light in his dark eyes was wonderful to behold.

"Something like that. Now, kiss me, Lewis!''

Without further ado, he did.

CHAPTER SEVENTEEN

PHOEBE WATCHED Lewis carefully work a small piece of tobacco to the front of his mouth and pluck it out between thumb and forefinger, with a sidelong glance at her.

"Oh, Lewis! Why don't you just give it up? Smoking's a bad habit."

"It's not a habit," Lewis said, lazily regarding the end of his home-rolled cigarette. "This—" he waved the smoldering butt in the air "—is the first smoke I've had in two weeks. That's not a habit. That's a…a ceremony." He grinned at her.

She grinned back. She didn't care what he did. He could keep his "ceremony," just as long as he wanted her back in his life. For good.

She listened to the rain pounding on the tin roof and admired the rings on her hand. Lewis had replaced the wedding ring on her third finger after they'd made love the first time. On, off, on, off. Maybe they'd stay there now. He'd whispered his vows, repeated them solemnly as he slid the rings onto her finger. Phoebe wished she could remember what she'd promised him. It had all happened in a dream, back in August. She'd meant what she'd said; she just couldn't *remember* exactly what she'd said. If they decided to go through with the ceremony for friends and family, she'd have another chance to promise all over again.

Lewis had stoked both stoves when he'd gotten up to get his cigarette papers and tobacco. He'd also lit two more candles. One burned on the shelf above the bed and another on the small table. The candles that had been burning on the table and the windowsill when she arrived had long ago sputtered out. It was peaceful in the cabin, nothing but the sound of rain and the crack and hiss of wood in the fireplace.

"Remember that place you fixed up in the barn?"

He glanced at her. "Yeah." He took another draw on his cigarette and blew the smoke over her head. "Crazy, huh?"

"Did you ever stay out there? Sleep there?"

"Sure. I stayed out there a whole week once, when I was flaming mad at Ma and—" Lewis suddenly stopped and frowned. He took another pull on his cigarette.

"And?"

"Oh, hell. Never mind. Kid stuff." He stubbed his cigarette out, half-smoked, in the bar-style glass ashtray he'd brought to bed. He was still frowning.

"What's the matter, Lewis?"

"Nothing."

"Is it something I said?" Phoebe hated it when he

got this closed, secret look on his face. It didn't happen often, but when it did, hell could freeze over before she could get him to spill what was on his mind.

He shook his head and raised his arms, clasping his hands beneath his head and stretching. "Forget I said anything. I was just thinking about, you know, kid stuff. Growing up out here, that kind of thing."

"Oh." Phoebe nestled down beside him again. She made little rivulets in his silky chest hair with her finger and hoped he had food for breakfast when the sun rose. Bacon and beans and pancakes. There was no fridge, of course. She was starving. Could she last until morning?

"Still, you had Billy," she said, returning to the subject of his childhood. "She was a lot older than you, though. Too old to play with. More like an older cousin, I guess, or an aunt."

"Or a mother," he said softly. Oddly.

"Well, hardly!" she replied. "A mother at fifteen or sixteen? I'll be twenty-four next April…"

He shot her a strange glance. "No. But it's different for you."

She frowned. "Different? How?"

"You've got a family, an education. You know where you're going in life. You've got…hell, you've got goals. No one could take advantage of you, make you do something you didn't want to do. Billy's, well, you know Billy. She's…"

"Weird? Unusual? Strange?" Phoebe grinned, but Lewis didn't smile back. Once, he would have.

Something was wrong.

"Anyway, what are we talking about?" she went on. "Billy's got a heart of gold, as my mother says, and that's all that counts. And I might *just* be a mother already, after last night. I hope not. I'm not ready to take that step. It's a big one." She smiled at him, and after a second or two of hesitation, he finally smiled back.

"It's no joke, you know," he said.

"I know that. You got any crackers or anything? Cheese?"

"On the shelf above the table."

Phoebe climbed out of the bed, over Lewis, and padded into the tiny kitchen area. She held the table candle on its ceramic tile higher, so she could see what was on the shelf. Sardines, kippers, smoked oysters, tuna—the fish family was well represented. There was a box of Ritz crackers, some wheat thins and a can of Danish brie, which Phoebe opened. She took gherkins out of a jar she found on the shelf and piled some on the plate, along with a handful of crackers and the brie. Then she picked up an un-opened jar of dry-roasted nuts and carried her snacks back to the bed.

"Here!" She deposited the food on Lewis's bare chest. "You be the table." She climbed over him to settle on her side of the bed, cross-legged.

"What if I get a coughing fit," he warned, his eyes on the food.

"You won't," she returned confidently. She cut some cheese and stuck it in Lewis's mouth. Then she popped a piece in her own mouth. "Mmm." She chewed and swallowed, then reached for a cracker. "I'm going to get fat, married to you. All this sex works up a girl's appetite. Hey!"

Phoebe grabbed for the plate, which had tilted dangerously as Lewis took a deep breath. This wasn't fun for him, for some reason. He wasn't laughing. Phoebe took the plate and lodged it on the duvet tucked between her crossed legs. There.

She'd wait it out. Eventually he'd tell her what was on his mind. In his own time.

"How was Calgary?" she asked, popping another piece of cheese into her mouth. That ought to be safe enough. She knew he'd been planning to see someone in the city the previous week, just before the weekend he was supposed to meet her.

"Fine." Lewis eyed the plate of food she was holding and selected a pickle. He chewed thoughtfully.

She stared at him. Just fine? That's it?

"Listen, Phoebe…"

"Yes?" She held her breath.

"I got some strange news when I was in Calgary. Some really strange news."

"Uh-huh?" She sliced off another piece of the brie.

"I mean, it's so weird I don't know if I should tell anybody. Even you." He tried to smile, to make light of his news, whatever it was, but he couldn't quite pull it off.

"Lewis," she began, then swallowed. There was a lump in her throat, and not just because of the snack she was eating. "You can tell me anything. Anything! I love you and we're married and that's all there is to it. You could tell me you were an alien visiting from…from Mars and I'd still love you!"

"Maybe Mars would be easier to figure out than what I'm going to tell you." He took a deep breath, then let it out shakily. "I found out that my mother's not Ma. It's Billy."

"Billy!" Phoebe wished she'd been able to hold back her shock.

"Yes. Apparently she had me just after she turned sixteen, and obviously the two of them, Ma—Mercedes—and Billy decided to keep it a secret. Sort of." He made a poor attempt at a laugh. Phoebe's heart squeezed in sympathy. "I guess they thought it would be better if it looked like Ma had the bastard—"

"Lewis!"

"—okay, illegitimate kid. I have no idea why."

"Have you talked to them about this?"

"No!" Lewis sounded vehement. "If they haven't

brought it up in twenty-seven years, there's no damn way I'm going to bring it up now.''

"I think you should. You can't just pretend you don't know. Maybe they've been meaning to tell you all along. Maybe they just need the right opportunity.'' Phoebe bent quickly and kissed Lewis's cheek.

He tried again to laugh. ''They've never had the right opportunity in twenty-seven years? Sure.''

"Look. I love you, Lewis. None of this makes any difference to me.''

"It should.'' he said violently. "Damn it, it should! Billy's...'' His voice wavered and Phoebe wanted to put her arms around him. "Billy's not much more than a half-wit, you've said so yourself. She's not someone you'd want to find out was your mother...'' Lewis's voice cracked. He seemed at a loss for words. "What about us?'' He looked tortured. "What about our kids someday? You could be pregnant now. What if we had a kid that...that turned out like her?''

"But, Lewis—''

"That's why I thought we should call this whole thing off. Forget about having kids, taking the risk. Get the divorce you were so crazy about getting last month, put it all behind us.''

"That's not going to happen.'' Her voice was steely. "We're married and we're staying married. And just because...'' She shrugged helplessly. "We can't worry about a bunch of *what if*s, Lewis. There's nothing really wrong with Billy, you know that. Not *wrong* wrong. She's just…just shy!''

''Shy!'' He threw back the covers suddenly and swung his knees over the side. ''That's putting it mildly.''

''Where you going?''

''To roll another smoke.'' He scowled and stalked toward the wooden dresser sitting against the opposite wall and wrenched out a drawer, then started pawing through the contents. Phoebe decided this wasn't the best time to rag him about his smoking, ceremony or no ceremony. He was in quite a state. No wonder. That was why he'd disappeared. He'd wanted to come to some kind of decision on his own. She supposed he'd told her because he'd decided to stay married to her—because she'd tracked him down and insisted on it—but he wasn't going to tell anyone else what he'd found out in Calgary.

Lewis rolled his smoke and lit it, then began striding back and forth in front of the fireplace. Four strides took him right across the tiny room. He was buck naked, with only the cigarette and a black frown on his face. It was distracting, to say the least. Phoebe reached for another cracker and a pickle. How the heck had he learned all this, anyway?

As though reading her mind, Lewis blew out a cloud of smoke. ''You probably wonder who told me, eh?''

Phoebe nodded.

"The guy I met in Calgary. The one who's been bugging me to join his company. He's my father!" Lewis took another deep draw on his cigarette and walked toward the fire. He poked viciously at the logs until sparks flew up the chimney. Then he threw another log onto the flames.

He whirled. "Did you hear me? I said my father told me, the bastard!"

"*Lewis!*"

"Well, what would you call someone who knocked up a fifteen-year-old, then blew out of town and left her with the bundle? Fifteen! That's jailbait. He had to know it, too. Bastard dropped off cash from time to time—I remember Ma getting it—but that's about all. He's been married twice...."

"Any kids?"

"Nope. That's why he wants me in his company. Needs an heir. Thinks he can buy me!" The dog, who'd been curled up near the fire, got up slowly and, with a cautious glance at Lewis, went to lie quietly under the table. "Apparently he's been tracking me for years. Knew all about the rustling thing. Knew about you—"

"Me!"

"Yep. Threatened me. Said he'd make it tough for you to get your scholarship renewed if I didn't agree to—"

"He did?" What kind of man was this? "Who is he, anyway?"

"Name's Bart Tanguay. President of Wild Rose. Fancy suit, fancy office, the whole works. I think he was the one who got Fred Billings into that hoity-toity club he wanted to get into in Calgary. The Devonian. So he'd owe him. Ha!"

Phoebe considered Lewis's news for a few minutes in silence. She couldn't help but be glad, somehow. She'd always thought it was a terrible thing that Lewis had no father, that he didn't even know who his father was. Not that this was the best outcome. Still, his father had turned out to be *some-one*—maybe a cad and a bounder, but a success in the eyes of the world. Someone Lewis didn't have to be ashamed of, the way he was with Billy.

Poor Billy. She'd never harmed a fly.

Phoebe thought of her own mother, so competent and efficient and friendly. Billy was shy and fearful, never said a word to a visitor. She was a wonder with animals, though, and had a magic touch with a garden. How could she have given up her son like that? And how could Mercy have gone along with it for so long?

MAYBE PHOEBE WAS RIGHT. She probably was; women had a sixth sense about these things. He should talk to Ma and Billy about this. There was no way he could think otherwise—Ma was his grandmother, yet he was so used to calling her Ma that he couldn't imagine anything else. And could he ever call Billy "Mother"?

Mom. He tried it mentally. Impossible. She was his weird older sister—fragile, gentle, wholly dependent, in need of protection from the slings and arrows of everyday life by him and by Ma.

But he wasn't discussing this with anybody else, just them. And Phoebe, of course. Billy would no doubt be horrified to discover that he knew. The last thing he would do was go public with the information about his real mother. Or father, for that matter. Nobody really cared, anyway.

Lewis doubted very much if Tanguay did, either. So there was no danger from that side, no matter what Tanguay threatened. Claiming Lewis as a long-lost son and going public with that information in their relatively small, close-knit, competitive industry would require a wholesale massaging of the facts that was beyond even Tanguay.

His father. Lewis tried that out in his head. Everything in him was repulsed by the knowledge, yet at the same time, strangely attracted. He'd been fatherless for so long it hardly mattered anymore. Yet it did.

He sighed and tightened his arm around Phoebe. He had to get some shut-eye before morning. At least the rain had stopped. All was peaceful in the cabin. Even the fire had died down to an orange glow, silent and flickering. His little home, his hideaway. With the woman he loved in his arms. He glanced down at Phoebe's russet head as she slept with her mouth slightly open on the pillow beside him. She snored gently. Just a little bit. Did he dare tell her? He smiled.

His lover. His woman. His wife. Here in his arms in his own cabin, a place he'd built with his own hands. What could possibly be better?

MERCEDES QUIETLY BEGAN her morning routine. She put on the electric kettle for a pot of tea, because the kitchen range was still cold and it would be a long time before she could boil water on it.

Then she bent over the wood box, picking out some chips and pieces of bark that had fallen from the split lengths. Good starter. She wadded up a page of the *Glory Plain Dealer* and carefully laid it in the firebox, together with the wood chips and pieces of bark and some kindling she'd cut the previous day. A wooden match completed the ritual, and in no time the kitchen fire was snapping and crackling cheerfully.

One page a day—by the time the week was up, the *Plain Dealer* was pretty much used up, too. Recycling, Mercedes thought with a mild snort. She didn't talk to herself—*yet,* she always added—but she didn't mind the odd laugh out loud when she thought of something humorous.

Right now, nothing in her life was humorous. Billy wasn't up, but that wasn't unusual. Mercedes generally took her daughter a cup of tea before she got out of bed. Sometimes Billy read in the mornings, in the bedroom she'd slept in all her forty-two years. Sometimes she'd daydream, looking out the window at the big maple, its branches waving in the wind, although Mercy didn't know what she had to daydream about. Sometimes she'd listen to the news on the radio. Or sing a little, to herself. Finally, about an hour or so after her cup of tea, she'd get up and get dressed and come down for a proper breakfast.

Mercy didn't mind. There wasn't much to get up for on days like this. The garden was long finished. There were chickens to be fed, eggs to collect, sheep to be fed and watered. But those tasks could easily be spread over the whole morning. In their many years together, mother and daughter had worked out routines, and they clung to them.

For instance, if Mercy took up a cup of coffee, instead of tea, the entire day would be ruined. Billy expected tea.

Today was washing. And she had a whole sack of laundry that Lewis had brought over yesterday. Imagine, a man of nearly twenty-eight bringing home his dirty clothes, just like a teenager! Lewis knew very well how to operate the machines at a coin laundry, but he also knew she'd be upset if he took his clothes to town, instead of bringing them to her. First off, Mercy didn't trust a coin-operated machine to do the job properly. Second, if she couldn't do a little laundry for her boy, wash his jeans, mend his socks, what was the world coming to?

It was rare enough that Lewis was even around. She had no idea why he'd holed up in that cabin of his for a week, or why he'd insisted she not tell anybody who inquired, but she was asking no questions, either. It was none of her business. She just hoped it wasn't trouble with the law. Either way, she was glad he'd come home to Bearberry Hill, to her and Billy. He'd always have a home here with them.

Mercedes decided to leave the mail on the table, where most mornings she looked over the wad of flyers that had arrived in the mailbox the previous day. She would attend instead, to sorting Lewis's laundry.

She dumped the pile of clothes onto the middle of the kitchen floor and separated out two pairs of jeans and some dark work socks. His shirts were light-colored, so she put them in a separate pile with his boxer underwear. A package of gum rolled out of a shirt pocket onto the linoleum. Men! Had he even cleaned out his pockets?

She thrust one hand into another shirt pocket and came up with a parking ticket, which she put on the table. Another hand into a jeans pocket yielded a two-dollar coin and more than a dollar in small change. That went into the jam jar she kept on the windowsill. Finders keepers.

She reached into a back pocket on a pair of black jeans. A slip of paper. Mercy looked at it—a check— then adjusted her reading glasses on her nose and inspected it more closely. Vaguely, in the back of her mind, she realized the kettle was about to boil, and she moved toward it, where the light was better anyway.

The check was from Bartholomew Tanguay. Tanguay! She took a quick painful breath and held it. *Lewis knew!* And the amount—there was a shocking number of zeroes on the check, and it was made out to Billy. Frightened, Mercy tucked it into her apron pocket. She'd have to talk to Lewis right away. It was past time. She'd let Billy put her off, delay for nearly six months.

Now someone else had spilled the beans—the worst possible person to have told Lewis anything at all, in Mercy's view.

She busied herself with making the tea, and when the tray was ready, she clambered slowly up the stairs, grasping the railing with each difficult step. She'd moved her own bedroom down to the main floor, after the accident with her hip.

"Billy?" She paused at her daughter's half-open door. "You awake, dear?"

"I'm up, Ma." They went through this ritual every morning. If Mercy had missed it…

Billy was sitting up in bed wearing a rose-sprigged flannel nightie that Mercy had sewn for her years before. It was faded now, but almost as pretty as ever, with cotton lace around the neckline and cuffs.

"Here's your tea, dear." She set the tray on Billy's side table and sat down heavily on her daughter's bed. She reached for her daughter's hand and patted it. "He knows, Billy. We can't hide it any longer."

Her daughter's involuntary cry pierced her heart. Mercy closed her eyes briefly—God give her strength—and then opened them again. "It's no use. He'll be around today to get his clothes. We have to talk to him."

"No!" Billy looked terrified. "We can't, Ma! It's been too long. I'm scared. I…what could we say?"

Mercy stood and settled the blanket cozily around her daughter's shoulders before leaving the room. Billy had always been weak, prone to chest complaints. She'd always been delicate, always needed extra care. "The truth, honey. We'll tell him the truth."

CHAPTER EIGHTEEN

PHOEBE APPROACHED the old farmhouse with some trepidation. It was early still, not quite nine o'clock. She'd awoken just after dawn and had climbed over the sleeping Lewis to quickly dress—her clothes had dried overnight—and to start the fires. Her fumbling efforts with the kitchen stove had woken Lewis, who'd lain there for a few moments watching her.

Finally, he'd offered her fire-starting advice. Soon both fires were blazing and sending welcome heat into the cold room.

They'd breakfasted on canned sausages—not very good—canned beans—so-so—and canned bacon from Denmark. Phoebe hadn't realized such products existed, but Lewis told her he also had canned butter on his shelf. It was food designed primarily for the old-fashioned outdoorsman or trapper who had no means of keeping butter and meat cold and fresh. Crackers didn't satisfy the way toast did in the morning, but all in all, it was a good homely meal, unlike so many they'd shared, in trendy eateries and fancy hotels.

This was more like really being married.

Ever since Lewis had told her about Billy, Phoebe had been thinking about it. How in the world could such a thing have happened in this day and age? Were people really so ashamed of an illegitimate pregnancy that they'd go to such lengths to conceal it? And what about the father—Lewis's father? This Bart Tanguay? Now that she'd had a chance to reflect, she agreed with Lewis—he'd been a bastard of the first order. At least he'd sent money from time to time, to help with expenses, she presumed. But that wasn't enough. That didn't meet his responsibility. That was no way for a father to act.

She thought of what might have happened in her own family, if she or Jilly had come home pregnant with no husband in tow. Her parents would be horrified, no question. They'd blame themselves for not bringing up their girls properly. They'd weep and rage and moan, and in the end, they'd offer whatever support they could. When the baby came, they'd welcome their grandchild with open arms and loving hearts. A couple of decades ago or so, a pregnant girl from a good family would have been expected to have her baby secretly in some Catholic home for unmarried girls and give it up for adoption. Not anymore. And, even decades ago, some families would have risen to the challenge of keeping both their daughter and their grandchild.

No matter what the neighbors might say.

Phoebe felt terribly, terribly sorry for Billy. She

was like a little bird, really. A fragile little bird. She
swooped and fluttered. Ma took care of her. Lewis
had always protected her. Bird in more ways than
one, Phoebe thought, remembering what her own
mother had said about Billy, how pretty she'd been
as a young girl and what a wonderful singing voice
she had. Her mother had shaken her head and wondered what had happened to change her so. Well,
now Phoebe knew. Billy had been seduced at fifteen
and left pregnant, to have a child at barely sixteen.
Then she'd conspired with her own mother to pretend
that Lewis was not her child at all.

Phoebe wanted to know the truth. She wanted
Lewis to know the truth, too. And she wanted them
to offer their love and support to both Ma and Billy.
It would be hard for Lewis, but he had to get used
to the idea. People made mistakes, but the past was
past. No matter what that past was, the future could
be different. If Phoebe didn't believe that, she didn't
believe in anything at all.

There'd been a frost overnight, after the rain had
stopped, and the footing was treacherous. Accom-
panied by Shep, Phoebe and Lewis picked their way
to the farmhouse on the path that ran through the
bluff, the shortest route. Two dogs ran out to greet
them, tongues lolling. The smoke from the chimney
of the ramshackle farmhouse was a welcome sight.
Phoebe squeezed Lewis's hand. She was wearing the
emerald, but they'd agreed to put the wedding band

away until they went through with their second ceremony. Lewis was hesitant to tell Ma and Billy about their plans until everything had been settled, right down to the last detail. She'd leave it to his judgment—she'd gotten both of them in enough trouble already with her impulsive schemes.

Mercy greeted them at the door. She seemed surprised to see Phoebe. No wonder, Phoebe thought; she'd left her car at the cemetery road and sneaked through the woods like a lover on a clandestine assignation last night.

"Come in! Come in! I was expecting you this morning," Mercy said to Lewis, with a smile for Phoebe. The old woman was dressed in faded baggy slacks and an old moth-eaten pullover. Her hair had probably been combed, but with the bad cut—Phoebe was sure the woman had snipped it herself—it was hard to tell. Reading glasses dangled around her neck on a shoelace. "I'm just in the midst of getting some laundry ready to wash, but I've got the teapot on and I've got a mess of porridge on the stove, waitin' for Billy to get up. You'll stay for breakfast?"

Mercy eyed them nervously, her eyes darting from one to the other. Did she know why they were here this morning? Phoebe wondered. She couldn't possibly!

"We've had breakfast," Lewis said, "but a cup

of tea would go down great. Or would you rather have coffee, Phoebe? I could make a pot.''

''Never mind! I'll put on a pot of coffee,'' Mercy insisted. ''I know how Phoebe likes her coffee and I know where everything is in my own kitchen. Sit down! I didn't realize you were here.''

''No. I left my car over at the church. I...I came last night.'' Phoebe couldn't see any point in pretending otherwise. Of course she was sleeping with Lewis Hardin. She was married to him! And even if she wasn't, Mercy Hardin wasn't born yesterday. She knew that Phoebe and Lewis had a relationship. A close relationship.

And, deep down, Phoebe did not believe that Mercedes Hardin was the type to sit in judgment on anyone. Not even her own daughter.

Mercy puttered about the kitchen, and Phoebe caught Lewis's eye over the scrubbed wooden table, nicely set with a red-and-white gingham square and a potted African violet in the center, just coming into bloom. Cream, sugar, butter, a milk jug and two cereal bowls with spoons were laid on the other two sides. The kitchen was warm and cozy, a sanctuary in the November chill.

Phoebe arched her brow and gestured with her head, indicating that Lewis ought to say something. Bring up what they'd come over to discuss. Maybe it was best that Billy wasn't around. At least not at the moment.

Lewis scowled. He seemed very ill at ease. Phoebe realized she had to back off. This was happening in his life, not hers. He had good reason to feel uncomfortable. His first thought had been not to say anything at all. Wasn't that just like a man?

But she needn't have worried. Mercy brought the subject up.

She came over to the table with the teapot and poured a cup for herself and one for Lewis. "Coffee'll be along in a jiff," she said, smiling at Phoebe.

Phoebe smiled back. She'd always liked Mercy Hardin. She'd been almost like a third grandmother to her, although of her two grandmothers, only one, Granny Longquist, was still living.

"Look here, Lewis," she said, rummaging in her apron pocket with a frown. She removed a slip of paper and held it out to him. "I found this in your jeans pocket this morning. I thought we should talk about it." She glanced at Phoebe.

Phoebe gripped the table's edge with both hands. "Would you like me to leave? Is this private?" she got out in a rush. She felt like a coward all of a sudden. Somehow she knew that Mercy was referring to something that had to do with Lewis's news.

Mercy glanced at Lewis now and he shook his head. He studied the slip of paper Mercy had given him. "No, Phoebe's part of this. She's part of my life now. I want her to stay."

Phoebe sat back, determined—above all—to keep her mouth shut.

"You've been to see Bart Tanguay," Mercy said. It was a statement, not a question. She sat down heavily in one of the empty chairs, by her teacup. She seemed very, very old.

"I have, Ma." Lewis's eyes were tortured. "I thought it was a business meeting. Then he told me about…about who he is. That he's my father."

Mercy nodded. Her faded blue eyes filled with tears. "I suppose he did." She sighed tremulously. "I have no idea, Lewis, why he should tell you now, after keeping out of it all these years. But it's my fault. I should have spoken to you myself. I wanted to, but—" She stopped, as if afraid to give Lewis any reasons. Phoebe instinctively felt that she was protecting Billy, as she always had. "You know how it is," she finished gently.

"I know, Ma. I know how it is." Lewis stared down at his hands, clasped tightly and resting on the table. He'd paid no attention to his tea. "He told me the rest, too, Ma. He told me that Billy was my real mom…" His voice broke and Phoebe saw his jaw tighten. She wanted to rush to him, to gather him in her arms. Her husband! Her strong, silent husband who'd never had a proper family, never had a proper mother or father!

Mercy stared at her hands for a long time. Finally she lifted her head and looked directly at Lewis. She reached out and covered his hand with hers. "It was a terrible thing we did," she said simply. "But I don't apologize." She shook her head. "No. It seemed like the best thing to do at the time."

Phoebe was aware that the coffee had finished percolating. Quietly she got to her feet and fetched the pot to pour herself a cup. It was so still in the farmhouse kitchen, only the crackling of the fire, and the officious tick-tock of the wind-up alarm clock perched on the windowsill.

"You're my grandson. You're not my son. I've always loved you as a son. So has Billy. We did the best we could. We raised you together, the two of us. But we've hurt you, Lewis, keeping the truth from you. I know we have. And for that, I'm sorry."

She bent her head again and Lewis quickly got up and put his arms around her bowed shoulders. "Don't cry, Ma. It's okay, really it is," he said, his voice thick with emotion. He cleared his throat. "Sure, it was a shock. But it doesn't change anything. You're…you're still my family, you and Billy. You're all I've got."

You've got me, Phoebe screamed silently. *You've got me.*

Lewis looked at her then and she knew that in his heart and soul, he'd included her, too.

Mercy pulled a tissue out of her apron pocket and blew her nose loudly. "You're everything to us, Lewis. You're the most precious thing that ever happened to either of us. A gift…'' She blew her nose again. Phoebe's heart ached for her.

''Never mind, Ma,'' Lewis said, patting her shoulder awkwardly. ''Never mind. We don't need to talk about it if you—''

''I *want* to talk about it. I want to explain, as best I can,'' the old woman broke in. ''Lewis, listen to me! For the love of God, sit down and listen to me! Don't put me off''

''Okay, Ma, okay.'' Lewis sat back down. His face was pale. Phoebe could tell he was hurting, not only for himself but for Ma.

''Your mother—Billy—was a lovely girl. She was the apple of my eye. She was sweet, she was innocent, oh, far more innocent than she should have been, growing up on a farm! We had no money back then, none at all.'' Mercy attempted a laugh that turned into a tremulous sigh. ''When she was fifteen, she got work with Mrs. Benjamin, across the other side of the bluff—''

''Benjamin?''

''Oh, they moved. They were on the Hawrylak place. She'd just had a baby—Nettie Benjamin had—and she was looking for someone to help with the children and the housework. She had a pack of young 'uns already when that last baby came. Billy took a job with her, Saturdays, and sometimes after school. To help her out, you know…''

Mercy looked to both Lewis and Phoebe. They

nodded. "Scrubbing floors, doing the dishes, baking bread, hanging out a wash, ironing, that kind of thing." Phoebe was appalled at the work that had been expected of a fifteen-year-old schoolgirl, but she said nothing.

"She'd take a shortcut over the bluff, comin' and goin'," Mercy continued. "It was a good half-hour walk even then, but we had no vehicle. I had no way of picking her up... Oh, Lewis!" She buried her face in her hands. "I blame myself, even now. If only I'd looked out for her better—"

"Shh, Ma. You did the best you could, I know you did," Lewis said.

"The money she earned came in handy. To buy the kind of things young girls like. Nice clothes. Extras. I never had cash for extras, you know that." Mercy was silent for a moment or so, then seemed to gather her strength. When she went on, her voice was firmer, stronger, as though she'd rehearsed the facts in her head a million times.

"Your father—Bart Tanguay—met her on one of her trips home. He offered her a ride in his truck. He was working for one of the oil companies that was drilling around here, and he took a shine to Billy. Told her all kinds of things. How she could make a career for herself singing. Modeling. How she could go to New York, Paris, I don't know what all he told her. Anyway, they...they became intimate." The old-fashioned term rang oddly in Phoebe's ears.

''The first time, I don't know, she says he took advantage of her in the Pattersons' cornfield, but it happened quite a few times, so it wasn't all his fault, I guess. Although he was older, nearly ten years older than her, and he should've known better, if she didn't.'' Mercy wiped at her eyes.

''Then…then he disappeared. He took off one day. I suppose his job was finished, and we never saw him again. Billy was expecting. I didn't realize it myself until she was nearly five months gone, and then the end of school was coming up. She hid it pretty well, and then…well, you were born, right here at home. I hoped Billy would go back and finish high school. I knew there was no hope for her otherwise, earning a living for herself, making a life. So I told her it would be best if I pretended that I'd had the baby, not her. I didn't want the kids at school to know anything. We never saw many people out here, and I don't suppose many knew much about me or how I lived or who I saw. Anyway, no one ever questioned it. That's how it started. And it just went on.''

''For twenty-seven years,'' Lewis said softly.

''Yes.'' Mercy wiped at her eyes again. ''It never made any difference, anyway, because she never went back to school. Wouldn't go. I guess he found out somehow, because we started to get money, cash money, in the mailbox now and then, and I always figured it was from him. He never got in touch with us until…until lately.''

''What do you mean, Ma, *lately?*''

''He called here a while back, not long after summer was over. He asked if we'd ever told you anything. I said no, we hadn't. He said…'' Mercy paused.

''He said *what,* Ma?''

''He said it was best that way, for all concerned.''

''The bastard!'' Lewis slammed his fist down on the table and the cutlery jumped. Mercy's eyes darted to his.

''Oh, don't blame him, Lewis. He sent money. He did what he could.''

''Did what he could! He's married two women since then, was engaged to one when he was carrying on with Billy. He's a bastard, Ma! A first-class jerk! Don't defend him.''

''Okay, Lewis, I won't.'' But Phoebe could tell she wasn't completely convinced. ''What about… that check I found in your pocket?''

''He wanted to buy Billy off. He wanted to repay what he called his debt to her.''

''But that's a lot of money, Lewis.''

''He owes it, don't you think?'' Lewis bit out savagely. ''He owes it for what he's done, doesn't he? The *bastard!*''

Mercy looked at Lewis for a long moment. ''He's your father, my child. He's your *father.*''

The kitchen was dead silent except for the busy tick-tock of the clock. Mercy smoothed the tablecloth in front of her, pressed the crisply ironed folds against the table with her thumb. Her nails were ridged and old, straight-cut. Her hands were worn, dotted with age spots. She wore no rings.

"Did you get your coffee, dear?" She turned to Phoebe, her eyes mild and inquiring. "Would you like something with that? Some toast? We've got—" She made an attempt at laughter, and it turned to a sob, a terrible, wrenching animal sound that came straight from her soul, then she dabbed at her eyes with her apron and began again. "We've got quite a lot of news for so early in the morning around here, don't we?"

Phoebe's heart ached for them both. And Billy. What a tragic story. Still, as Mercy said, Lewis was part of this story. He was their gift, their precious gift. Hers, too. Her eyes filled with tears and she got up to put more hot water in the teapot for Mercy and Lewis. The porridge was steaming on the range, so she took off the lid and gave it a stir. Then she came back to the table with the teapot. "I'm sorry you had to hear all this, Phoebe," Mercy said.

"Oh, Mrs. Hardin! I...I wanted to be here with Lewis. He..." She glanced over Mercy's head to Lewis, who looked grim. "He told me about his father, that part," she went on softly, "and Billy. I hope he can put it behind him now. What's past is past.''

Mercy laughed, a soft, knowing laugh. "Is it, dear? Is the past ever past? I wonder.''

Lewis looked startled at her words, as though he'd seen a ghost. Just then the door to the hallway creaked open and Billy entered. Lewis's face went pale again. Billy smiled shyly at them, seemingly oblivious to the dramatic tableau they must have presented, and went directly to the stove where she gazed into the porridge pot. She didn't say a word. She carefully put the lid on and turned to them at the table.

"Would you like some tea, Billy?" Phoebe said, standing up and taking charge. *Now what?* "Or there's coffee.''

"Tea's fine,'' she said in a small voice. "Thank you.'' She came toward the table, to her place already set—bowl, plate, cup, spoon.

"Billy, honey, sit down,'' Mercy ordered. Billy sat and turned wondering, fearful eyes to her mother. "Lewis knows all about everything. I told him and…and his father told him.''

Billy looked at Lewis and her mouth trembled. Her big blue eyes suddenly overflowed with tears. Lewis got up—Phoebe could see his hands shaking at his sides—went around the table and put his arms around Billy. She gave a small strangled sob and put her arms around him, too. Around her son.

"Never mind, Billy," Lewis said. He patted her shoulder gently. "It's okay."

Phoebe felt her own tears start to fall, and she sniffed loudly. No one noticed.

"Never mind," Lewis repeated in a hoarse voice. "I know everything now and we'll do whatever you like. We'll keep it our secret if you want, or we'll tell the world. It's up to you. I...I don't care. It's all the same to me."

There was no point now in setting any record straight, Phoebe thought. It would only lead to more questions and more trouble and misunderstanding in the community. Twenty-seven years had gone by. What was the point of correcting the error now? The people who mattered knew—Lewis and his mother and grandmother. And his father, of course.

And her, his wife.

"Is the porridge ready?" Billy said, stepping back from Lewis's embrace and looking at her mother. "I'm hungry."

Phoebe went to Lewis and flung her arms around him. He kissed her lightly and smiled. It was a tight, anxious smile. His eyes were bleak with pain. She laid her head on his chest, hugged him then stepped away. Billy was oblivious. Had they expected anything else? She hummed softly to herself. Mercy had dished her up some oatmeal and she was spooning sugar on it, as though today was just another day.

"I don't think we should say anything, son,"

Mercy said to Lewis and Phoebe, over her daughter's bowed head. Her eyes were dark with a pain all her own. "She doesn't really understand. She's been so afraid of everything all her life. Ever since…well, you know when."

"What about the money?" Lewis asked. He felt in his shirt pocket, as though just then remembering that Mercy had given him the check.

Mercy stared at him. "I don't know," she said. "I just don't know about that."

"Billy?" Lewis stepped up to the table. It looked as if he was going to keep on calling her Billy, just as he called Mercy Ma. Old habits were hard to change.

"Yes?" Billy smiled up at him. Phoebe wasn't so sure Billy didn't understand what was going on. She had a serene, calm look and seemed happier than Phoebe had ever seen her. Things were going on in her brain. She was attending to this knowledge, that her son knew her secret and had forgiven her, in her own private way. In her own private world.

"My…" Lewis hesitated. "My father gave this check to me to give to you. It's yours."

"What is it?"

"It's a check. It's money. It's made out in your name. I guess he…felt he owed you or something. For everything that happened."

A cloud passed over her fine blue eyes. She stared

down at her porridge, then up again at her son. "A check?" She looked at her mother.

"It's a check, Billy. Like the money that Lewis sends us all the time."

"How much money?"

"Fifty thousand dollars."

Phoebe gasped—she couldn't help herself. This was some news. Lewis hadn't said a word about the check to her.

"Oh." Billy seemed to think that over. "My, that's a lot of money. Do we need money now, Ma?"

It was a simple question from someone to whom money, or the lack of it, had always had some importance.

Mercy laughed. "Heavens, no! I've got more darn money stashed away in my calico sack than we can ever spend. Money from Lewis. It makes me nervous. What do we need money for? We've got everything a body could want!"

Billy smiled. "Then throw it away, Ma. Put it in the fire."

And, to Phoebe's enormous shock, that was exactly what Mercy did, opening the lid of the firebox and dropping the check in before Billy could take another spoonful of her porridge.

Guilt money, that was all it was, Phoebe thought. Blood money, according to Lewis's thinking. Still, fifty thousand dollars...

"Is there any more milk?" Billy held up the

empty jug, and Mercy took it from her and crossed to the refrigerator. She refilled the jug, glancing out the window as she walked back to the table. Lewis and Phoebe were still standing in the middle of the kitchen, Phoebe with her arm around Lewis's waist. She was so proud of him. She was so proud of all of them.

Mercy smiled. "Looks like a fine day, after all, don't it? That storm overnight blew in some clear weather. I think I'll let the sheep out into the orchard this afternoon. They've been agitatin' for a good run and some fresh air."

Lewis turned to look outside, as his grandmother had indicated. He stuck his hands in his pockets and squared his shoulders. "Yep. Fine day."

Billy bent to her porridge, spooning it up slowly and methodically until every last bit was gone. Then she put down her spoon and sat quietly, smiling at her empty bowl.

Mercy poked at the fire again and Pretty, the cat, yawned and stretched and got up from the pile of Lewis's clothes on the floor, where she'd been snoozing, and wound herself around Mercy's legs.

The clock ticked busily on.

And that, Phoebe realized, was that.

CHAPTER NINETEEN

CHRISTMAS, HER FIRST with her husband—although, of course, no one knew—was wonderful. They decided on a wedding at the end of December, which left the usual fuss and festivity of Christmas unchanged. But this Christmas, Phoebe and Lewis were spending the holiday in their own home—Lewis's cabin in the woods. Her parents knew and probably didn't approve but Phoebe was sure they wouldn't say a word.

The condo she and Lewis had bought in Edmonton was in the process of being repainted by the firm Lewis had hired, and coming home to Glory—Swallowbank Farm, the Hardin place and Lewis's little cabin—for the holidays after her exams were finished in early December seemed the most sensible option.

Phoebe was glad they had. It snowed a week before Christmas, and all the visits they made to neighbors and friends had that special feeling that a fresh snowfall always brought. They spent Christmas Eve going to midnight Mass with Phoebe's family, and the next day sat down to a late-afternoon Christmas feast in the Hardin-farmhouse kitchen, featuring roast goose, sauerkraut and apples, fried parsnips, beet pickles, creamed kale, mashed potatoes, gravy and mince pie—at least that part was familiar!—with Mercy and Billy. Mercy said they never used the dining room unless the prime minister came to visit and he never did, so...

Phoebe didn't care what they did or where they went or what they ate as long as she was with the man she loved.

Once the date was settled and the invitations had gone out, Phoebe and Lewis could start planning for their new life together in the condo in Edmonton, which they planned to move into after the marriage ceremony. Lewis had told her she'd invite his father and his wife to the wedding over his dead body. Phoebe didn't really believe him so she sent an invitation, anyway.

She received a very nice, very formal handwritten reply—which she shared with her husband—saying that Mr. and Mrs. Bartholomew Tanguay would be unable to attend, as they would be away on holiday, a Mediterranean cruise, at the time of the nuptials. However, Mr. and Mrs. Tanguay wanted them to be aware that arrangements had been made to deliver a cherrywood dining-room suite to the couple's Edmonton address early in the new year. In conclusion, Mr. and Mrs. Bartholomew Tanguay extended their warmest wishes to the happy couple.

"What do you think of that?" Phoebe exclaimed after she read the note aloud to Lewis.

"Think?" Lewis had gotten over his initial shock that she'd gone ahead and invited his father to their wedding and was pacing the cabin floor in front of the fireplace. Phoebe recalled a recent, similar scene, with Lewis wearing nothing but a frown and a cigarette. This time he only had the frown. "I think he's up to something, that's what. A dining-room suite!" He snorted. "What kind of weird wedding present is that?"

"It's your father's kind," she said firmly. "Expensive, impersonal and bound to make an impact. We can hardly ignore a dining-room suite, can we? And actually, we need one. I hope he's got good taste."

"What if he'd accepted? What if he'd shown up at the church with his fancy wife on his arm? With Ma there, and Billy?" Lewis was outraged, but she could see the warm light of appreciation in his eye, too. He realized she'd scored a tremendous coup for him, whether he approved or not.

"If they'd come, well, then, we would have dealt with it somehow," she said airly. "Graciously, of course." She had no regrets. She knew she'd done the right thing.

Lewis muttered something she couldn't hear. Phoebe was certain he was coming around to the idea that his father wasn't a complete ogre. That maybe

Bart Tanguay had had second thoughts, too, about the way he'd handled things, and this was a peace offering to the man who, after all, was his only child. He'd realized he couldn't bully his son—talk about a chip off the old block!—and he was trying another tack.

He was a sensible man, Phoebe believed. A practical man. And eventually her husband would have to face that reality. If *she*—Harry and Nan Longquist's brainy daughter—could accept the possibility that she might just find herself balancing motherhood and a career from a ranch house in southern Alberta someday, her husband could accept the possibility that his own father might have had second thoughts, too.

Honestly! Men could be so difficult sometimes.

THE DAY OF THE WEDDING couldn't have been finer. The fresh snowfall the night before had covered the landscape with a pristine blanket of white, which clarified and muffled sound at the same time. Shouts were clearer and louder, traffic noise more muted.

At first, Phoebe and Lewis had wanted to rent the Glory community center for their big party. Deep down, they knew, that was what it was—a chance for the entire community to share in their joy. A secret wedding, no matter how romantic, meant they'd missed out on all the excitement of what others called a "real" wedding.

This way, they had both.

In the end, they settled on the hall next to Saint Augustine's. It was smaller than the community center, but handy to the church, and the Women's League would be catering. Phoebe told her parents there was no option—she and Lewis would pick up the expenses for the reception and dance. Of course, she had a fight on her hands with her father, and it was still undecided. At first, Nan Longquist was all for organizing her friends and relatives to bring squares and cakes, but Phoebe put her foot down firmly. This was a time for Nan to relax and celebrate, too, not be relegated to the kitchen brewing vast urns of tea or worrying that this or that catering detail might not go right.

Phoebe assigned wedding flowers to her mother, which made Nan happy. She and Jilly and Renee and Phoebe's aunt Catherine spent the morning of the event decorating the church and the hall with masses of winter flowers—chrysanthemums, gardenias, hot-house lilies and, of course, poinsettias, which, as Nan pointed out, were still perfectly good and suitable for a winter wedding.

Renee was in seventh heaven, convinced she'd had something to do with her big sister's romance with that "hot" guy from up north somewhere.

Phoebe was more excited than she'd expected to be. She had a new dress, a lovely soft apricot velvet gown, calf-length, which she'd chosen, instead of the traditional white. After all, she was already married and she was certainly no virgin.

Lewis, she knew, was wearing a new suit he'd had made by an Edmonton tailor. Dark navy-blue, and very, very suave. He'd taken Ma and Billy shopping at a mall in Lethbridge and they'd both bought new outfits, at his expense, he'd reported. At his insistence. At first, Lewis had told her, Mercy had been quite sure they both had dresses that would "do," but he had said, no, new dresses all around. Shoes, purses, hairstyling, the works.

Actually, he'd told her, they were thrilled to bits about the wedding and about her. Ma said she'd always known the Longquist girl was going to get their Lewis in the end. Lewis's plans for the day included shepherding Ma and Billy to the hairdresser in the early afternoon and then bringing them to the church.

Phoebe understood completely. They were shy, even though they'd know most of the people coming to the wedding and reception. They'd feel more comfortable if Lewis was with them.

The ceremony itself was to be short and sweet. No long prayers on their knees, no long sermons about married life, no long admonitions about duties and requirements.

This was the part Phoebe still wasn't entirely happy about. She was already married to Lewis. What was the point of this reenactment? Was it only to expedite the truth, to move smoothly from the concealed marriage to the public one? If so, that was pretty cowardly—even though it *had* been her idea. On the other hand, her parents were thrilled about the wedding. Phoebe realized how much the secret marriage had robbed her family of something that was very important: presenting their daughter to the community as a married woman; publicly welcoming Lewis as their son, joining themselves forever with the Hardin family.

This was what ceremonies were all about. They weren't just about the two people getting married. They were about the whole community, the society in which they lived.

Not much could be done at this stage, Phoebe thought, pulling on her gossamer silk stockings; she hadn't even known there were such things as silk stockings anymore. Lewis had ordered them for her from some secret supplier that only he—or all men!—knew about.

She stood and examined herself in the mirror. Freckles—there were some things you just couldn't do anything about. Her hair looked great, though, thanks to Jilly's careful ministrations. Phoebe lifted the flower garland—Jilly's suggestion—and settled it on her head. She'd been afraid it would look tacky, but actually, it looked lovely.

Half an hour, and they were due at the church. Trevor was driving and Renee was sitting in the passenger seat, with Phoebe and her parents in the back.

After the ceremony and the reception, she and Lewis planned to drive to Edmonton. The condo was fine for now, Lewis had said, until they moved to the country or needed a bigger place. Phoebe knew that wouldn't be necessary for a while; she wasn't pregnant from their encounter at the cabin. She was happy to be moving out of the residence and into a real home with her husband. They'd been married nearly four months and they'd hardly done anything resembling normal married life.

Honeymoon? Moving into their own home. That was Phoebe's idea of a wonderful, romantic time. Starting the new year right.

The parking lot at the church was jammed. Friends and neighbors from all over the district, as well as the town of Glory, were there. This, Phoebe thought, was the most exciting part. She'd see Hannah, the librarian she'd adored when she worked at the library. Her best friend from high school, Natasha Jarvis. Tim, the guy her uncle hired regularly each summer—he'd recently gotten married himself, to a girl from Tamarack. Phoebe had had a crush on Tim once, so long ago she could barely remember. She was quite sure Tim had never suspected. Of course, Lindy would be there, although Boyd had declined, as had Bethany Cook. She and Reg were going to Reno to take in some shows, she'd told Lewis. Phoebe was rather relieved to hear it.

Lewis's car arrived at the church just behind them.

Phoebe's heart soared and ricocheted in her chest. She was so in love with her husband she couldn't believe it. To think she'd had cold feet only three months before.

Lewis's eyes were glowing as he watched her emerge from the car with her mother's help. Trevor was getting their father's foldable wheelchair out of the trunk.

"You look fabulous, honey," Lewis whispered, and kissed her cheek softly. "Almost good enough to marry—again."

"I feel odd about that, don't you, Lewis?" Phoebe whispered back. "I mean, we're already married. This is so dumb!"

"Admittedly not one of your better ideas," he said with a grin. "The party will be fun, though. What the heck."

Phoebe noticed Billy and Ma standing off to one side.

"Mrs. Hardin!" Phoebe hugged the older woman, feeling tears in her own eyes as she watched the faded blue eyes fill with moisture. "You're looking terrific, you and Billy both!"

She hugged Billy, who'd had her hair stylishly cut and was wearing a blue dress with a gray coat over it. Very modern, very spiffy. Mercy was wearing a pantsuit of some sort, with a navy jacket. They both had purses and matching shoes, and Mercy's hair had been permed.

What a transformation!

"How shall we go in? Lewis first?" Nan asked. "Oh, we have to hurry. I think we're late."

"We're not late, Mom." Phoebe hugged her mother. If she only knew!

"Let's go in together," Lewis suggested. "All of us."

Phoebe quickly agreed. She knew Lewis didn't want to leave his mother and grandmother to enter the church alone.

"That's not the way it's supposed to be," Nan wailed.

"Never mind, Mom. That's the way we're going to do it."

"Suits me, Mother," Harry growled from his wheelchair. "I'll take Phoebe's arm and just wheel down beside her. We can sort things out once we're in there."

Nan nearly swooned. This was *not* the way things were supposed to be done, and no doubt her sister, Catherine, would have something to say about it later.

The party entered together. Everyone stood to watch them come up the aisle. Lewis walked in front with Ma and Billy on one side, Nan on the other. Phoebe held her father's hand as Trevor pushed the chair. Renee skipped along behind, bright eyes darting everywhere, her finger in her mouth.

No one, it seemed, could stop smiling. At the front

of the congregation, Lewis saw that his mother and grandmother were seated, then escorted Nan to her place. Harry pulled up in the aisle and Trevor took his place at the other end of the pew. Jilly was sitting elsewhere with friends who'd come earlier, as was Ben. The church was packed.

"Oh, Lewis!" Phoebe grabbed Lewis's arm as they turned to face the priest at the front. "I don't feel right about this."

"Oh, man! Not again, Phoebe," Lewis groaned quietly.

"I don't mean being married. I just mean…you know, going through with all this again. It seems so phony!"

The priest cleared his throat and beamed at them. He was ready.

"Phoebe," Lewis said patiently, out of the corner of his mouth, "what do you suggest?"

Phoebe could hear her mother's quiet "shh!" behind her. The organ music had stopped. They weren't supposed to be talking at this stage—arguing even, which was how it must have seemed to the people behind them. They were supposed to be looking at the priest and getting started on their marriage vows.

"Lewis?"

"What, baby?" Lewis was smiling happily. She could tell he didn't care; he didn't give a damn about anything. He was smiling at her as though he'd never loved anyone the way he loved her and never would again. As though they were here all alone, and there was no one else in the world but them. As though she was the woman for him and always would be. Just as he was hers, and always would be. No matter what.

"Let's just tell everybody," she whispered. She squeezed his hand. "Why not?"

Lewis gazed at her for a few steady seconds. Then he grinned. "Why not, indeed?" He bent forward and spoke to the priest, who looked surprised but then beamed and nodded his head vigorously.

They turned, holding hands, and the crowd buzzed. Were they calling it off? A scandal!

"Friends and neighbors," Lewis began in a loud voice, "we have something to tell you, Phoebe and I. We're standing up here to get married, as you can see and as you've all been invited to witness, but the fact is…we're already married."

There was a collective gasp from the crowd. Phoebe noticed that her mother had clapped her hands to her cheeks and her mouth was wide open. Her father was looking interested, to say the least. Renee had thrust her tiny fist into the air in a "yesss!" gesture.

"The fact is, Phoebe asked me to marry her last August—" a roar of laughter from the congregation "—and I did. We were married by a magistrate in Lethbridge—I can prove all this! And for some crazy reason that I can't quite remember now, we decided not to tell anybody.''

Lewis looked at her. She knew she was blushing furiously. She squeezed his hand again.

''So, there's not much point in doing this again, unless it's a renewal of our vows, which is fine with me. I'm just as keen on marrying her now as I was then. Anybody else want to join us? Step right up, folks, and then we'll go next door and have a he—'' Lewis caught himself in time. Had he forgotten where he was? ''—er, a heck of a party.''

The crowd went crazy. There was laughter and talk and discussion and people mopping their eyes, some with tears and some with laughter.

''Oh, sure, why not?'' from one side of the church. ''Excuse us!'' from the other side as couples made their way to the aisle and then up to the front.

Phoebe saw half a dozen people come down the aisle to join them. Cal and Nina Blake, her uncle Joe and aunt Honor, a couple from town that Phoebe didn't know well, friends of her mother's...

In the end, five couples—six, including them— lined up in front of the priest and, amid much laughter, renewed their wedding vows together. This wedding, Phoebe thought, as she left the church in a daze of happiness, would go down in Glory history.

The party was an enormous success. First, Lewis danced with his bride, to the strains of the traditional

"Wedding Waltz," played surprisingly well by a five-piece Kinsmen band from High River.

"Happy, darling?" He smiled.

"Couldn't be happier!" she said. "Maybe we could do this again sometime?"

"Any time, Phoebe. Any time at all."

Then the other couples who'd renewed their vows joined them on the floor for another rendition of the "Wedding Waltz."

After that, Phoebe took to the floor with her oldest brother, Ben. Her father smiled proudly from the side. Of course, he couldn't take that first dance with his married daughter.

And Lewis danced with Billy. She glowed in his arms, danced beautifully, and people said they hadn't seen her look so pretty in years.

Of course, they said, he'd have danced with Mercy first, as custom dictated, only, Mercy had a bad hip. He could have danced with the mother of the bride, instead, as he very properly did the next dance.

But Billy was first. Wasn't it wonderful, everyone said, that Lewis thought so much of his only sister?

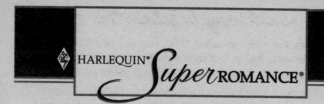

HARLEQUIN *Super*ROMANCE®

*They look alike. They sound alike.
They act alike—at least
some of the time.*

THE REAL FATHER by *Kathleen O'Brien*

(Superromance #927)

A woman raises her child alone after her boyfriend,
the father, dies. Only his twin knows that his brother
isn't the real father....
Available July 2000

CHRISTMAS BABIES by *Ellen James*

(Superromance #953)

One twin masquerades as the other. Now they're both
pregnant. Did the same man father both?
Available November 2000

Available wherever Harlequin books are sold.

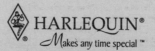

HARLEQUIN®

Makes any time special ™

You're not going to believe this offer!

In October and November 2000, buy any two Harlequin or Silhouette books and save $10.00 off future purchases, or buy any three and save $20.00 off future purchases!

Just fill out this form and attach 2 proofs of purchase (cash register receipts) from October and November 2000 books and Harlequin will send you a coupon booklet worth a total savings of $10.00 off future purchases of Harlequin and Silhouette books in 2001. Send us 3 proofs of purchase and we will send you a coupon booklet worth a total savings of $20.00 off future purchases.

Saving money has never been this easy.

I accept your offer! Please send me a coupon booklet:

Name: _____

Address: _____ City: _____

State/Prov.: _____ Zip/Postal Code: _____

Optional Survey!

In a typical month, how many Harlequin or Silhouette books would you buy <u>new</u> at retail stores?

☐ Less than 1   ☐ 1   ☐ 2   ☐ 3 to 4   ☐ 5+

Which of the following statements best describes how you <u>buy</u> Harlequin or Silhouette books? Choose one answer only that <u>best</u> describes you.

☐ I am a regular buyer and reader
☐ I am a regular reader but buy only occasionally
☐ I only buy and read for specific times of the year, e.g. vacations
☐ I subscribe through Reader Service but also buy at retail stores
☐ I mainly borrow and buy only occasionally
☐ I am an occasional buyer and reader

Which of the following statements best describes how you <u>choose</u> the Harlequin and Silhouette series books you buy <u>new</u> at retail stores? By "series," we mean books within a particular line, such as *Harlequin PRESENTS* or *Silhouette SPECIAL EDITION*. Choose one answer only that <u>best</u> describes you.

☐ I only buy books from my favorite series
☐ I generally buy books from my favorite series but also buy books from other series on occasion
☐ I buy some books from my favorite series but also buy from many other series regularly
☐ I buy all types of books depending on my mood and what I find interesting and have no favorite series

Please send this form, along with your cash register receipts as proofs of purchase, to:
In the U.S.: Harlequin Books, P.O. Box 9057, Buffalo, NY 14269
In Canada: Harlequin Books, P.O. Box 622, Fort Erie, Ontario L2A 5X3
(Allow 4-6 weeks for delivery) Offer expires December 31, 2000.   PHQ4002

If you enjoyed what you just read,
then we've got an offer you can't resist!

Take 2 bestselling love stories FREE!

Plus get a FREE surprise gift!

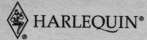

This Christmas, experience
the love, warmth and magic that
only Harlequin can provide with

Mistletoe Magic

a charming collection from

BETTY NEELS

MARGARET WAY   REBECCA WINTERS

Available November 2000

HARLEQUIN®
Makes any time special ™

Visit us at www.eHarlequin.com   PHMAGIC